The Poem *Prince Bitch* was contributed by the poet Anthony R. Randle of Chicago, Illinois

Cover design by Gregory McNeal

I0653523

Copyright ©2009 by R. Bryant Smith
All Rights Reserved

First Edition: Effusses Enterprise, August 2003
ISBN #:0-9758787-0-0-0
Second Edition: Effusses Enterprise, September 2009
ISBN#: 978-0-578-03580-2

Let It Be Real

A Novel By R. Bryant Smith

Effusses Enterprise

Austin, Texas

Acknowledgements

Just in case the Lord shall come before we get together again,
I'll meet you! Yes, I'll meet you on the other shore!

A special thank you to the following people who continuously go the extra mile in making certain that I continue to write and I continue to be me.

All praises to God for His awesome wonder!

A special "Thanks" with endearing appreciation is extended to my parents: Ms Barbara Ellen Chaney, Mr. Roy B. Smith, Jr. and Mrs. Marilynn P. Smith. Truly you are the world's greatest parents.

I send "shout outs" to: Ms. CasSandra D.S. Anderson, Ms. Crystal D. Hickerson, and Ms. LeKeesha Weathers for being the world's greatest sisters.

I send "shout outs" to: Mr. Ryan B. Smith, Mr. RaShad B. Smith, Mr. Russell B. Smith, and Mr. Clayton P. Smith for being the world's greatest brothers.

Also, I'd like to extend warm wishes to my brother RaShad and his new bride Nikka Sewell Smith. This is the match, Lil Brother.

A special "Thank You" is further extended to me dearest friends: Mr. DeAnthony J. Banks, Mr. Andrew Bradford, Mr. Marvin Hooper, Dr. & Atty. Carlos & Kerri Thomas, Prof. Bryan Keith Thomas, Dr. Victor Anderson, Rev. Harold K. Gause, Mrs. Patsy A. Coleman, Mrs. Patricia T. White, Ms. Stephanie Harris, Ms. Stephanie Watkins Pitts, Mr. Bryant Tyus, and Mr. Maurice Jones for being the best friends anyone could ever ask for.

How wonderful it is to have a collection of other artists who encourage you. I extend warm "thanks" to Rev. J. Ricc Rollins, Mr. Lorenzo Robertson, Mr. Darios Omar Williams, Mr. Greg McNeal, Mr. Timothy Hampton, and Mr. James Earl Hardy who are also friends who constantly encourage me along this journey of writ.

Last, a special "Thank You" is extended to other friends that I have met along the way.

May His peace be with you until we meet again!

Dedication

In Memory of
Mrs. Gertrude Hickerson Chaney
"Momma Gert"
March 15, 1909 – August 15, 1996

On all of the pages of my life, Granny, you have been there! I thank and praise God for the years He allowed you to be in my life! You have been the inspiring force for many of my accomplishments in life. I thank you for your watchful spirit that forever surrounds my well being and me. I shall meet you in Heaven one day... until then, thank you and I love you!

In Tribute to

Mrs. Barbara Ellen Chaney
Mr. Roy Bedford Smith, Junior
Mrs. Marilynn Perry Smith

My three amigos: My mother, my father, and my step-mother. All three are unique yet are a wealth of love, knowledge, compassion, and understanding. Thank you all for the roles that you play in my life and always know that I love you.

Let It Be Real

A novel by R. Bryant Smith

Prologue

No one in the small Northwest Tennessee city of Fairhaven could believe that such tragedy of rape apparent rape and murder could enter its borders, yet it had! The chilly hand of Death had slowly choked the life from the fragile body of Frederick Perry one Saturday evening. His bed had become his "cooning board" and his sheets became his "winding sheets" as he was ironically discovered lying peacefully in bed with his eyes open and his mouth slightly ajar as if his last words had been: *"Why?"*

Now, many within the area had come to pay last respects to an icon of the community. Frederick was to Fairhaven as any pillar was to any society.

A young and vivaciously attractive small framed man; it was evident that Frederick had been overpowered in his tiny apartment that yielded his tragic death. He was by all means the town "fag," "sissy," or "punk." He had accepted his identity and embraced himself in comfort, solace, and nurturing when no one else would. Thus, he was considered "weird," "strange," or "different" by the people from his hometown and neighboring communities. Frederick met no strangers as he befriended everyone that he met. This further complicated his murder. His entourage of friends was left prostrate with grief on discovering his remains the evening he was scheduled to perform in his first pageant as a drag queen.

As the hand of time closes a chapter on one episode, it opens a new chapter on yet another. Saddened by the death of their friend, Melvin, Bradley, Desmond, Douglas, Xavier, and Howard listened to Reverend William Barnes deliver a very profound eulogy. None of them could believe that death would enter their entourage of friends yet Death had forged its cold hand upon Frederick which forced them to rely upon friendship as grief encompassed the group.

Melvin sat stoically and began to tune everything and everyone out as he began to reflect upon his own existence. To him, this day was unimaginable. He was not yet thirty and was burying a person who had, through time, become a friend. He thought about how both he and Frederick were small, petite, caramel colored men who had chosen two very different paths. Melvin never found a great need to wave a rainbow flag or run down the street proclaiming his sexual orientation to the world. Frederick, on the other hand, did not mind letting you know exactly where he stood. He was indeed gay. Both men were industrious. Although Frederick had worked for a local nursing home as a Certified Nurse's Assistant, he had lived a full life without pretense. His life was totally different from Melvin's. Melvin felt that he himself had finally "arrived" as he had now taken his position among the elite members of Fairhaven's African American Society. Melvin had, by southern standards, done the admirable thing. He graduated college and shared his wisdom and knowledge in the city of his birth thus making Fairhaven a more modern element of social well being. Although he was a homosexual man living within the rural south, he, unlike Frederick, did not mention his sexuality to anyone except his close circle of friends. Often, this annoyed Frederick. Frederick felt that Melvin lived a lie and thus had bound himself in a prison built by no one other than himself.

Bradley, who had been deemed the group whore, had tone down considerably after a series of events and adventures in Atlanta, Georgia and abroad. Still a towering, well defined, muscular young man, wisdom gained through years of experience could be seen clearly in his eyes. He was indeed a worldly man, which taught him to be practical. Practicality, however, he could not conceptualize the justification of Frederick's murder. Bradley had tolerated Frederick and Frederick's shenanigans on the strength of association and friendship. Bradley was handsome and had the looks of an average straight African American man. He prided the fact that those who pursued him were actually in pursuit of their own personality. Hence, Frederick often posed himself as an offense to the methods in which Bradley could and did acquire his "trade." However, Bradley repeatedly ignored the fact that he disliked Frederick's "beat out" face, arched eyebrows, filled and painted finger nails that had been manicured at the local manicurist, or his supposed unisex clothing that had actually been bought from a women's petite section from any women's clothing store.

Desmond and Douglas, the two college drop outs, were now successful business men in three West Tennessee cities. Douglas has begun to bald slightly in the top of his head as years of laborious work had finally begun to settle on him. Desmond, on the other hand, yo-yoed in size due to continual moments of depression brought on by the new order of world vanity. Desmond's body was not chiseled like Bradley's nor was he small framed like Melvin or Frederick. He was tall, big boned, full figured, and pudgy in all of the wrong places. The new American look required one to have muscles rippling off of more muscles. Desmond did not possess this. Although Douglas constantly declared his adoring love for Desmond, nothing could suppress Desmond's fear of not being accepted by society because of his weight and size. Everyone thanked God that Douglas was in Desmond's life during the tragedy of Frederick's death. Pound cakes, homemade pies, fried foods of all kinds, cooked vegetables dripping in pork juice would certainly send Desmond's newly discovered blood pressure sky high let alone tragic news. Yet, when Desmond went on an eating spree, only he could manage to stop himself from the rage. Desmond had always accepted Frederick for the unique individual that Frederick was. He never thought of Fredericka s being nothing more or less than another human being who was attempting to cope with life in any manner in which he could. Douglas understood Frederick's harsh life, hence, he could not judge it, ridicule it, or make fun of it. Although Douglas had chosen a completely different life than Frederick had chosen which led him to success, he never felt that Frederick was beneath him because of the path chosen.

Xavier, the high yellow, high cheek bone, wavy hair, Creole vixen from Baton Rouge had become a gospel recording artist. Xavier's music had gone double platinum twice within a period of three years after his graduation from college. He had begged Frederick on several occasions to leave Dyer County and at least tour with him in order to see more of the world than West Tennessee. Frederick declined because he had no love for airplanes or trains. Xavier refused to ride the *Greyhound* bus anywhere. Long gone were the days where he had to travel on any type of bus in order to get to a performance. He refused to revert back to that mode of transportation for anyone. Nevertheless, Xavier was always fond of Frederick because they both possessed unparallel skill in "cussing a mug out!" Often, when Xavier wanted true encouragement, he would call Frederick. Seldom could people understand Xavier's apprehensions in life but Frederick did. Frederick would always give Xavier a good "cussing" out and then end the conversation with *Now that I've given you your normal cussing out, I want you to know that I still love you, child!*

You have no reason to be upset! You have everything that any gay man could want. You have a career, a beautiful home, and most importantly... a wonderful man. It ain't often that a black gay man can get all of those things without a hell of a lot of sacrifice and problems to accompany them. You are human! Since you are human, honey, you will bear just as many burdens and problems as everybody else. So, welcome to the world of being human, honey. Now get the hell off my phone!"

Howard, the first love of Frederick, would not smile his gorgeous smile again for six months after the discovery of Frederick's corpse. A man normally full of laughter had been stripped of it in one moment. He had loved Frederick beyond their break-p and beyond death. Unfortunately, he was young and unwise. His youth would not allow him to be ready and willing to commit to a monogamous relationship until it was too late. Frederick had been everything that Howard liked in a man. Frederick was feminine, petite, and shapely. Those elements in a man always immensely turned Howard on. Howard loved sex and could not limit himself to one partner yet Frederick wanted monogamy. Because of Howard's lust for many men, when the time presented itself and he was finally ready to settle down to one individual, it was too late. This fact became his cross to bear such that he refused to ever date another man that even remotely reminded him of Frederick.

William, a tall, dark, slender man was indeed attractive. When he smiled it seemed as if sunshine spread across the land. After graduating Vanderbilt University's School of theology, he had become a very celebrated minister in Memphis, Tennessee, known for the dutiful work his congregation did within the community.

William first became pastor of a traditional African American Baptist church in Memphis, Tennessee. After years of battles with his congregation, the congregation bordered splitting. Unbroken, however, William continued with the vision that God had given him. Straying away from the Baptist doctrine, he resigned as pastor of the Baptist church and founded his own nondenominational congregation...The Universal Morning Star Nondenominational Church. It was a first of its kind in Memphis. A church that was all affirming. His new congregation began with less than thirty members but rapidly grew. Hence the congregation was forced to relocate thrice within four years until a decision to build a new edifice was made. The church bought and secured four acres of land. On this land a sanctuary was erected and could seat twelve thousand comfortably. The church was built in the center of all of the other buildings that were owned by it. An HIV/AIDS hospice that could house two hundred was erected on the northern corner of the site. A shelter that could house at least forty homeless families was erected on the southern corner of the site. An educational facility was erected on the western corner of the site and a concert hall was erected on the eastern corner of the site. The catch phrase of the church was: A morning star in the time of despair- a place to be free from earth's hurtful wear."

A totally non-traditional congregation, Morning Star welcomed recovering alcoholics, drug addicts, dope dealers, homosexuals, transgendered, and countless other people within society that society had deemed "misfits." The church, under William's leadership became internationally known for its work within the community. After buying the property and building cites, the church employed its own members to work within the infrastructure. The over-all mission of the church far exceeded William's original vision. He was elated when several of his associate ministers left Morning Star and established their own congregations in other cities using the same methods of the mother church. Hence, it was known throughout West Tennessee and abroad that The Universal Morning Star Nondenominational Church was the safe haven for anyone who hurt.

Melvin's mind continuously flooded with scenes throughout the course of the recent past. He thought about walking into Frederick's apartment on that dreadful evening. The memories choked the words that came from William's mouth out of his ears. The picture was too vivid.

They knocked on Frederick's apartment door.

No answer.

They beat on the door for five solid minutes.

No answer.

"Fuck this," Howard said as he turned the doorknob.

To his amazement, the door was not locked.

The three entered the apartment cautiously.

"Frederick," Melvin called out into the hollow apartment.

Still there was no answer.

Howard investigated the kitchen.

Bradley walked into the bedroom.

Melvin glanced around the room. He saw the dresses were hung neatly on hooks that had been recently installed on the walls. On top of the sofa were hatboxes that had been neatly stacked beside shoeboxes. Assortments of purses were piled high in a corner chair. Three caddies bearing make-up, brushes, and an assortment of facial products lay on the coffee table on the front living room sofa.

"He's dead," Bradley said. "Don't touch a thing. Call 911."

Melvin motioned to call the number when Bradley abruptly hung the telephone up.

"What the hell are you doing?" Melvin asked as his eyes began to water.

"We've got to get this shit out of here before the paramedics get here, Melvin," Bradley said as he eyed the room.

"Have you been smoking that shit, Bradley?" Melvin sobbed. "He needs help! What do you think, Howard?"

Howard could say nothing as he began to wail pathetically.

"Close the goddamned bedroom door, Howard," Bradley instructed as he shoved Howard onto the sofa causing one of the boxes of shoes to fall to the floor. Bradley closed the bedroom door without looking inside at Frederick.

"We have to call the police, Bradley," Melvin whined.

"We are going to call the police after we get this shit out of here, Melvin," Bradley said as he grabbed Melvin firmly by the shoulders and looked into Melvin's eyes. "I know he was murdered and it was in a terrible way at that but Frederick deserves a police investigation. If the paramedics and police comes into this place with all of these damned gowns and shit all over the place they will say that it is just another faggot who got himself into trouble."

Melvin remained silent. Howard held his head in his hands as his weeping began to slowly subside.

"I know Frederick was out and all but we have to think about our place in this small assed town," Bradley continued. "You work at a bank, for goodness sake, Melvin! Do you think that once the scandal of it all hits the town then Frederick will get some glorious funeral? Hell, no! Everyone will say that he got just what he deserves and I am not standing for it! Get those damned dresses and put them in the car this instant!"

"But..." Melvin attempted.

"But my ass," Bradley grumbled. "Get the shit and hurry up! It's still dark enough where no one can see our coming and going. Thank God he chose an apartment that did not have easy visible access or we would be fucked! Howard, get the hell up and get those shoes and anything that has to do with the pageant and go and put it in the car. When we finish, you drive Melvin's car to his house and put it in the garage. Get my car, drive it back over here and pick us up when all of this is over."

An hour later, when everything had been removed including Frederick's extensive video pornography collection, pornographic magazines, and multiple dildos, Melvin was allowed to telephone 911. Howard had driven Melvin's car back home and had come back in Bradley's car as instructed.

Twenty minutes after the telephone call to 911, the police and paramedics arrived. Melvin noticed the look on the paramedics faces after they pronounced Frederick dead. Melvin almost snapped when he realized the look was not a look of sorrow or sympathy but instead it was a look of utter disgust for the life and life style of the individual. The police were no less sympathetic. Melvin, Howard, and Bradley were all escorted to the police station for questioning. They were, however, released immediately.

William took the podium and waited for the congregation to settle down after Xavier had finished singing his rendition of *Move On Up A Little Higher*.

He then began his eulogy:

This is a very hard task, which is before me today. Nevertheless, I will begin by saying that Frederick is in the hands of a just God. I'm so glad that we don't have a heaven or a hell to put him in. There is but one thing that I am totally aware of and most certain of: **The most important thing in this life is that we have a personal relationship with our Maker.**

The Apostle Paul tells us in his Second Letter to the Corinthians:

"We have this treasure in earthen vessels, that the Excellency of the power may be of God, and not of us. We are troubled on every side, yet not distressed; We are perplexed, but not in despair; Persecuted, but not forsaken; Cast down, but not destroyed; Always bearing about in the body the dying of the Lord Jesus, that the life of Jesus might be made manifest in our body."

So many times in the hustle and bustle of daily life, we forget to take the time to stop and enjoy the beauty of the dawning of a new day or the majesty of a day's closing. We seldom make time to simply smell the aroma of the rose. We are too busy to pause and notice how majestic the hand of God is. When we consider an artist, how creative he or she may be, the artist's best work pales in comparison to the art found within the multiple shades of color that God sprinkles across the earth.

When I think of how this same God who created the universe created such a beautiful being as a human, my spirit is touched by the ugliness that surrounds today's occasion. I had the opportunity to meet Frederick on several occasions. I am reminded of his ability to remember just how fragile life is. Because of this, he enjoyed every moment of life. Frederick was not afraid to laugh at himself with others. Frederick was not afraid to cry with you and for you. Frederick was definitely not afraid to "cuss you out" either when he felt that you had stepped on his toes or he felt that you needed a good "cussin."

"Amen!" a young woman yelled which caused the congregation to laugh slightly.

Frederick had a practical religion. By that I mean that he didn't mind going out of his way to get to church! He would simply tell you: "I know that my Redeemer lives and I ain't with all of that other stuff that you are talking about." Frederick didn't mind letting you know that he had something that surpassed all of our understanding. He had a treasure that people couldn't give him which allowed him to stare in the face of public ridicule and declare… "I am what I am!"

"Say that, preacher," Xavier said as he sat stoically on the front pew beside Melvin. Xavier crossed his long legs which only made his foot stick farther out into the aisle. Bradley, who sat on the opposite side of Melvin, looked at Xavier from the corner of his eye. *"He's such a queen,"* Bradley thought as he readjusted himself in his pew.

In knowing God, Frederick could stand and declare:

You may try to press me down on every side, but you cannot crush my spirit!"

"Yes," an elderly woman shouted.

Often I have overheard conversations where Frederick would talk about how perplexed he was about a situation. I can praise God that Frederick would not despair over it.

"Have mercy, Lawd," one of the mothers who sat in the traditional Mother Board/Amen Corner" moaned. Tears began to roll down Bradley's face as he attempted to blot out the recent memory of Frederick lying in his bed… dead. At noticing the tears flow steadily from Bradley's eyes, Desmond began to make a snorkeling, growling, snorting sound.

"Blahka mahka crucka mahka blahka," Desmond sounded off. Bradley gazed in astonishment at the noise on his immediate left. Douglas patted Desmond's shoulder gently. Desmond coughed and then became silent.

It is a strange thing how family can abandon you,

"My, Lawd," a robust lady who sat in the Amen Corner next to Etta, Melvin's mother, grunted.

Friends can abandon you,

"Yes they will," declared one of Frederick's co-workers. Bradley stiffened in his seat. He thought about seeing Frederick lying in the bed on the night of the pageant.

Your job can abandon you

"It sho' can, preacher," a deep voice from the left of the sanctuary hurled the words into the air.

But when you know that God will not abandon you, who can come against you?

"Say that, preacher," Douglas commented as he thought about the many times that he secretly loaned Frederick money to pay rent, electricity bills, or telephone bills prior to Frederick obtaining employment at the nursing home.

Even in this terrible tragedy, some may feel that Frederick was struck down but I have come to tell you today that in all that was done to Frederick, he still wasn't destroyed.

"Amen," the congregation shouted. "Thank you, Jesus! Hallelujah!"

The Apostle Paul tells us in his first letter to the Corinthians in the fourth chapter that if this earthly house of this tabernacle were dissolved, we have a building of God, a house not made with hands, eternal in the heavens. It's good to know that Frederick is in the hands of a just God!

"Yes it is," someone yelled.

It's comforting to know that Frederick doesn't have to be troubled anymore!

"No, sir, preacher, sho' don't!" someone yelled. Tears streamed down Xavier's face. He thought about the many hours that he and Frederick spent on the telephone. He thought about the many warnings that he gave Frederick about the company in which Frederick kept. Xavier despised the folk who had begun to frequent Frederick's apartment. In Xavier's opinion, they didn't have a pot to piss in or a window to through it out of but always managed to hang around Frederick in order to beg, or borrow, or constantly be looking for some "spare change."

He doesn't have to be perplexed anymore.

"Not at all, preacher," another person shouted.

He doesn't have to be persecuted anymore.

"No mo'," a dark, lanky woman who sat in the balcony yelled.

He certainly can't be cast down anymore!

"Never!" one of the Fraternity members roared from within his pew located in the middle aisle of the sanctuary.

The blessed assurance is that He found the other building of God. The building that is not made by man's hands!

"Thank You, God!" a gruff voiced woman groaned.

If Frederick were here today, he would tell you: Don't lose your heart and get caught up in the midst of sorrow. If you did wrong towards him, time will not afford you the opportunity to apologize now. If you didn't get the opportunity to tell him that you loved him, time has passed you by. Frederick would agree with the apostle Paul and tell you that our outward bodies are all slowly wasting away but our inward spirit is renewed day by day if we have a hope in Christ! Frederick's light and momentary troubles only achieved him an eternal glory that far outweighs all of the struggles that he had to endure while on this side of Jordan.

"You preachin', preacher," another woman in the amen corner yelled.

William paused. He looked into the congregation and then he looked into himself. He swallowed.

The question before us all, however, is to answer this:

Who kiiiiiiiiiiiiiiiiiiiiiiiiiiiiilllled Frederick?

A hush fell over the sanctuary. The words seemed to loom in the air.

What was the reason to kill him?

The congregation remained quiet in astonishment.

Why?…

"Why?" Desmond screamed as he sobbed in tears. Douglas firmly gripped his shoulders.

"Lawd, why he ask that question? Here this one goes," Bradley thought as he stiffened in his seat and sat straight up. Melvin's body was present but his mind was aloof. Melvin merely stared straight ahead. Xavier began to fan emphatically.

Why?…………..

"Have mercy, God, Why?" a mother in the Amen Corner screamed in a loud yet piercing wail.

Why?…….

"Why?" the congregation moaned sadly in response to William.

Why take this life of this lodge member?

"Why?" the congregation moaned.

Why take this life of this man who served dutifully on the usher board?

"Why?" a member of the usher board screamed as another usher attempted to console the sobbing woman.

Remember entering Mt. Carmel and being greeted by Frederick? Remember the wide grin? Remember the black suit?

"Oh yes," a choir member snorted. Xavier grunted slightly. Everyone knew that Frederick was not coming to church "any type of way." Frederick respected the old customs of "dressing up" for church. Therefore, every year, he always bought a new black suit to usher in as part of his church decorum.

Remember the white gloves?

"Yes, yes, yes!"

Remember that one arm folded behind him?

"Um hum!"

Remember that polished brass usher badge?

"Yes, sir" Bradley chuckled as he thought about how neither he nor anyone could forget Frederick's gleaming usher's badge. Unlike everyone else, Frederick insisted on wearing an usher badge that had a five point star on it as if he were an officer of the law. He would not mind flashing it at you to give special emphasis to the position that he held. When in discussion on what a person did in his respective church, Frederick didn't mind telling you that he was the proud vice-president of "Ursher Board Number 1." *"Yes,"* Bradley thought fondly. *"I remember!"*

Remember how Frederick would greet you every Sunday morning with a "Good morning, saint, how you doin'?"

"Yes," the congregation responded endearingly.

Remember how Frederick could remember your name, your family, and everything about you whenever you came to Mt. Carmel?

"Uh hum"

Remember how Frederick could remember your aunt's cousin's sister's child who was sick?

"Yeah," a woman yelled out in the congregation as individual members nodded and smiled. "I remember dat!"

You know, Frederick didn't say much, but you knew you were welcome at Mt. Carmel.

"Yes, you was," a member of the choir cried out.

He was ours!

"Yes, he was ours," a sobbing usher wailed as she wiped tears from her eyes.

That man, that person, that usher, who greeted us, you know the one we all adored...

"Yeah," the congregation responded.

The one who made us feel at home at Mt. Carmel...

"Um hum," the congregation moaned.

That man is also the person whom many of us met with suspicion...

"Umph," an elderly woman grunted as the congregation sat silently in confusion.

Lodge members, remember the silence? Remember accepting dues and donations for your civic causes? Frederick was ours! The same person who we accepted money from who seldom rocked the boat... He was ours!

"Umph," one of the fraternity members grunted.

Yet, the question that stands before us today is now how we only want to remember Frederick but... who killed Frederick?

"My Lawd," one of the mother's from the Amen corner groaned as a hush fell once again on the congregation. William's question seemed to float slowly across the sanctuary yet swiftly fill the ears of the wading congregation.

Was it our gossip?

"Have mercy, Jesus!"

Was it our back biting?

"Lawd have mercy, was it?"

Was it our peculiar looks when he wanted to work with our youth?

"Have mercy!"

Was it us?

"Was it?" a robust woman guffawed from the rear of the sanctuary. Bradley stared straight ahead as his lips began to skew up in the corner of his mouth. He wanted desperately to scream out: **"Hell naw, it wasn't me! It was cheaper to lend this bitch money rather than to bury her!"**

*I've come to tell you today that we **all** killed Frederick!*

The congregation stood still. Desmond's eyes bulged outward as his mouth dropped open. Xavier began his litany of fanning himself in an attempt to calm his nerves. Melvin stared straight ahead avoiding aloof of the question or the reaction of the congregation. Bradley grunted. Bradley thought: *"I didn't kill that crazy bitch!"*

We killed Frederick through gossip and snide remarks.

"My Lawd," one of the mothers in the Amen corner groaned.

We killed Frederick by passing him on the street as we drove by in our fancy cars and he walked.

We killed Frederick by omitting his name from our social registers.

You know, we live in a society where we have to slave at a job eighty hours per week, own a huge house with a huge mortgage, and own several vehicles before we can consider ourselves important.

"Oh yes," several voices range out in unison from various sides of the congregation. Bradley grunted again. Xavier looked around Melvin in a chastising manner at Bradley. Bradley rolled his eyes at Xavier. Desmond cleared his throat. Bradley looked squarely at him. Desmond's lip twitched. Bradley turned his head away when he noted the tears welling in Desmond's eyes.

We live in a world where we judge a person's worth be their wealth.

"You preachin' now," an old deacon groaned.

Frederick didn't fit into this box of grandeur. No, he was no school teacher. He was no banker. He was no lawyer. He was no judge. He was no doctor.

Desmond wailed out loudly and began to cry and snorkel loudly and emphatically.

Frederick was his own man.

"Yes, he was."

Frederick worked!

"Sho' did, preacha," an elderly woman yelled from the balcony.

Again, I say, Frederick worked!

"Say that now,"

Frederick had a job!

"Um hum!"

Frederick worked diligently at the nursing home!

"Yes, he did," one of Frederick's co-workers exclaimed.

Frederick supported himself!

"All right now," Xavier yelled and then began to fan himself.

A black man who supported himself...

"Come on, now" someone yelled as the organ began to agree with the words of William in musical response known as "preacher chords."

He served his community silently.

Douglas clapped his hands.

He served his church to the best of his ability.

"Yes he did," the congregation shouted.

He was bold enough to keep on pressing toward the mark of higher calling!

"Preach, preacher!" someone yelled from the choir loft.

He realized that if this earthly house is destroyed, that's all right, because there is another building he can obtain. Another building not made by man's hands. Another building that is eternal!

"All right now, preacher," a lady who sat by Melvin's mother yelled.

Ain't that good news?

"Yes," the congregation shouted.

"I said, ain't that good news?"

"Yes," Douglas shouted as several ministers who sat in the pulpit rode from their seats in affirmation of the question posed by William.

"Ain't that good news, saints?"

"Yes, sir, good news!"

Frederick can now take up the words of Lizzie DeArmond and Homer Rodeheaver and exclaim with joy... When comes to the weary a blessed release, when upward we pass to His kingdom of peace, when free from the woes that on earth we must bear, we'll say Good night here but Good morning up there!

"Thank you, God," a woman screamed out.

Frederick can now say "Good morning" up there where Christ is the Light!

Bradley squeezed Melvin's hand as tears began to stream down his face.

He can say "Good Morning" up there where there is no longer this thing called night!

"Yes, sir," the congregation shouted as the music began to respond to William who, at this point, had taken the microphone from its receiver and began to walk down into the aisle and in front of the casket. He looked into the audience and proceeded to preach in his "Baptist" hum.

Frederick stepped from this earth to God's heaven so fair.

"Yeah," the congregation thundered as Desmond began to wail and snorkel louder. William walked directly in front of the casket and waved his hand as if in a salute.

And said, "Good night," down here...

"Good night," the congregation shouted.

But we can praise God that Frederick said "Good Morning" up there...

"Thank you!" a woman yelled over the thunderous shouts of the congregation.

I'm leaving you now, Fairhaven, with this assurance...

Frederick lived a life.

"Well, well, well."

Troubled but not distressed!

"Come on with it, preacher," Douglas roared and rose to his feet.

Perplexed but not in despair!

"Yes," the congregation shouted.

Cast down, ho, but not destroyed.

It's mighty good news, saints!

"Mighty good!"

It's mighty good news to know that you have another building

"Yes," Xavier shouted as he stood up and waved his handkerchief in the air.

Another building not made with earthly hands....

A building prepared by a magnificent God....

A God who is all seeing and all knowing....

A God that prepared a building rent free...

"Preach, Barnes," Bradley found himself yelling as he too also stood up from his seat.

Frederick has worked on his building!

"Yes, yes, yes!"

He paid for it through laboring down here!

"Yes!"

Ain't that good news?

"Good news!"

No more weeping!

"No more!"

And no more wailing!

No more!

Everyday

"Every day!" Desmond gurgled as he screamed, waved his arms in the air, folded them, waved them in the air again, folded them again, and then began a loud gurgling wail.

Every day is gonna be "Howdy! Howdy!"

"Thank you," someone in the balcony screamed and began to run around the balcony.

Never, never, never good bye!

"Never!"

That's mighty good news!

"Mighty good news," the congregation responded as William walked back to the pulpit, placed the microphone in its receiver, and continued his eulogy.

Frederick was ours!

"Yes, he was," Etta said.

And we were his!

"Yes," Howard cried as he emphatically played on the organ.

He had to say "Good Night" to us for a little while....

"Good night," the congregation yelled. Bradley sat back down in his seat as a sobbing sensation hit him.

But it's mighty good news to know...

"Yeah," one of the ministers on the roster yelled.

It's might good news to know that Frederick said "Good Morning" to God!

"Thank You, Jesus," a woman screamed - Her voice lifting over the congregation like a shrilling shriek rather than a praise.

That's mighty good news, children!

"Good news," the congregation shouted.

Mighty good news!

"Yes," the crowd shouted as William took his seat and the musicians began to churn out *Hold On, Help Is On The Way* for the choir to sing. The choir sang softly as the morticians prepared for the final stage of the funeral... the viewing of the remains.

When the congregation began to view the murdered body of Frederick, the choir began to sing *It's An Uphill Journey To Glory.* Various people screamed "Good night" as they viewed the remains for the last time.

Desmond wailed like a tortured animal throughout the viewing. He constantly screamed out Frederick's name as if through screaming, the dead would arise. When it was his turn to view the remains, Douglas and several other men had to hold him to keep him from climbing into the casket. After he knocked down several floral sprays and potted plants, the group of men finally managed to calm him enough to sit him down. Various fraternity members ushered Bradley out after he viewed Frederick's body. He could not control his emotions or tears. It seemed as if a flood gate had opened in his face. Although he did not create such a public display of emotion as Desmond had, The Rev had directed several fraternity members to be on standby to usher people out of the sanctuary. Melvin fainted upon viewing the body and was taken into the pastor's study by members of the fraternity.

As the lid on casket was slowly being closed for the last time, the choir sang *I'm Working On My Building*. Frederick's casket was rolled out of Mt. Carmel Baptist Church with the choir singing a new rendition of *When All God's Children Get Together*. A host of friends joined in the procession and followed the casket, flowers, and pall bearers to the cemetery where Frederick would indeed rest from labor eternally in the Mt. Carmel Baptist Church Cemetery. He was in earthed beside his grandmother, Jewel Temples.

Chapter One

Someone To Care

Melvin met his friends coming from the burial sight of their beloved Frederick. As he looked at Bradley, Desmond, Douglas, Xavier, and even The Rev, it was hard to imagine that ten years had swiftly passed them all by. They were no longer the teenagers and young adults from yesterday. It seemed as if their youth would not stand still long enough for them to enjoy it more each second. Melvin realized now just how important life was. He also realized just how important it was to be included in a group of men who understood him.

It seemed that a dark and eerie cloud hung over Fairhaven and Dyer County. A murderer was on the loose and yet life must go on. Melvin could not fathom this new life in which he now led. It seemed as if he had transformed over night when just what appeared to be weeks ago, he was only beginning the journey.

"I'm starving," Bradley said in a very bass yet gruff voice. Frederick's death had hurt him deeply. After all, he was the last person to literally see Frederick alive. He had not eaten in days nor had he slept. Melvin insisted that he stay at his home rather than alone until at least after the funeral.

"If you are hungry, then you need to eat," Xavier said. "You look rugged, child."

"Alright frivolous," Desmond laughed. "Pastor Barnes just preached about vanity."

"I told you all that Xavier doesn't listen to William when he preaches," Douglas laughed. "He is still sitting there goo goo eyed."

"If we weren't on church grown I'd tell you something, Douglas," Xavier laughed as he grabbed Bradley's left arm and began to lead him into the dining hall of Mt. Carmel.

The group entered the cafeteria of the church that seemed bustling with activity. The aroma of fried chicken, greens, macaroni and cheese, spaghetti, lima beans, pinto beans, corn bread, homemade rolls, and an assortment of casseroles greeted you before you could enter. If Bradley didn't have an appetite, Melvin certainly did.

"Child, don't knock me over," Xavier said as he looked up at Melvin who had inadvertently began to push his way toward the long tables that held a variety of food on it.

"Ya'll are walking too slow," Melvin laughed as he forged his way to a closer spot in the front of the line.

"Now, Melvin, you see all of these people in front of you," a reprimanding voice said.

Melvin looked up at The Rev and began to laugh.

"I'm hungry and these people are taking too long to get something to eat," Melvin laughed. "But thank you for letting me get in front of you."

The Rev laughed as he allowed Melvin to break in front of him.

Melvin finally managed to fix himself a plate of food from the buffet style tables that were set for the awaiting crowd. He found a vacant seat on the far side of the room and sat down and began to eat.

"Some folk could wait on everybody else," Bradley said as he sat down next to Melvin.

"Well, where do we go from here?" Desmond asked as he sat down at the table followed by Douglas and Xavier.

"We eat, honey," Melvin said as he continued his litany.

"I hope you gain ten of the twelve pounds that I'm getting ready to gain just for eating a few bites of this food," Desmond laughed.

"Are you back on that weight tip, child?" Xavier asked as he looked up from the side of his face at Desmond in disbelief.

"Yes, I'm on a weight tip," Desmond said. "It is easy for you all to say something because you will not gain a pound from eating anything that you want but I can just look at food and I might as well go on to the store and buy a new pair of pants a new size larger. I'd give anything to have my waistline from high school again."

"I don't here Douglas complaining?" Bradley commented as he slowly nibbled his food.

"I've already told Desmond that he can get as big as a house and I ain't going nowhere," Douglas said as he looked affectionately at

Desmond. "If he gets as big as a house, we'll just have to buy a bigger house, that's all."

"I just can't stand ya'll!" a voice from behind the group said.

The group turned around to see who had said this. Melvin continued to eat. Desmond prayed secretly that there would not be a confrontation on this day.

"Who you talking to?" Xavier asked preparing for battle before he could turn around to place a face with the voice in which he recognized.

"I'm talkin to all of you all," the short, bald man who was impeccably dressed said with such a zest and zeal until everyone at the table stopped eating.

"Hardaway?" Xavier said as he rose from his seat and hugged this new face to the group.

"Um, Huh, child, just listen at you all, so concerned with negativeness and how you look and what I see before me is a table full of strong, handsome, successful black men. Stop all of that talk, child and be blessed."

At this point, Melvin stopped eating to actually listen to what this man was saying.

In lieu of the tragedy that had occurred, this guys was telling the truth. So often this same group in whom he had become close to seemed to love to wallow in self-pity when in fact the gentlemen's words were correct. There was a table of very diverse but very attractive African-American young men.

Xavier hugged the man's neck and presented him to the gentlemen who sat at the table.

"Everybody this is Hardaway, my friend from Memphis," Xavier said with glee. "We used to sing together out on the road in days gone by for me now but he still is on the battlefield."

"Child, with you singing *Move On Up A Little Higher* in the manner in which you did today I know I can rest my weary bones and sit a spell."

"Do join us?" Bradley said as he pointed to a vacant seat at the table.

"Well, how have you been doing, Hardaway," Xavier began before Hardaway could sit down. "I haven't seen you since our first show together years ago."

"Child, I am yet holding on, blessed and highly favored but I'm on a mission now."

"At this point, I believe we are all on a new mission to at least find the murderer of our friend," Melvin said causing a great hush to travel across the entire cafeteria.

Bradley stopped eating.

Desmond braced himself for impact of what response anyone could give at this moment.

"Well," The Rev said as he took a seat at the table. "It looks like we will just have to bide our time and be careful."

"I'm still just in shock that such a terrible tragedy could occur in this little place," Hardaway said. "When I heard the news, I knew I had to be here because I remember how sad Frederick was at times and now this."

"You knew Frederick?" Bradley asked in amazement. He was not amazed that Frederick could be known but he was amazed that Frederick knew many celebrities within the social arena of the day. All of who seemed to have come from out of the wood works for his wake and funeral.

"Child, who didn't know Frederick," Hardaway laughed. "On the few times that I ever went out to the Apartment Club, I could always count on seeing him there."

"I heard they were closing it?" Bradley commented wryly.

"Honey, it's closed."

"That's an end of an era," The Rev commented with a slight laugh.

"It sure is," Melvin said. "Lord, I really had some good times up in there in my life time."

"Ain't that where you first fell in love, honey?" Xavier chuckled.

"Don't go there," Douglas snickered. "You fell in love the same night, if I can recall correctly."

Everyone at the table laughed but only Bradley, Douglas, Desmond, Melvin, and Xavier knew why they laughed. Their minds drifted back to the night when Xavier left them to meet William and they all rode to Memphis with Douglas.

Tears began to swell in Melvin's eyes as he began to think about the night. He could not forget how Frederick had "read" him for not accepting him as he was.

"Child," Hardaway said as he began to rise from his seat. "Don't you start crying now because I will go forth if you do."

"Where you going?" Xavier asked Hardaway.

"Well, I've got to get back to Memphis. I am actually on tour right now but had to fly in to come to the funeral out of respect of Frederick."

"Well, it was truly a pleasure meeting you," Melvin said.

"Why thank you and I hope to keep in contact in the future with you all," Hardaway said. "Just be strong and keep the Lord first in
your life. We'll make it through this too!"

Xavier walked Hardaway to his brand new *Cadillac Coupe Deville*. Hardaway placed a wide Panama straw hat on his head as he exited the cafeteria and strolled out arm in arm with Xavier.

"Now how are things going with you, child?" Hardaway asked Xavier as they reached the *Cadillac*.

"I'm living, baby, and that's good enough for me," Xavier replied. "I truly thank you for being here for us and if I had known that you were going to fly in I would have made certain that they put you on the program to sing a solo."

"Honey, you all did just fine. I enjoyed sitting in my respected corner and listening for once."

"I love you, First Lady Hardaway," Xavier said as he hugged Hardaway again.

"I love you too First Lady Barnes," Hardaway said as a tear trickled down his cheek.

"You are so encouraging and yet so misunderstood," Xavier laughed.

"Xavier, if these folk don't catch on to the vision in time, it will be too late. We have got to get the message spread that God is a God big enough to love everybody. I'm tired of coming to funerals of friends and acquaintances for needless things."

"I know this and you know this but the children here in the rural communities don't have a clue, child," Xavier said as he finally released Hardaway from his grasp.

"Well, the mission begins with us and if we don't spread the Word who will," Hardaway said as he opened his car door and stepped inside with such grace and eloquence, one truly would know that to enter into his presence one was in the presence of royalty. "Oh, yes, William preached a wonderful message. Please give him my regards and tell him that I wished that we could have seen one another on this trip but when I get back in town we can all do lunch or something."

"Oh, I'll tell him," Xavier laughed. "He is going to be hot as a wet hen if he finds out that you were here and he didn't know it. But, you are so true, we do need to come together and somehow unify our brothers."

"There are too many African-American gay men who are hurting out there," Hardaway said as he cranked his engine. "If I can help just one somebody, then this old life of mine won't be in vain."

"Yes, I know," Xavier smiled. "That's why we must continue the good work because if we don't care, who will?"

"There is someone who cares, child," Hardaway said. "Be blessed and keep the Lord on your side."

He pulled off as Xavier waved him goodbye.

Chapter Two

Summer Time 1998

Another year had passed by and the murderer of Frederick had not been found. Life in Fairhaven had gone back to normal. Melvin had recently been promoted to branch manager of the new bank that had been recently opened in Newbern, Tennessee. Fairhaven's one bank, The First Bank of Fairhaven, had finally moved up in the world. Melvin was elated to receive the promotion and welcomed being away from the main office. Bradley had begun a new quest. Because he had made quite a name for himself as a seamstress in Dyer County and he had new connections with new fashion designers in New York and Paris, he stepped out on faith and opened a clothing store in Dyersburg, Tennessee. Thus, *Frederick's Fashions* was opened in a very strategic location on Highway 51 By-pass.

The summer of 1998 was scorching hot in Dyer County. Most all of the farmers had become agitated with the weather because there had been no rain for two solid months. Crops had begun to burn up which caused a slight panic across the land. The prices for food had begun to increase due to the draught. Yet, bar-b-quest and picnics were a constant during the extreme heat.

"Thank the Lord for air conditioning!" Melvin said as he walked into Bradley's clothing store.

"Child, God is still good all of the time," Bradley laughed as he brushed the wig on one of his mannequins that would be used in a window display.

"I would say," Melvin said as he looked around the shop. He could not help but admire how chic the entire place looked. It actually looked rather out of place because it was fabulous. One would expect a store of this caliber to be found in New York City on Madison Avenue or in Time Square not on what was known as the stretch in Dyersburg. Nevertheless, Bradley had again pursued a dream and made it come true.

"Since we are the only people in here, I am dying to know something," Melvin began.

"What, child?" Bradley asked a bit irritated, as the hairstyle he was trying to achieve would not work on this mannequin for some reason.

"How did you afford this?"

"Now that's a crazy question."

"Considering who I am talking to, no it isn't but you can always tell me it is none of my business."

"Child, as many dresses and gowns and suits that I have made in the past three years, believe me, I've paid my dues to be here."

"Thank the Lord."

Bradley stopped piddling with the mannequin to stare at Melvin for a second. He could not believe the insinuation that was being brought forth by his best friend and yet it was once again... happening.

"If you are asking me if I fucked to get the building, no, I actually worked by the sweat of my brow and the labor of my hand to accomplish this."

"I didn't mean to make you angry or anything but you know you..."

"Yeah, I know me but for once I set a goal for myself and did not want to rely on any man to help me achieve it. Hell, look at my hands," Bradley said as he showed Melvin his hands.

Melvin stared in disbelief. Bradley was always a man who insisted on having perfectly manicured hands in the past and now they were callused from laborious work.

"What on earth?" Melvin asked in disbelief.

"It's called working for a living, child. I have worked on those temp jobs in the factory for so long now until I couldn't keep polished nails to save my life. After I would get off from one of those fly by night jobs then I would sew for the public. Everything from formals to suits. Now, I am going to rest for a little while."

"Well, I can't say that I cannot relate," Melvin confessed. "I've been working solid seventy hour weeks for well over seven months now. But, hey, I got promoted so I guess it was worth it in the end."

"Honey, those white folk don't give a damn about you and that's why I have my own shit," Bradley said wryly as he pushed the mannequin into the window.

"You have been so bitter since Frederick's death until it is unreal, child, what has happened to you?"

"Absolutely nothing has happened to me except that I woke up and realized that I will soon be thirty and I'm no longer that hot diva that I used to be."

Melvin was totally in awe now.

"Don't look at me like I'm crazy, hell, I have grown tired of the rat race as we know it."

"Correction, baby, as you know it, remember, I have never sold my body in exchange for sex."

"Oh, really?"

"Yes, really," Melvin said as he glanced the beauty of the store again.

"Child, I'm not even going to argue with you today about it, what brings you here anyway?"

"I just stopped by to see if you were coming to frat meeting tonight?"

Bradley walked to the counter, withdrew a checkbook, and began to write in it. Melvin watched him and said nothing.

"Here," Bradley said. "Take my dues, I'm not much into going cross town tonight and I really don't feel like putting up with OPT tonight either."

"Well I wasn't going either, to be honest; I was actually coming by to see if you wanted to go to the Casino tonight with me and this new guy I met today at the bank."

Bradley laughed.

"Honey, I don't want to be a third wheel or even a chaperon on a date tonight, you go ahead and have a good time."

Melvin laughed this time.

"You have it all wrong, Bradley," Melvin said. "We are just going over to eat and maybe enjoy a drink or something but this guy does not want me."

"Well, who the hell is it and why would I want to go?"

"Child, it is The Rev's partner."

Bradley's eyes became wide as saucers.

"The Rev?"

"The Rev!"

"How did you find out who The Rev was dating?"

"He came into the bank today to open a new account. Well, everybody was gone, so I went on and did the paper work for him. Child, I could not help but notice the big rock that was on his hand. So, I asked him, where he got it."

"And he told you The Rev gave it to him?"

"Not exactly."

"I'm curious now," Bradley said as he placed a CLOSED sign in the window and began to turn lights off in the building. "How did you discover it was The Rev's partner if he did not say that?"

"Honey, on the bank statement, it is a joint account. So I asked him if he knew The Rev and he said quite intimately."

"Hell, yeah, I'll go to the Casino with y'all." Bradley laughed. "I'm interested in seeing this person."

"He actually teaches at our alma mater."

"Dyersburg High?"

"No, child, Fairhaven Elementary."

"Get out of here!" Bradley laughed. "What grade and what subject does he teach?"

"He teaches seventh grade Mathematics. He replaced Miss Washington."

"Alright, then," Bradley laughed. "Child please tell me he has not met that crazy ass Billy Linen who teaches Special Education over there?"

"I'm sure he has because you know if there is a pass to be made, Billy will be the one to make it."

"Honey, I just want to see what this man looks like." Bradley confessed. "Hell, as long as you tried after The Rev, guhl, please. Give me five minutes to let this register run so I can make my night deposit."

"Cool, I'll call him and tell him to meet us at the Mall and we can all ride in one car."

"Cool, you do that and then take the dues to the Omega Complex and I'll meet you all at the Mall by seven-thirty."

"Bet," Melvin said as he walked out of the store and quickly walked to his car, stepped in, and turned the music up full blast.

At seven thirty on the nose, Bradley, Melvin, and the new mystery man pulled up onto the parking lot of the Dyersburg Mall. Bradley always laughed at the thought of Dyersburg calling this building a mall when it was basically a one level, indoor, shopping center. He had grown accustomed to being able to walk around a mall and actually become tired of walking because the mall was so large. Not so in the Dyersburg Mall. However, it was the only mall within a 50-mile radius of anything.

Bradley was shocked when the man stepped out of the car. He could see why The Rev chose this guy. Although, the man was short, he was fine as hell. He was an inch shorter than Melvin was. Like Melvin, however, he was petite in weight. His golden brown eyes could captivate any audience on any day. His hair was cut close to his head but a mound of waves gave it the added touch needed to genuinely call him perfect. He had a very confident attitude about himself, which made both Bradley and Melvin warm to him instantly.

"Good evening," he said as he stretched forth his tiny hand. "I'm Maxwell Quest."

"Hi, I'm Bradley Kelly." Bradley said in awe as he extended his hand only to receive a very firm handshake from this little man.

"It's nice to meet you," he said. "I've heard a lot of good things about you since I've relocated to this area."

"From The Rev?" Bradley asked.

"Yes," Maxwell laughed. "He actually thinks you guys are the greatest. He is at the Omega Complex right now hacking away at fraternity business and I just needed to get away from Dyer County for a minute to relax."

Bradley felt a bit guilty now because he knew that he could have attended the meeting but he just could not bring himself to listening to the same old tired business.

"He is dedicated," Melvin said to break the ensuing silence.

"Well, are you all ready to go?" Maxwell asked.

"Sure, who wants to drive?" Melvin asked.

"I don't mind, you all can ride with me," Maxwell said.

"Why not, I'm tired anyway. Just point me to the back seat and I'm fine," Bradley said.

To both Bradley and Melvin's surprise, Maxwell drove a 1999 Candy Apple Red *Ford Explorer* that appeared to be custom built. The size of the vehicle actually made Maxwell look even smaller yet this was his pride and joy.

Melvin rode in the front passenger side and Bradley stretched out in the back seat.

"Child, this is fresh," Bradley said as he entered the sports utility vehicle.

"Oh, it is a birthday present to me this year," Maxwell chuckled. "By me, of course."

"Honey, I understand," Bradley laughed as he thought about the various "gifts" he received down through the years from his previous partners which allowed him the opportunity to spend lavishly on himself.

Maxwell turned his CD player on and began to blast Celine Dion.

"Guhl," Bradley said as he jumped up. "Have you gone mad and lost your mind?"

Melvin laughed against his will.

"What's wrong?" Maxwell asked as he turned the music down to a more comfortable level.

"Shit, I ain't used to a lot of loud noise after I get off of work and you scared me," Bradley confessed which made Melvin laugh the more.

"Oh, I thought you didn't like Celine or something," Maxwell giggled.

"She ain't my favorite but I can live with her," Bradley laughed as he shuffled in the back seat again.

The drive to Caruthersville, Missouri was rather short with Maxwell behind the wheel. The normal twenty-minute drive took Maxwell eleven minutes from the Mall parking lot to the casino parking lot in Caruthersville.

"Shit, let me outta here," Bradley said when Maxwell pulled into the Casino parking lot.

"Do you like to gamble?" Maxwell inquired. Melvin turned to see if Bradley was faring well from the ride.

"Hell," Bradley said as he shook his head slightly, "Child, you don't have to drive fast to impress me. Damn!"

Both Maxwell and Melvin laughed at Bradley who staggered slightly for a moment.

"I've rode a many thangs in my life time but I don't do roller coaster rides in the car unless a fine ass man is in the car with me. Maxwell, you cannot drive me that fast on the return trip. I know this is your car and all but, hell, child, the speed limit is 70 and I know you had to be doing at least 90."

"OK," Maxwell laughed, "I can respect that. The Rev always fusses about my riving as well."

"Hell, honey, give him a heart attack in the bedroom not on the street behind the wheel of a car." Bradley said as he straightened his clothes and began to walk toward the casino opening.

"Child, you have to excuse, Bradley, he is getting cantankerous in his old age," Melvin laughed.

"Honey, The Rev is cantankerous enough, believe me, I know" Maxwell laughed. "I bought this Explorer against his will because he felt that I didn't need a sports utility vehicle because I drive so fast. He says I need something heavy and then picked out this old 1985 2 door Sedan and I was like, pahlease!"

"Well I don't give a damn," Bradley said. "I just want to live long enough to bury a husband or better yet be able to have a funeral where they can view my remains. Hell, as fast as you be driving my child it would be my luck to be decapitated."

Maxwell and Melvin laughed.

"Child, couldn't you see it now," Bradley continued. "They roll my body in and some bitch asks: "Well where is his head?" and this crazy bitch beside us would tell them: Oh, yall know how grand Bradley is, his head will be here in a few minutes in another coffin. No, honey! I don't need the publicity."

The three of them laughed as if they had known one another for years as they entered the casino.

"Are we going to gamble tonight or just eat?" Bradley asked.

"Well, I don't gamble so I'll just eat," Maxwell said.

"Honey, you know I don't gamble," Melvin said. "The food here is excellent, though and that's the only reason I come over here."

"Liar!" Bradley said as he looked out of the corner of his eye at Melvin with a "yeah right" look on his face.

"That is the only reason I come over here," Melvin insisted as the three entered the restaurant and found a comfortable seat.

"Child, you know you be looking for a husband when you come over here." Bradley interrupted.

"Well, it's better than finding him in church," Melvin said as he picked up a menu.

"Well, that's a whole nother story," Bradley laughed. "And Xavier would not appreciate the comment."

Melvin and Bradley laughed.

Maxwell looked at them.

"Child, Xavier is one of our mutual friends who met his partner in Melvin's church," Bradley laughed.

"Oh," Maxwell said.

"Well, I am dying to know," Bradley began.

"Child I hope you are not getting ready to ask him what I think you are." Melvin said in somewhat disbelief.

"Yes I am because I want to know," Bradley said point blankly.

"What do you want to know, Bradley?" Maxwell asked.

"How did you and The Rev meet and so on and so forth," Bradley said.

Melvin's heart felt a twinge of jealousy as he looked at the starry eyes of Maxwell who was prepared to deliver a full account. Melvin did not know if he wanted to hear this or not. After all, he had wanted The Rev for years and now this pretty, high yellow boy has him. *"Damn him!"* Melvin thought as he looked across the table at Maxwell. Somehow, Melvin could not bring himself to hate Maxwell.

"I met The Rev about two years ago when I was in College,"

Maxwell said as his eyes lit up with love as he began to think about meeting the man of his dreams.

"I was a hot 19 year old junior and he was a sexy 29 year older but I wanted that man and I was determined that I would get him and there was nothing he could do to keep me from getting him either." Maxwell said with honesty yet with a slightly wicked sense of victory.

Bradley's mouth twitched as he looked at the expression on Melvin's face. Bradley wanted to laugh so terribly but forced himself to be quiet to listen to the story while he saw Melvin squirm.

He was on campus conducting business that day when I first spotted him." Maxwell continued. "I was talking to a friend girl of mine and when I saw him he took my breath away. I told Deidra that he was going to be my next husband but I had to find a way to get introduced."

A sweat formed on Melvin's face as Maxwell continued the story. Bradley placed a napkin on his mouth to contain his laughter. As Maxwell continued, Bradley's body would jump a bit as he suppressed his laughter.

"Well, Deidra worked in the President's office and I worked in the Business Office and it so happened that he was the President's accountant."

"Wait a minute, what school did you go to, Maxwell?" Bradley asked as he began to think about the name of the president of the college as well as the name of Deidra.

"I went to Dreaded State Christian College For Christ-like Employees For Christians which is in Alamo, Tennessee."

"Is that the full name?" Bradley asked with a wondrously loud laugh.

"Yes. DSCCFCEFC are the initials," Maxwell proclaimed with a helliscious look on his face.

"Was the young lady named Deidra Kelly, by chance?" Bradley asked.

"Yes, do you know her?"

"She's my first cousin," Bradley laughed and finally released a bit while Melvin almost became white as a ghost. "Please forgive my interruption, go ahead."

"Anyway, come to find out, The Rev was dating one of the professors on campus but Deidra told me that things were terrible between the two of them. So, she arranged a meeting. After I found out that he would be on campus for at least a week, I made sure that every time that he saw me I was dressed to kill. So, one day, from out of nowhere, he was in the Business Office at my desk asking for information about something or another. And honey, I let my mojo do the rest."

"And what exactly is your mojo?" Melvin asked contritely.

"I looked that gorgeous black man square in the face and said: Hello, may I help you?"

Bradley could hold it no further. He laughed until his sides hurt.

Melvin was not amused in the least.

"Do continue, I'm curious?" Melvin said.

"Before I continue, let me ask a question," Maxwell said as he looked Melvin squarely in the face.

"Shoot," Melvin said.

"Am I offending you?"

"How do you think you have the power to offend me?"

"Child, don't answer that because Melvin does not want to know the truth," Bradley laughed.

"Huh?" Maxwell questioned.

"Maxwell, Melvin wanted to meet you because for years he has been in love with the man that you are in love with."

"I don't appreciate you revealing that, Bradley," Melvin growled. "Further, I am not in love with The Rev."

"Then why are you mad?" Bradley asked.

"Dogs get mad and I am not mad," Melvin said hotly.

"Maxwell, have you ever seen a mad dog before?" Bradley asked

"No, I'm from Memphis."

"Well, behold a mad dog before you," Bradley roared in laughter. "This bitch is mad as hell."

"I'm not mad I'm just coping," Melvin confessed.

"Why are you coping?" Maxwell asked genuinely.

"I just don't understand how life is truly a fucking bitch and then you get ice water thrown into your face."

"Child, calm down," Bradley said. "Maxwell didn't know that you wanted The Rev. He is not part of your issues."

"I'm just sick of being alone," Melvin confessed. "And it seems like any worthwhile man in this area is already taken."

"What makes The Rev so damned worthwhile?" Bradley asked.

"Because he is a perfect gentleman at all times," Melvin said as tears began to fill in his eyes. "I always wanted a man with that type of strength who knows how to give me the love that I deserve and want so fucking bad."

"Guhl, you do have issues," Bradley said as he looked at Melvin in pity. He passed Melvin a napkin. "Wipe your face."

"The Rev has his bad points, you know?" Maxwell attempted to comfort Melvin. "And I live with this so-called perfect gentleman, so I beg to differ on that one."

"Oh, you have done nothing wrong, Maxwell, and I am honestly happy for you and The Rev," Melvin stated as tears began to flow heavily down his face. "I just don't understand why I am not good enough for men to like me."

"What are you talking about?" Bradley asked. "Men like you, you just don't like the men who like you, that's all."

"I don't want a loser." Melvin said as he wiped the tears from his eyes.

"What is your definition of a loser?" Maxwell asked.

"Some uneducated Negro who doesn't want anything out of life except a cold beer. Someone who can sleep with you but cannot even kiss you. Someone who can love to fuck you but hate themselves so much until they will kill you like they killed my friend Frederick and I'm so goddamned tired of this shit until I could scream!"

"Well, Melvin, I really don't have a lot of words to make your hurt go away but the only thing that I know is this: Keep The Rev off of a pedestal. Yes, he's a good man but he has faults like any other man. You say you want a relationship with The Rev, well, baby, you had better be willing to take a back seat to his projects.":

"Are you willing to go through that again?" Bradley asked.

"What projects?" Melvin asked.

"The Rev is fine and all of that; I will not discredit myself by not recognizing those attributes, but when he involves himself in all of these clubs and work and whatever. And that fraternity, child I don't even get in the way of him and his beloved Omega Phi Theta. Believe me, there are a lot of times when I had to be secondary to him or listen to him bitch for hours on end and I'm the only bitch in my home!"

"You go, bitch!" Bradley laughed and hi-fived Maxwell.

"Melvin, you also have to realize that there are a lot of good men out there and there are a lot of bad ones out there. Sometimes the good ones are turned bad because of the bad ones. I was shocked to know that The Rev did not love his last partner but was merely there."

"So you managed to bring happiness into his life?" Melvin asked wryly.

"I think that is a question for you to ask The Rev because I'm not The Rev, I'm Maxwell," Maxwell stated firmly. "But I can say this, however, The Rev brought a hell of a lot of happiness into my life so I will not just let him go."

"Child, you better hold onto your man," Bradley chuckled.

"You are so young," Melvin interjected.

"Age is a number," Maxwell said. "I've always wanted one thing in life and that is to be married to a man and before the year 2000, I will be married to The Rev."

Both Melvin and Bradley gasp at this declaration. Two men married in the rural South was totally unheard of. The country was already at unrest because of gay marriages and now Maxwell dared speak this into existence.

"Has he committed to marrying you?" Melvin asked.

Maxwell lifted his hand to reveal a very ornate diamond ring.

"Jesus keep me near the cross," Bradley gaped.

"You go boy," Melvin laughed. "When is the date?"

"I'm working on it but he has until December 31, 1999 to profess his undying love to me before God and an assembly and to say the words "I do" to the phrase: have and to hold, for richer or poorer, in sickness and in health, in good times and in bad times, 'till death do you part!" Maxwell said as he seemed dreamy eyed. Bradley noticed his eyes flicker before he continued. "If he doesn't, you'll be free to have him Melvin because I will be gone."

"Wait just a minute," Melvin said astonished. "I don't want your leftovers."

"It's not the matter of leftovers," Maxwell said. "I just will not allow myself to love a person, live with him for an eternity, and not present myself before God and the angels."

"Child, sounds like a winner to me," Bradley laughed.

"You all are not going to do it in Dyersburg, I hope?" Melvin asked as he thought about the headlines of the local newspaper if such an event occurred.

"Hell, naw," Maxwell laughed. "But we will make certain that plenty of Dyersburgians are on the guest register for the grand occasion."

"Child, you are too many things for me," Bradley laughed as he finished his meal and enjoyed the company of the young men at his table.

Chapter Three

The Living Is Easy

Bradley woke to the noisy sounds of *K97* radio blasting in the background. He silently laughed as he recounted the expression on Melvin's face the previous night. Although he loved Melvin dearly, he never could fathom Melvin's infatuation with The Rev. The Rev was an attractive successful African-American man by Dyer County standards. He was not a millionaire by any means but he could afford a few simple luxuries that the norm could not. This gave him a few extra liberties that others generally would not receive in Dyer County, especially if they were African-American. Bradley could not help but shake his head when he thought about the mere fact that the turn of a new decade, century, and millennium was just around the corner and African-American people in Dyer County owned less property and businesses than they did at the turn of the Twentieth Century. He had witnessed the sell and dispersal of his beloved Rock Spring Community piece-by-piece and bit-by-bit. Slowly, the original African-American inhabitants sold the land choosing to move North, East, or West yet never reinvesting in the land for which the great founders of Rock Spring built.

He could not help but feel sad when he realized that not less than fifty years prior The Smith-Kelly Clan had owned property for several miles in the RoEllen area. In 1998, however, only a precious handful of those descendants owned a fraction of what was always known as Rock Spring. He witnessed watching the colored cemetery where all of the Smith-Kelly Clan was buried grow up into weeds. He watched as the old Rock Spring School was sold for $17,000 without in as much as a notice to the descendants. The Smith-Kelly Clan is large enough whereas each descendant could have donated $10.00 each and The Rock Spring School would never have been turned into a five-bedroom home for a Caucasian family. He witnessed the Rock Spring Cumberland Presbyterian Church in America hold its final worship service as The Cumberland Presbyterian Church. Because there was little attendance and the martyrs of the church finally died completely out in the late 1980s, there were not enough willing relatives dedicated to remain as members of the historic congregation.

Hence, the building was leased monthly to a female evangelist/preacher who desired a home for her "wading" congregation of ten people.

No one seemed to mind. The only stipulation was upon funerals of Smith-Kelly Family members; the building would be used to hold the services there and would yet be called Rock Spring Cumberland Presbyterian Church rather than Tabernacle of God Evangelical Church.

"Well," he thought aloud. "I'm not going anywhere. This patch of land will outlast me and somebody else will have to fight over who gets it when I'm gone."

Bradley's trailer was no ordinary trailer. It was a triple-wide trailer that had been bricked in the front. A wide patio was attached to the East entrance while an attached hallway had been built to lead from his backdoor to his sewing room.

He chuckled at the thought of loving the place he had hated so much as a young man as he walked into his kitchen and began to brew a pot of coffee.

His ensuing trip down memory lane was interrupted by the telephone.

"Hello," he answered on the second ring.

"How's my baby this morning?" the all too familiar voice said.

"I'm doing wonderfully, Josh, but I'd be doing a hell of a lot better if I had a check in my hand right now," Bradley said wryly as he poured himself a cup of coffee and sat down at the kitchen table.

"Damn, Brad," Josh growled. "What do I have to do to make you understand that I love you?"

"Keep my damned bank account satisfied," Bradley said tartly.

"What has happened to you, Bradley, you are all about money now when I can remember the time when you were actually a nice person to hang out with."

"Yeah, yeah, yeah, so I'm an old bosom buddy now. Skip the dumb shit, Josh, what the hell do you want? Time is money and you are wasting mine."

"I just got in from Atlanta and wanted to know if you wanted to get together?"

"Make the check payable to Bradley Kelly or bring cash if you think your shit is going to bounce because I don't mind beating you down, niggah."

"What has happened to you?"

"What the fuck has happened to you?"

"Man, you trippin. I just wanted to get together for old time sakes that's all."

"Like I said, earlier, time is money and money it time. Where's the wifey?"

"Keisha's visiting family."

"Why don't you visit the family and do the family thing while you are here, Josh?"

"I don't deal with Keisha's family and you know that every time that I come home my family begs me so much until I can't get anybody's rest."

"Time is money and again, you are wasting mine."

"Bradley, please, I need you and I need you badly."

"My price has not changed and you are already on the clock. You know I will get mine one way or the other."

"So, I take that as I can come by?"

"You know it costs you more if you don't bring your wife," Bradley said as he crossed his legs with a wicked smile. He grew to enjoy torturing Josh.

"You know I can afford anything you ask, niggah, don't play me," Josh grumbled.

"Am I detecting anger in your voice?" Bradley chuckled. "Well, let me get out the old calculator because this is very definitely extra."

"Are you gonna let me in or what?" Josh asked.

"Where the hell are you?" Bradley asked in bewilderment when he noticed a shadow at his kitchen door.

"Just let me in," Josh laughed.

Bradley stood up and opened the door. He looked at Josh and his ego staggered a bit. Josh Curbie was still gorgeous! Yes, life had been great to this fine specimen of a man. He was still tall and ruggedly handsome yet he now possessed a polished and refined look. The boyish look was no longer prevalent. Josh had come of age and was indeed a man.

"Is this how you treat the man who you professed your undying love for years ago?" Josh laughed as he stretched his wide arms wide and gave Bradley a hug.

Bradley could have melted but he knew if he faltered he would go down a long road once again that he had not traveled for years. Bradley managed to twist out of the embrace, the deliciously familiar smell of his first love, the familiar embrace of his first experience.

"How is life in Atlanta?" Bradley finally managed to ask as he looked Josh over once again before returning to his seat and cup of coffee. At this point he wished he smoked in order to calm his unsettled nerves.

"It's life," Josh said as he sat down directly in front of Bradley spreading his huge muscular legs wide open to reveal the gift that God had given him.

"On all days, why in the hell did you choose to wear shorts today?" Bradley asked as he began to sip his coffee. Are you trying to tempt me or something?"

"You know you want to let me tap that ass," Josh said as he fondled himself.

"Why in the hell can't you tap your wife's ass?" Bradley said hotly. "She does have one doesn't she?"

"It will never be as good as yours," Josh grinned.

Bradley shook his head as sweat began to form on his head. He knew he was becoming weak but he had to keep his defenses up.

"Why are you all here?" Bradley asked in order to change the subject. "I thought you never spent summer in Tennessee since you began coaching."

"Keisha's momma is sick and she wanted to be here for the surgery and I had to come home to check up on a few family matters. You know my crazy assed brother is out of control again."

"Since when has Jeremy not been out of control," Bradley said as he thought about the wasted life. "He's such a fuck up."

"Those damned drugs have really fucked his mind up and now he has been stealing everything at momma's house to get a damned rock," Josh said. For the first time Bradley noticed the worry and concern in Josh's face. He, for the first time, looked worn and tired of an endless situation.

"Well, why don't you move your momma to Atlanta away from that crazy motherfucka?" Bradley said with contempt as he thought about Jeremy. Jeremy, like Josh, had earned a scholarship to play ball at a major university. Josh worked hard and went on to get drafted by the Atlanta Falcons. Jeremy, who in all essence was a far better ball player than Josh ever could be, was kicked off of the basketball team for failing to pass a drug test. He came back to Fairhaven angry at the world because he had blown his own chance to fame. In his guilt and shame, he turned to drugs and went to no end to get them. What few good looks he had dispersed over the years of abuse to his body yet he managed to maintain a perfectly chiseled physic. One night during a brawl at a local tavern, a man sliced into his face with a razor. Jeremy beat the man relentlessly. It took eight men to pull Jeremy off of the man. The scar made him look more intimidating to Bradley. The word spread across town quickly that Jeremy Curbie was psychotic; hence, he acquired the nickname "Psycho."

"Momma doesn't want to leave her house here and I do have a family of my own," Josh said.

"Yes, I almost forgot," Bradley commented softly.

"Are you never going to forgive me for marrying Keisha?" Josh asked in a very pitiful voice.

"Why hell no," Bradley said. "I left Fairhaven and everything that had to do with Fairhaven for you years ago when you were nothing."

"Yeah, I've heard the story before," Josh groaned.

"Well, you're going to hear it again and again until I get tired of saying it." Bradley said. "And I won't get tired until they bury me."

"Why won't you let it go?"

"Because, when I told you that I loved you," Bradley began. "You told me that you could not return the feelings and maybe I should get paid for what I do because I was so good. Well, I did and you still came back and I was the fool because every time you came back with that pitiful ass story I accepted your sorry ass back."

"Well, you didn't complain too much as long as I made sure that you had one of the most expensive apartments on Buford Highway in Atlanta," Josh returned. "Nor did you complain when I made sure that you wore the best rags in town and drove the best cars."

"And that was your fucking compensation for love?"

"You were one of the grandest punks in Atlanta what else did you want, bitch?"

Bradley became furious.

"I was one of the grandest bitches in Atlanta because I chose to be, mothafucka," Bradley raged. "Furthermore, those fucking pennies that you gave me every week weren't about shit."

"You're a damned lie!"

"You're another one," Bradley returned. "And furthermore it was not your ass who kept me it was George and you very well know it. I walked out of a man's life that gave me everything for you and what did you have the damned nerve enough to do to me? Invite me to your fucking wedding."

"That was not my idea it was Keisha's," Josh defended. "After all, she did attend every got dammed Omega function with that punk ass Melvin for years but he never was man enough to be a man."

"Don't you talk about Melvin," Bradley raged. "Just because he didn't want that desperate ass fish didn't mean you had to go marry her."

"You will not talk about my wife like that to me," Josh yelled.

"Or what," Bradley yelled and rose to his feet. "You gonna try to kick my ass in my own house? Niggah you really trippin now!"

Josh rose to his feet in a rage only to meet the "you better not think about it" gaze in Bradley's eyes.

"Get bad, if you want to," Bradley said. "Ass whippins come a dime a dozen in these parts."

Josh could no longer resist. He grabbed Bradley and kissed him passionately.

To his surprise, Bradley twisted free of his embrace and hit him in the face. The lick was so hard until Josh stumbled backward and fell on his behind.

"Have you lost your damned mind," Josh growled angrily. "Man, I'll…"

"You'll what," Bradley said with such venom until Josh blinked.

"What has happened to you, Bradley?" Josh asked in utter amazement. He knew that he could never out match Bradley's strength. Bradley was equally as muscular as he was and equally as stout. However, never before had Bradley responded to him in this manner.

"I just don't want your mothafuckin hands on me," Bradley said as he began to cry uncontrollably. "I just don't want no man to touch me ever again. I don't want to be like Frederick"

Josh had never seen Bradley like this before. Above all else, Bradley was a strong African-American man who had overcome the many obstacles of life. He had overcome being an African-American gay man living in the rural South. He had overcome poverty although by very unconventional means. He had overcome. Now, he was a sad, frightened little boy.

For the first time in the existence of a relationship/ friendship/ partnership, Josh felt true compassion for Bradley. He sat next to Bradley on the floor, placed his large muscular arms around the sobbing man and allowed him to cry.

Bradley cried for the first time in his life tears that he seemed never capable of shedding. He cried for the life of Frederick, the loss of Frederick, and the memory of Frederick. He cried for the years of ridicule and ostracism he had been subject to living in the rural South as a gay man "out of the closet." He cried for being misunderstood sexually. He cried for being misunderstood Spiritually. For once in Bradley's life, he cried.

"Let it all out," Josh whispered as he held Bradley tightly. "Let it all out, baby boy."

Bradley had not been called baby boy since he was a child. Strangely, the last person who called him this was his father, which made Bradley cry all the more.

"It's going to be all right," Josh reassured him as he held him tightly allowing Bradley to release.

Thirty minutes later, Bradley sighed and there were no more tears.

"You feel better," Josh asked him as he continued to hold him.

"Much," Bradley said weakly. "I'm sorry. I don't know what came over me..."

"Hey," Josh said as he put a finger to Bradley's lips to silence him. "You needed to get that out of your system. I heard about how Frederick was murdered. They also told me that you were one of the people who found him."

"Yeah," Bradley said as he sat limply in Josh's arms. "They still haven't found the person who did it and I just can't imagine dying like that."

"I think whoever the son-of-a-bitch who did it should be hanged," Josh said in disgust. "Frederick was wild but he didn't deserve to die like that."

"It had to have been someone who knew him but we just don't know who," Bradley said absently.

"Things have changed so much around here until this doesn't even feel like the hometown that I grew up in. I'm used to shit happening like that in Atlanta, Chicago, New York anywhere but in Dyersburg or Fairhaven or RoEllen."

"Child, since those damned drugs have come into this city you can trust no one anymore."

"So you don't trust me anymore?" Josh asked as he looked Bradley in the eyes with loving compassion.

"You walked out on that trust years ago, Josh," Bradley admitted against his will. "I loved you so deeply until I became a whore to make sure that we would both survive in Atlanta. I gave some of the best years of my life to faceless, nameless men in order that I could be with the man that I fell in love with so many years ago."

"But you knew that I could not love you and have a career too," Josh lied.

"If I had done a *Vesta* and bust into your wedding singing *Congratulations* then you would have snapped out of the madness," Bradley laughed. "But you have been good to me down through the years attempting to pay for the mistake."

"She almost found out that I had been sending you money," Josh said sadly.

"As I told you when you married her," Bradley said as he slowly began to pull completely out of Josh's grasp. ""I would never come cheap again."

"Did my money buy this home and your business?"

"My, aren't we nosy," Bradley laughed. "Unfortunately, I hate to burst your little sweet and precious ego, but no, your money was barely enough for me to wipe my ass on, niggah."

"What do you mean?" Josh asked in bewilderment.

"Honey, after your betrothal I gave in to George, moved into his condo and really lived the life of Riley. It was so sad that as hard as I tried I just could not love him."

"So what happened to George?"

"Hell, ten stocks and twelve bonds later, I just couldn't fathom waking up to him next to me any further."

"So is that when you came home?"

"Child no, I met Arthur who was wealthier than George," Bradley laughed. "Child, I just worked at *Macy's* and came home. We had a maid and a cook but he became too damned possessive. So, I asked him to buy me a piece of land in Tennessee and we could build a summer home here."

"He fell for that one?" Josh laughed.

"Well, it wasn't altogether that simple but after I had the deed in my hand I announced that I just could not live in Atlanta any further so I was moving home. Then, I moved here and bought this trailer."

"How much money did you accumulate in Atlanta?"

"Enough as to where I would live a comfortable life in the sticks," Bradley chuckled. "I accumulated enough to make me forget about someone who rocked my world *many* years ago and told me that I was so good that I should put my stuff on the market."

"Well, it seems it worked," Josh laughed.

"Yes," Bradley chuckled. "I guess it did and now I am closed for business."

"So you mean that you can resist me now?"

Bradley looked into Josh's puppy dog eyes and smugly said: "You better believe it. Go home to your wife, Josh. Hell, at least be an honorable husband if you aren't anything else. Why did you marry her if you felt that five years later you would come to Fairhaven and try to sneak around with me?"

"You are the only person that keeps me in touch with my past."

"Child, you have a brother who can keep you in touch with your past."

"That bothersome bastard," Josh grumbled as he thought about Jeremy. "I'd rather not even have to see him again. The loser."

"You triflin, you know that?" Bradley said in disgust and amazement.

"If the niggah stay off of drugs long enough maybe he could get a damned job somewhere with his lazy ass," Josh said with such resentment until Bradley stared at him in astonishment. "I begged him to come to a treatment program in Atlanta and he took the damned ticket I sent for him and cashed it in for money to get more drugs. That's how much he thinks of me."

"But he is your brother," Bradley managed to interject.

"He's a fuck up and mark my word, he is going to do something that will get him in a world of trouble before it is all over with."

"Josh," Bradley said softly as he gently ran his fingers through the top of Josh's soft hair.

"You gonna give me some?" Josh whispered as he closed his eyes at the touch of Bradley's fingers.

"No, you are going home to your wife," Bradley said and stood up, walked to the door, and opened it for Josh.

Josh opened his eyes, blinked, and sadly walked out of Bradley's home.

Chapter Four

Fish Are Jumping

"You told him what?" Melvin roared with laughter on the telephone as Bradley recounted the entire story that had taken place so early in the morning.

"Child, I told him to go home to his wife, hell, that is why he married her," Bradley laughed.

"I told her not to marry him," Melvin said as he thought about his friend from years prior.

"The woman loves him and in his own way he loves her too."

"Then why was he at your home if he loves her so much?" Melvin questioned earnestly.

"Because I have always been available to him," Bradley confessed. "It really wasn't until today that I realized that I really love me and I am really pissed off about a lot of the choices that I have made in life up to this point."

"Oh my God," Melvin exclaimed in disbelief. "Are you sure you didn't give him a piece, Bradley?"

"Did you give LaKeisha a piece?"

"Hell no, I don't do fish," Melvin laughed.

"Then why is it so hard to believe that I resisted that fine specimen of a devil called a man?"

"Because of that exact reason," Melvin laughed. "Hey, the frat is supposed to do a Memorial Service tonight for all of the deceased members, are you going?"

"Nope, I gotta work."

"What a surprise," Melvin laughed. "It used to be we couldn't stay out of the Omega Complex and now we barely go into it for anything."

"I personally wish they would go on and turn it into a private club or something that is opened to the public."

"They do that twice a year, I think."

"When have you heard from Xavier and William?"

"O.K. for changing the subject, but anyway, I talked with them on yesterday and they are doing fine. Xavier is on tour again this month which keeps him on the road a lot but otherwise, they are fine."

"How quaint!" Bradley said. "How about Desmond and Douglas?"

"Child, pick up the telephone and call them," Melvin laughed. "Hey, you didn't forget my fish fry tonight, did you?"

"No, Melvin, for the umpteenth time, I'll be there."

"The Rev and Maxwell are supposed to stop by after the Memorial Service."

"Well good for them." Bradley teased. "I hate to admit it, though, they are a cute couple."

"They actually are."

"Now I'm shocked!"

"At what?"

"At the fact that you don't hate that guhl for laying it on thick the other night about how much he is in lurv with The Rev?"

"Well, if they are happy I am happy."

"Well, they are certainly happy."

By eight o' clock in the evening, cars and trucks lined the street that lead to Melvin's house. There was nothing like an old fashioned "fish fry" in the South. Melvin hosted his fish fry in the same manner as countless other people in the area. A huge black pot bellied cooker was filled with lard, shortening, and oil and then heated. Because of the size of the contraption, it usually took an hour for the oil to heat up to a friable temperature yet when it did, the festivities began.

Melvin could no longer rely on his grandfather to fish three to four days per week and catch a mountainous amount of fish to be cleaned and cooked, so, he was forced to run to a nearby fish market and purchase cat fish, buffalo fish, and crappie that were already cleaned. He loved the joy of just preparing for a gathering in his home. For years it had become the gathering place for many of his friends and traditions are traditions.

It was Melvin's tradition to host a summer fish fry for his friends whereas he could work himself into frenzy in preparation of the event. He loved the rewards and benefits of guest feeling welcome and free.

He did not mind frying all the fish, supplying the slaw, hush puppies, spaghetti, white beans, corn-on-the-cob, green beans, and iced tea provided the guest bring at least a covered dish and/or a case of beer and a bag of ice.

The heat of the South would not permit a summer outdoors activity to begin prior to dusk without causing a heat stroke. Hence, it was not strange to hear of fish fries or bar-b-ques being scheduled late in the evening. No one wanted to fight the heat especially when the convenience of air conditioning made life so much easier for all.

Melvin's heart swelled with pride as he looked over his back yard to see it filled with laughter. Several card games were being played at once. Those who played Spades were at one table while those who played Tonk were at another and still a third table was set up for those who played Bid Whiz. Music floated softly into the air like an aphrodisiac. Certain songs would play and blood curdling screams would be heard from someone who had a brief reminisce of falling in love or making love or being in love. From Luther Vandross' sexy tenor "doo doo doo doo doos" to Marvin Gayes' smooth and mellow "Sexual Healing" to Anita Baker's sultry altoing "Rapture" to the high pitched yells of the Artist formerly known as Prince, someone would always think back! And just when they began to think back, the designated DJ for the evening would through on Betty Wright and work the entire crowd over in a full chorus of *"Think back to your very first time!"* Then, as always, someone would complain about the slow music and ask for something that everybody could dance to be played before they had to "knock the DJ out for workin' their nerves."

The best way to move any rural Southern crowd at any gathering is to play the *"Electric Slide."*

Melvin couldn't contain his laughter as he realized everyone of his guest had formed eight lines and begun to dance.

"This is living, damn I miss it down here," Josh laughed as he popped a can of beer opened and joined into the dancing line.

It totally amazed Melvin at how regardless of where a person began, as long as one person began to dance, everyone else could always fall into place immediately when the *"Electric Slide"* was played. What amazed him more was the fact that his fish fry was inclusive of gay people, straight people, old people, and young people and everyone was having a good time. The Rev and Maxwell were the major topic of private conversations for the evening although Desmond and Douglas were part of the crowd as well. Melvin was so happy to see LaKeisha again for the first time since she had married Josh five years prior. He advised against it but could never destroy her happiness when asked the question: "Well, why shouldn't I marry this man whom I love completely?"

Melvin was utterly happy to see Howard again. It was Howard's first public appearance beside church since Frederick's death. Somehow, Howard did not look older but younger, fresher, and more renewed.

Melvin laughed when he looked at what he called the "mother board" - The ladies who were mothers regardless of where they were. They could not help themselves. This fish fry was no exception. Melvin's mother, Etta, The Rev's mother Ellen, Maxwell's mother, Jean, and several other ladies were in and out of circles as quick as lightening making certain that food was properly seasoned, cooked, and served.

It sometimes shocked Melvin how closely knit the entire community was. Yet it was. This made him happy. This was truly the first time in one year's time since the death of Frederick that he had friends and relatives in his presence that was happy. It was almost like times that had seemed to have gone by when neighbors loved their neighbors and their neighbors' children. When people respected people for who they were and not for what they were. There was no fear of violence brought on because of the misuses of drugs and narcotics. Although there was plenty of drinking going on even the normal drunks were tolerable.

"This is a very nice party," Maxwell congratulated Melvin.

"Why I do thank you and I look forward to seeing more of you in the future, Mr. Quest," Melvin laughed.

"Oh, indeed," Maxwell laughed as well as he gave Melvin a hug. At first, Melvin did not know how to respond to the hug. Maxwell hugged so genuinely and yet so tightly and he held on to a person for such a long time until it unsettled Melvin's nerves. Melvin did not feel a sexual energy but energy of friendship, loyalty, and camaraderie. Melvin now understood how The Rev could love Maxwell yet Melvin was not content on assumptions.

Melvin strategically sought out The Rev and managed to steal him gently away from a conversation in which he was casually participating.

"Rev, may I ask you a question?" Melvin asked as he and The Rev walked slightly away from the gathering.

"Sure, go for it," The Rev said in his normal straightforward manner that always turned Melvin on, plus the slight smell of rum on The Rev's breath mixed with his *Perry Ellis Original Cologne for Men* always had an effect on Melvin.

"Are you sure that you won't be offended by the question?" Melvin asked.

"If you are sure you won't be offended by the response," The Rev replied.

"What is it that you see in Maxwell?"

"My entire existence," The Rev responded.

"Shit, that wasn't the response I wanted," Melvin thought to himself.

"I mean what was it that made you know that this was the man of your dreams?" Melvin asked genuinely. "I mean, it is no secret that I have had a crush on you for years and somehow, I let you get away or I did not pursue you the right way or just tell me what it was that made you know Maxwell is the man for you."

The Rev looked at Melvin in his unique little way, raising his left eyebrow as a slight grin appeared on his face.

"First, Melvin, let me say this," he said. "I truly do think you are an adorable man worthy of a honorable man. I really need you to take me off of your pedestal and accept me as a friend rather than some figment of your imagination or some hero guy that I am not."

"Don't flatter yourself, Rev, you know you are a bitch," Melvin said absently to which The Rev laughed a hearty honest laugh. "And stop laughing at me! And stop evading my question."

"I'm not laughing at you I just haven't been called a bitch in years and that was by The Sponge," The Rev said as he quickly reminisced the high school years.

"Well, The Sponge was no angel either," Melvin laughed "But the answer to my question is?"

The Rev took a deep breath and then a swallow of his rum and coke and then for what seemed to be an eternity, allowed the liquid to slowly flow through his system as he began to look dreamily into the stars and recount his story.

Arthur Mulberry, president of Dreaded State Christian College For Christ-like Employees For Christians hired The Rev's accounting firm to do his personal taxes. Daily The Rev felt as if he were being watched but never could place to whom the attention came. As time would tell, The Rev found himself in a position whereas he met Maxwell Quest.

"Hello, I'm Maxwell Quest," the young man said with a flicker in his eye that seemed as if a thousand diamonds had been dropped on a carpet of hazel velvet.

"Hi, I'm The Rev," The Rev replied as he attempted to continue to do his work and not pay attention to the young clerk.

"If you need anything, just let me know," Maxwell said as he sashayed into another office.

Two minutes later, Maxwell reappeared.

"Look," Melvin said, "I've heard all of this before, God have I heard all of this before, get to the good part, what made you fall in love with this man?"

"Oh, you want to know what made me fall in love with Maxwell," The Rev said as if some new question had been posed to him.

"Duh?"

Finally, Maxwell got The Rev's attention and peaked his interest, somewhat. The Rev could not help but notice the perfect ensemble the young man wore: a three-piece navy blue suit, bold blue tie, and a sparkling white starched shirt.

The Rev after three days of bombardments by Maxwell yielded.

"Would you like to go to lunch this afternoon?" The Rev asked.

"Actually, I won't be free for lunch but if you make it dinner I'll make it worth your while," Maxwell said.

"Deal, so do I pick you up or would you prefer to meet me?" The Rev asked.

"Where do you live, I live here in the Dreadful Dorms?"

"Well, I haven't seen a dorm room in years but anyway, I live in Dyersburg," The Rev said as he passed Maxwell his card.

"Do you cook?"

"I learned from the best," The Rev boasted.

"Good, then I'll meet you at your house for dinner at seven and you can plan an appropriate dinner." Maxwell said as he spun on his heels and walked away leaving the Rev feeling as if someone had just sold him a new used refrigerator and had beaten him out of his money.

At six: fifty-nine, The Rev's doorbell rang.

"Damn, he's prompt," The Rev complained slightly.

The Rev opened the door and his breath was taken away at the sight that was before him. Maxwell now wore a pair of black jeans that hugged his bubble butt, a gold V-line sweater that revealed no more than the silver chain around a smooth and voluptuous neck. He seemed somewhat taller which made The Rev look downward only to see a pair of gold snakeskin Cuban heeled boots on a pair of the smallest feet The Rev could remember seeing on a man.

"Good evening," The Rev greeted. "Welcome to my home."

"Good evening to you as well," Maxwell returned. "And I felt that since you cooked the least I could do was bring something. So here."

Maxwell then presented The Rev with a single red rose.

"Wow," was the only word that could come from The Rev's mouth.

Maxwell smiled at his second victory of the evening.

"I thought you would like it, you seemed poetic to me," Maxwell teased.

"You know the symbolism behind the single red rose, don't you?" The Rev asked.

"No," Maxwell replied. "Why don't you tell me about it over dinner. I'm famished."

"Follow me," The Rev said as he led Maxwell to his dining room.

Maxwell noticed how large the apartment was yet he also noticed the disarray of it. Within his own mind he thought "*I belong here and this feels like it should be my home as well and he feels like the one I want to marry.*"

The dining room was fabulous. A long mahogany dining table was filled with a full course meal yet there was a table setting only for two at separate ends of the table.

"I'm not sitting way down here," Maxwell protested. "Maybe in the future when we have guest but never just for regular dinner."

The Rev listened to Maxwell's choice of words but attempted to disregard them.

"Fine, you can sit closer to me, let me just adjust the music."

The Rev walked into another room and turned soft jazz music on which floated softly over the entire house. The music gave the setting a comfortable tone.

The Rev and Maxwell ate and talked for hours before they had realized it.

"I would like to know something," Maxwell asked. "Why are you not involved with someone?"

"I'm recently out of a relationship," The Rev commented without remorse.

"What a shame," Maxwell said. "Well, I'll be honest, I'm happy you are not involved because I want you and have wanted you since the first time I saw you on campus three months ago."

The Rev was shocked. He normally felt a vibe when someone tried to get involved with him. He just could not picture this person.

"When did you see me on campus?"

"The first day you came on campus, you wore a navy blue suit with a light yellow tie with a really pretty design on it and the handkerchief matched. You had a black brief case and had on a navy blue hat that matched your suit."

"Damn," The Rev laughed. "You've described me to a tee."

"Do you need time?" Maxwell asked.

"Time for what?"

"To consider becoming my husband?"

"I haven't even kissed you and.."

Maxwell kissed him before he could finish the phrase.

A mighty wind rushed over The Rev. It seemed as if the stars, the moon, and the sun all stopped while the night and the day played havoc on which should come first. Suddenly, The Rev felt rejuvenated, carefree, wild, excited, elongated, passionate, compassionate, and ready for whatever road would lie ahead.

The Rev returned the kiss.

Maxwell wrapped his tiny arms around The Rev's broad shoulders until his hands settled around The Rev's neck. The Rev's tongue slowly began to enter into Maxwell's upturned, thin, pink, lips and The Rev began to plunge his tongue forward and Maxwell began to follow The Rev's lead and extend his tongue.

At that moment, The Rev felt as if lightning had struck him. He had not felt in tune with another individual in so many years until he had forgotten the true meaning of passion and desire.

He stood and lifted Maxwell in his arms as he kissed Maxwell's lips, neck, cheeks, nose, eye brows, chin, head, ears - anything his lips touched seemed to become more intoxicating than the previous. Maxwell moaned. The Rev groaned. Maxwell screamed. The Rev shouted.

"Oh, damn!"

"Huh?"

"Oh, I'm sorry?"

"What's wrong?" Maxwell asked.

"Nothing, I don't think," The Rev said. "Excuse me for just one moment."

Maxwell became bewildered as to what had happened and why the sudden stop when it seemed as if everything was going wonderfully.

The Rev came back into the living room where he had somehow carried Maxwell during the previous episode.

"What's wrong?" Maxwell questioned. "Did I do something wrong?"

"Hell, no," The Rev said as he attempted to catch his breath for the nine hundredth time.

"Then what happened?"

The Rev attempted not to laugh but could not contain himself.

"I would like to know what the joke is?" Maxwell asked impatiently.

"In all of my life," The Rev began as he sat next to Maxwell and began to slowly caress him in his arms as he gently began to nibble on Maxwell's ear. " In all of the years of my life, in every relationship, through every fling, NO ONE has ever made me cum by just kissing me until just a moment ago."

Maxwell was floored. The battle was almost won at this point for Maxwell.

"You came?" Maxwell asked disappointedly.

"Yes," The Rev laughed wickedly. "But not for the first time tonight. Do you think you can handle me?"

"Hell, if you just came, I know I can handle you," Maxwell teased.

The Rev suddenly became a hot, passionate, wild, creature unlike any that Maxwell had ever seen in his life. *"Thank You God!"* Maxwell thought as The Rev slowly began to caress his entire body from head to toe. Back and forth, forth and back. Up and down. Down and up. Circular. Semi-circular. The Rev kissed Maxwell and Maxwell returned his kisses with hot, passionate kisses and moans of pure ecstasy.

The blue silk shirts peeled from broad shoulders revealing a paper sack brown flesh that could only be given to this African King. The gold sweater peeled from the smooth Carmel shoulders of this African Adonis falling amidst the carpet to study war no more. This African King's tongue glides slowly across the streams, lakes, rivers, and oceans of this African Adonis tasting the sensual nectar of life in each follicle and fiber of flesh that the Great God Jehovah bestow upon such as could be called a human. And in the background Luther croons:

"The time is right, you hold me tight, and love's got me high... "

A whirlwind, a tornado, a hurricane lifts this African King and this African Adonis into the gentle beat of the heart of the air and silently, softly, tenderly, sensuously yet oh so slowly the great tribunal drums of the past beat as Cuban heels run to Cuba and Italian loafers run to Italy for fear of the avalanche of the deep black hue of denim as it slides slowly down or the soft earthen tone of khaki falling to face Mother earth.

And Luther kept on sangin':

"Moooooove a little close to me, you owe it to yourself"

The world is without form and void as the African Adonis tastes the sweet yet forbidden fruit of the African King. Darkness covered everything as the African King sojourns on a voyage throughout the universe obtaining more precious gifts than platinum, gold, or silver. And when it seems to be ending… it just begins!

And Luther kept sangin':

"And I will selfishly take a little for myself"

The African King pulls from within his soul in search of the one thing lost years ago. Somewhere, somehow, some place, far in a distance. And what? The African Adonis holds this great treasure before the African King and graciously gives it to him. And the African Adonis is slowly encompassed with passion. The heavens move and the earth quakes.

"Oh, yeah"

"Yes,"

And time stays still as the African King plunges through mountains high and valleys low on a peaceful expedition the land of The African Adonis. When alas, when like the plates of the earth when rubbed together forms the volcano in its explosive beauty…

The African King and The African Adonis become one. The African Adonis King. The battle had been fought and the victory had been won.

"Woe," Melvin said. "That's deep."

The Rev remained starry eyed as he thought about the beginning of his relationship with Maxwell.

"Well, Rev," Melvin said genuinely. "You deserve him and I am no longer jealous."

"There was no need for you to be jealous anyway. The Lord will send you somebody greater than I ever can be to you but you don't realize this yet."

"Man, after Julian, the creeps I went out with don't even compare. They all talk a good game but fall so short."

"Don't compromise your standards for b.s."

"When is the wedding?" Melvin asked with a twinge of envy.

"Maxwell is setting that date."

"How will it affect you social role here in the rural South?"

"We are going to take things one day at a time."

"Please, try not to make it public because it will ruin you socially, Rev."

"Well, Melvin, let's face it. I'm gay. I'm in love. Fuck folks."

Melvin hugged The Rev.

"You will not change, dude, that's why I love you."

"And I love you as well."

Chapter Five

Mother Bowed

Mother's Day Saturday morning at Flora's Beauty Parlor in Newbern was always a festive time for Desmond. It was the one time of the year that he was certain to catch many of the divas that had shaped his life, patronized his aunt's salon, and was quick to offer any advice needed. Success had surely come to him without a degree from Lane College yet it had its price. He did own two successful salons in two very different cities - Douglas & Desmond's *House of Hair* on Lafayette Street in Jackson and *Flora's Beauty Salon* on Main Street in Newbern. He employed stylist and barbers at both yet business always led him to Newbern on the Second Saturday of every month. Being Mother's Day always fell on the Second Sunday in May, this afforded him the opportunity to see many of the ladies that he would not normally see on his regular visits.

As always, every chair was filled when he arrived. This made his heart swell.

"Child, you are getting as big as a house, come here and gimme a hug," one of his elderly patrons cackled. He loved Mrs. Williams but he could have gone without the greeting. He did not have to be constantly reminded that he no longer wore a size thirty-two in the waist and seventeen in shirts. He had come to accept the fact that regardless of the endless diets and other forms of self inflicted torture, he wasn't going to be a small man. *Slim Fast* got old quick and he knew this.

He hugged Mrs. Williams and slipped her the usual Mother's Day Card with the usual 10% discount coupon in it.

He spoke to the other patrons and passed them the same gift as he walked into his office.

In his office it was business as usual for him. His day began with a dozen glazed donuts, two Twinkies, and a diet coke. He always laughed at the irony of the diet coke yet would always silently chuckle to himself: "Calories... calories."

As the day began to move swiftly on, he overheard the conversation of a few of his clients which interested him enough to crack the door to his office and turn his music and calculator completely off.

Desmond listened contentedly to the voices of Ellen, the mother of The Rev, Jean, the mother of Maxwell, Etta, the mother of Melvin, and Delores, the mother of Bradley as they were in the height of Saturday morning beauty parlor talk. All four women were from a totally different background but were all held together by a common bond, their sons were gay.

"Well," Ellen continued her dialogue. "I can't say that I do agree with my son's life style but I can say that at least I have a relationship with my son. To me this is more important than who he sleeps with,"

"I agree fully, girl," Jean chimed in. "Hell, I was ready to kill your son when I discovered that he was attempting to date my son."

"Do what?" Ellen asked as she looked Jean fully in the eyes amidst the hands of a stylist. Ellen, who was now a retired Civilian Personnel Administrator, had recently moved back to the Dyer County area to be closer to family. She was yet an attractive diva for the age of fifty-two. She was continuously flattered when she and her son would go places only to be asked if she was her son's sister rather than his mother. Over the years, she had begun to put on weight and was no longer the size six that she had been when she had attended the historic Bruce High School in the 1960s as one of its cheerleaders. She was now a size sixteen and cared less about it. Her hair was now salt and pepper yet still as unmanageable as it was when she pressed and rolled it when she was a teenager. Her features were distinct while her dimples were her trademark.

"Oh, don't look so surprised," Jean laughed. "My son did not tell me he was gay when he and your son got together. I didn't bump your son's lifestyle because it was his but my baby is my baby."

Jean was a typical strong willed African-American woman from the South. She, like the other mothers, had survived segregation in the South yet she never knew she was still living in a very racist world created by her own people. She refused to wear long hair and gloried in keeping her hair short and closely cropped. Like Ellen, her smile was legendary and her dimples could charm a rattlesnake if she decided to charm a rattlesnake. She was a retired Executive Secretary who made the extreme rural part of Brownsville, Tennessee her home.

After the death of her second born child, Brownsville became her refuge and place of solace and healing. She did not mind cutting the entire world off from her because, as she always admitted, Life is what you make it and life can be as beautiful as you make it.

"Child, you were going to kill The Rev?" Etta laughed as she attempted to imagine the sight.

"As dead as he could have been killed," Jean exclaimed. "Maxwell had told me one fictitious lie and when The Rev called the house one night I became offended and was ready to strike out at anyone and anybody who was trying to turn my baby gay."

"Well, what changed your heart and mind?" Delores asked. Delores was Delores. She was who she was and cared less about what anyone else felt, thought, or did but always attempted to understand other people. She just thanked God that she raised a child who loved and respected her and could care less about his preference. She, unlike the other women, refused to leave her job at the factory. She had been there for twenty-seven years and could not imagine giving up her profit sharing and other benefits. The day she was hired at the Coleman Factory in Fairhaven was the day life changed for her and she let nothing change the life she had established for herself without the aid and support of a man.

"Honey," Jean laughed. "The day after I threatened The Rev and cursed him out real good, Maxwell and I went for a walk."

"Girl, you have plenty of room to walk and think down in Brownsville," Ellen laughed. "Have you all been down there yet to see all of the space Jean has down there. It is a beautiful and peaceful place."

"I went last week and was astonished," Delores laughed. "I thought I had it good here in Fairhaven, it is too peaceful down there."

"Anyway," Jean continued. "Maxwell tells me: 'Mom what would you say if I told you that I was going to marry a man?' and so I looked at him and knew then what was in his heart."

"Ooo, child," Etta laughed. "I wished I could have been a bird in a nearby tree to see the expression on your face."

"I was too outdone," Jean laughed. "Now here it was I had cursed a man out thinking he is trying to take my child into some web of deceit and my child is gay all along."

"How did you deal with it?" Delores asked.

"Shit, it wasn't anything to deal with because he moved out the next day," Jean said with a bit of pain I her voice. "I just wasn't willing to lose another child to the bullshit that I had been taught all of my life. Once you have lost a child then you will understand what I am talking about."

"Well, at least you are there for him, girl," Etta said.

"Hell yeah, I'm there for my baby," Jean exclaimed proudly as she thought about Maxwell. "Honey, he packed his glad rags and brought some girl up to the house claiming he was moving in with her when this girl had a small child and I know that Maxwell hates to be around children too long except for when he is working at school."

"Girl you don't mean to tell me he claimed he was moving in with a woman after that revelation?" Delores laughed.

"He certainly did," Jean continued. "So I went along with him and asked for a contact number so I could get in touch with him and he squirmed like a fish out of water."

All three ladies laughed.

"But I'll give him credit," Jean said as she thought fondly back to the day. "He had his lie in order and covered well. Do you all know what he told me?"

"What?"

"He told me that they didn't have a phone yet but it would be turned on in a few weeks where he would then call and give me the number which to this day I still don't have."

"So, what did you do?" Ellen asked.

"I called The Rev's house and asked to speak to him."

The women roared in laughter.

"What on earth did he do?" Ellen asked.

"He went along with the lie and pretended that Maxwell lived with the girl until I finally got tired of the situation and busted both of them."

"How did you bust them when they seemed to have had everything covered?" Etta asked as she tilted her head to allow the beautician freedom to roll her wet hair.

"Well, after thinking about a lot of things, I realized my child is a young man who has to make his own decisions. I don't necessarily care for his choices but he has to meet life head on at sometimes. I certainly did."

"Child, I was out of the house as soon as I graduated high school," Ellen laughed. "You know that in the sixties that was the easiest thing to do was get married and get out of our parents homes."

"Girl, wasn't those old folk hell to deal with?" Delores laughed. "And to think our children were spoiled by these same folk who would beat our asses for the least of things."

"Ellen do you remember when we all got arrested for participating in the sit-in at Woolworth's in Dyersburg?" Etta laughed.

"Child, how could I forget it," Ellen laughed. "Mother beat my behind and put me on punishment for a whole week for participating in that contribution to African-American history. She could care less whether or not we were served at the front door or back door."

"I know that's right," Etta laughed. "I'm just happy that no one was killed and that the judge and lawyers and things attempted to understand our reasoning."

"Well, Dyer County did not really participate in the Civil Rights struggle in the fifties and sixties but they surely did reap the benefits from it," Ellen said wryly.

"That's only because our ancestors really were not for integration, if you remember it well," Etta said. "Integration meant that many of our businesses would fold."

"Well, that certainly occurred," Delores said. "You scarcely see many black businesses in our community anymore when there was once a time when you crossed those tracks in Dyersburg and Black Dyersburg bustled with activity. Everyone made their way here as well."

"Child, I remember Bobby Bland, B.B. King and all of the great blues singers singing on The Hill or The Switch," Etta laughed. "I also remembered how we did not even really care to shop downtown

Dyersburg except for maybe shoes or an overpriced outfit that was years out of fashion by the time we could afford to buy it."

"Well, I certainly am proud of Bradley for opening up a store on the stretch in Dyersburg," Jean said. "We need more black businesses in these areas."

"Well, speaking from experience," Etta said. "I have found that it takes being rejected and getting your feelings hurt to be reminded that you can do what you wish in your own community."

"Well, I guess that is easy to say being you are the wife of an undertaker," Delores laughed. "That's basically it for black business in Dyer County. You can count on your hands the other few businesses that are black owned here."

"That is precisely my point," Etta said. "Clarence's business is a business that he knows will sustain him for a lifetime and he will not have to rely on outside help from white people to keep the business going but the only reason his funeral home is patronized is because black folk will not go to a white funeral director to get buried unless they work for them."

"I feel you," Jean laughed. "In the same token black people will not support black business a lot of times because so often you cannot rely on black business people to effectively produce quality work and when they do black people will do their best to pull the people down."

"Well I will support black business only if they are timely and efficient," Ellen said. "In other words, don't give me a product two days after my deadline and expect me to patronize you again. That makes me look bad and your business look bad as well."

"And we also need to teach our people to stop being late for everything," Etta laughed. "I tell my church members all of the time, if I am going to preside over any function that starts at three o'clock, don't come in at four o' clock and think you are going to lead the congregation in the Opening Hymn of Praise because we will be ready for the benediction by then or we will be so close to the benediction until you will question if we had a program at all."

Delores laughed.

"Child," Delores chuckled. "She's telling you all the truth because whenever Etta has sponsored a program she always begins promptly and has refused to allow certain women to sit with the organization if the program has already begun."

"Honey, I don't need you to come in dressed to kill to march in the parade when the parade is down the street," Etta laughed. "Get your white on and get pinned up with your corsage before we begin otherwise don't sit with us. I don't have time for grandness"

"Now that is a gay phrase," Delores laughed.

"I'm learning," Etta replied.

All four ladies laughed as Hortence Perry entered the salon. Instantly, the mood changed.

"Praise the Lord, saints," Hortence greeted as she entered the salon. Hortence was a beautiful African-American woman as well. She wore a denim skirt, cotton socks and what was known as "baby girl" tennis shoes, a multi-colored, long sleeved blouse, and a straw hat that had a huge sunflower on the front of it.

"Good God, what an entrance," Delores whispered slightly maliciously to the seated group.

"Hello, Hortence," the ladies responded.

"That's Evangelist Perry," Hortence beamed as she sat next to Etta.

"What church do you belong to again, I forgot the name?" Jean asked.

"I'm a member of The Pearly Gates House of Power and Deliverance Full Gospel Apostolic Church of the Lord and Savior Jesus Christ," Hortence smiled with glee. "And Sunday I will be ordained an Evangelist."

"I'm ready to get under the dryer," Ellen commented to her stylist symbolizing that she no longer wished to communicate with the group at present.

"I think I'm ready as well," Delores said feeling the same passion of resentment rise within her soul as well.

"We're sorry ladies, everything is full at present but we will get you all under a dryer as soon as possible," the attendant said.

"What a glorious day to become an Evangelist as well, Mother's Day Sunday," Hortence rattled. "The Lord surely is a great and awesome God and His wonders to perform."

"Child, you are too many things for me right now," Delores commented as she looked at Hortence.

"And just what does that mean?" Hortence asked. "You mean to tell me that you don't believe that the Lord is the Rock of our Salvation and that He cannot supply our every need?"

"I believe in God, Hortence, I just have a slight problem believing in you right now, that's all," Delores said as she obtained a copy of *Essence Magazine* from a nearby table.

"I understand how people can't accept the fact that I am saved and sanctified and filled with the precious Holy Ghost and fire and that many of you all are going to hell for not being filled with the Holy Ghost whereas you will speak in tongues but I still love you anyway, sister," Hortence said as she pulled a Bible from her purse.

"I will kick your holy ass in her today, woman," Delores said as Ellen, Jean, and Etta looked up at Delores rising out of her chair to stand in front of Hortence.

"Girl, she ain't worth it," Jean said as she stood beside Delores and patted her should.

"I don't understand what all the commotion is about anyway?" Hortence said. "But the Bible does say that people will be jealous of the Spirit that you have within."

"Hortence, the Bible also says that without Love you can have the gift to in as much as raise the dead but it is in vain if it is not in love," Etta said gently.

"The Bible says also to not be unevenly yoked and I know what lives you all live so I can stand a bit of persecution from the unsaved when I know you all are going to hell anyway."

"Now just a minute, sister," Etta said as her face flushed with fury. "I don't bump whatever your beliefs are but you are not coming in here with a lot of senseless mumbo jumbo about who is and is not going to hell. Actually, I think that you need to re-evaluate whether or not you are going to get there."

"Oh," Hortence commented as she crossed her legs. "I know I'm on my way to Heaven to meet the King and if you all want to get there I would turn away from my wicked ways and come on over and listen to Bishop Ickles."

"Bishop Ickles!" Jean, Ellen, and Delores said simultaneously.

"That crook," Delores said as she shook her head, laughed and sat down on the opposite side of the room from Hortence.

"My pastor is not a crook," Hortence defended. "He is saved, sanctified, and filled with the precious Holy Ghost and fire and walks in the statues of Christ."

"He's a damned jackleg preacher if I have ever seen one," Delores laughed.

"I'm praying for you sister," Hortence said as she began to look upward towards Heaven, clasp her hands, and begin speaking so rapidly until no one in the room could understand a word she said.

"What is she doing?" Ellen asked Jean.

"Girl, she calls herself praying in tongues."

"Oh."

"In your prayer, honey," Delores yelled. "Pray for the young men who paid for your son's funeral."

Hortence stopped mid prayer and looked at Delores with such hatred until a noticeable unpleasantness filled the room.

"I prayed for that person you called my son but he refused to change his demonic ways and God destroyed him," Hortence said with such conviction until the four ladies all gasped at the same time.

"I don't understand," Etta finally said attempting to understand Hortence for the first time since Frederick had been murdered. She attempted to understand any woman who would not love a child unconditionally but to hear this woman frightened her a bit.

"I asked Bishop Ickles to pray with me about that person," Hortence said. "We did. And his life style was ungodly so God erased him from the earth because of it and I thank God for doing it."

"Your own child?" Jean asked. "What kind of religion is that?"

"The Bible tells us about Sodom and Gomorra and how God destroyed two whole cities because of that type of sin," Hortence said. "And God is going to destroy all of those people living in that abomination before His sight if they don't turn from their sin and go back to Him."

"You really believe what you are saying too, don't you?" Etta said as she looked at Hortence in disbelief.

"I believe in God's Word just like my pastor preaches it," Hortence said. "And I know that child went straight to hell and I won't ever see him again so I disowned him."

"You have a mental problem," Ellen said as she walked into another section of the beauty salon.

"God loves you too, sister," Hortence said and continued her speech. "I heard about how people gave him a big church service and defiled the House of God by allowing his remains to enter in it."

"You need prayer, girl," Jean said. "That young man did not deserve to die in the manner in which he did and he was well deserving of the funeral that was given to him."

"It don't matter what kind of funeral he had," Hortence continued. "He still went to hell."

No one saw Desmond standing in the door listening to the conversation at this point.

"How can you say that about your own child?" Etta asked." He came from your womb?"

"I didn't raise such a thing to go around and mock God by trying to be something he was not and I was glad that God eradicated such sin," Hortence said.

"Get the hell out of my salon," Desmond said as uncontrollable tears streamed down his face.

"What?" Hortence asked as she noticed Desmond for the first time since she began her dialogue.

"I don't want your business and don't ever come into my establishment again or I will call the police on you," Desmond said.

"You can't put me out of here," Hortence said as she stood up with her Bible clutched in her hands as if it were some type of shield. "I've been coming here for years to get my hair done and…"

Desmond took his cell phone from off his side and began to dial a telephone number.

"Hello," he said. "Yes I need an officer at Flora's Beauty Parlor on Main Street. I have an irate customer who will not leave the premises… Thank you. I'll be here waiting."

"I know you didn't just call the police on me," Hortence said as fury began to fill her. "I know that your punk ass didn't just call the police on me!"

Etta, Jean, and Delores turned and looked at one another and then at Hortence and Desmond. They could not believe that she had cursed nor did they believe that she had just insulted the owner of the beauty salon.

"I just called the police and they will escort you out of my establishment," Desmond said. "And as for being a punk, I would rather be a punk any day than to be a hypocrite like you."

"I'm telling Flora," Hortence protested but did not move an inch.

"Girl, Flora has been dead for two years now," Etta laughed. "And I know because my husband buried her."

Hortence became engulfed with rage as the police pulled up to the salon and walked in.

"We just received a call," one of the officers said as he walked into the beauty salon.

"Yes, sir," Desmond said. "This lady refuses to leave my property and I would like her to be escorted off the premises."

"You mother fucker," Hortence yelled. "I can't believe you!"

"Who is this doing all of this cussin'?" Ellen asked as she returned to the room to see what was going on.

"Ma'am," the officer said as he placed his hand on Hortence's shoulder. "I don't know what is going on but if he asked you to leave then it would be wise that you leave or I will have to arrest you for trespassing."

"Get your damned hands off me," Hortence yelled. "I'll leave this damned place but I'm coming back with my pastor."

"Ma'am," the officer said. "It would be best that you just don't come back."

"Fuck you," she said as she stormed out of the beauty salon.

"Ooo," Delores laughed. "I surely would like to hear what your pastor has to say about you cussin' like a sailor the day before you get your Evangelist license."

"Go to hell, bitch," Hortence yelled as she walked toward her car.

"Girl, if I go there I would join you," Delores laughed.

The ladies laughed and returned to their seats inside of the salon. The officer left and Desmond walked into the area where the ladies sat.

"Child, you have to look over her," Jean said. "You see she is gone."

"I just hate people like that. Especially her," Desmond confessed.

"There's no room for hating your enemies, child," Etta said as she patted his shoulder. "Just pray for her. I certainly do."

"I almost busted her out about Bishop Ickles, though," Delores laughed.

"What about Bishop Jackleg, girl?" Ellen laughed.

"The reason Hortence has such faith in the Bishop is because I hear she has been his mistress for years now," Delores laughed.

"Well what does the wife say about it all?" Jean asked.

"Nothing. I hear he beats that poor woman merciless," Delores explained. "Hortence is allowed free reign in that little church."

"And she says that Frederick is going to hell," Desmond laughed. "It seems to me that she would be more concerned with her own soul."

The ladies laughed.

"I actually pity her," Jean said. "She is so busy chasing a man until she has missed some of the most precious moments any mother could have with a child. Personally, I'm happy to be a part of my two sons' lives."

"Two sons?" Etta asked.

"Yes, The Rev and Maxwell," Jean laughed. "I love them both because they love one another."

"Girl, I continuously pray for my baby," Etta laughed thinking about her Melvin and how lonely he seemed at times.

"If it were not for our mother's prayers," Desmond said. "I don't feel that any of us could make it."

"I'm proud to have you as a son as well, Desmond," Etta said gently as she hugged him slightly.

"Thank you, Miss Etta," he said boyishly.

Chapter Six

Just Over My Head

Melvin reviewed the final figures on the accounts for the day and decided everything was in good standing. He was proud of his little branch office in Newbern. No doubt, his office was no larger than a small bedroom in his home but he was content. He was the first African-American man to hold the position of manager in a bank in Dyer County. This was an accomplishment in itself. He felt privileged to sit among the notable greats such as Bradley who owned his own clothing store, or Grimlock who owned his own restaurant in the middle of the notorious East side of Dyersburg. As far-fetched of an idea as it would seem to be, Ann's House of Wings was a thriving black business and was supported for miles around. Another African-American finally hosted his own television talk show while yet another was in the making of writing his first novel. Howard took charge of a now nationally known community choir. As the grand age of thirty slowly crept upon Melvin, he could honestly say he was pleased.

With all of this pleasure, however, there was yet one thing lacking in his life, which often made everything else seem in vain. He was yet alone. He was alone even though he was attractive, intelligent, and able to pay his bills on time with an occasionally slip. Melvin hated receiving "past due" bills in the mail, hence, he would strive to always keep his bills paid on time but even he had to admit that on occasion he too would slip and be late at times. With all of his capabilities, even he had to borrow money from his parents at times. Yes, he had an adequate paying position at the bank yet he still had a federal student loan to repay. He still had an annual property tax to pay as well as homeowner's insurance. In all of his glory and magnificence, he like everyone else still had bills. Yet, he was "O.K." with this.

On this hot June evening Melvin decided to go the gym. This would be the first time in ages that he had decided to work out. Although he really did not have to work out, he always wanted to maintain some form of healthiness. The gym tended to provide a form of Spiritual completeness. It offered his body the opportunity to commune with his soul.

Melvin looked around the gym as he began his exercise regime. He was pleased. Within the room he was finally the finest looking guy there. To his left was an older man with an extremely huge and grotesquely fat figure. The man did not seems as if he were really applying any great knowledge of health and fitness to any particular exercise regime as the man sat in a corner reading the evening newspaper. To Melvin's right were two middle-aged men who did look great for their ages. They were perfectly toned, fit and trim yet one man grunted and groaned after ever stretch, lift, or pull while the other man complained about the least thing.

Melvin politely placed his earphones on his ears and began to stretch to the sounds of Michael Flatley's *Lord of the Dance.* The music took him completely away. Soon, he became lost in the music as well as his exercise program. Occasionally, he would close his eyes as he began to pump iron to the beat of the music becoming totally absorbed in the excitement and drama of the music.

It was wonderful, exciting, refreshing, and replenishing as his body, mind, and soul became one forgetting everything and everyone around. It was one of the few times that he had felt complete. Sweat began to pour down his face as his adrenaline began to flow as he continued hit litany. He felt great. He was so proud of himself for actually returning to the gym again after so long. It was a time for him to release his hate for the murderer of Frederick. It was his time to actually grieve in a different manner for Frederick. It was his time to vent his anger and frustrations at African-American men, those who were gay and for those who were straight. He was sick of the games African-American gay men played. Consequently, he was sick of the ignorance of African-American straight men. The African-American gay men that he encountered had so many issues with just being gay until it would take a sifter the size of the Empire State Building to shake the craziness free or they would be so insecure with themselves until it would take God himself to raise them from the pit of sorrow from whence they had fallen. Even he was tired of holding a platinum membership card in the *"I Can't Find A Man"* **Club**. The African-American straight men that he had encountered were so dingy with ignorance until he never ceased to be amazed at how stupid they could actually be. If he heard the question: "Why don't you like pussy?" just one more time, he would shoot the person who uttered it. Now really, was this an appropriate question to ask another individual if you did not have a problem with your own sexuality? To Melvin, that was like asking someone: "Why don't you like to sleep at the head of the bed instead of at the foot?" Who gives a shit?

Just as Melvin continued to review the atrocities of life in his mind, he smelled a very familiar sent. A unique sent that always sent shivers down Melvin's spine and back up to his neck and back down to his penis. He had not smelled the smell since he had dated Julian and prayed to God, the Angels, and the entire host of Heaven that when he opened his eyes, Julian was not standing anywhere near him.

Slowly, he opened his eyes, thanking Jesus, God, the Angels, and the entire host of Heaven that it was not Julian. Instead, it was the blackest man Melvin had ever seen. Indeed, the man was as James Weldon Johnson once wrote: "blacker than a hundred midnights, down in a cypress swamp." Melvin's heart jumped when the man tossed one of the most gorgeous smiles Melvin had ever seen in his life at him only revealing thirty-two of the whites, straightest, smoothest teeth. Before Melvin released it, he commented to the man: "Shit, your smile is so pretty you should market it to the dentist."

The man laughed and sat directly beside Melvin.

"Well," he said. "That's a first."

Melvin attempted to review his mind quickly and thoroughly attempting to remember the face of this beautiful man before him. Dyer County had so many new people moving in and out until he could no longer keep track with the old guard from the new members of the historic society. He had never seen the man before - not in Dyersburg, Newbern, Fairhaven, RoEllen, Trimble, no where!

Melvin noticed that they were the only two people in the entire building at this point. In his work out, he had not realized that everyone else had left him.

"Well, hi," the man said and offered his hand for the perpetual Southern introductory handshake. "My name is Eric, Eric Curbie. I'm new here."

"*Sweet Jesus,*" Melvin thought to himself. A Curbie - and you know the Curbies are packing and for the most part...trade!

"Hi," Melvin said in a strange voice. "*What the hell,*" he thought as he cleared his throat. "I'm mean, hello, I'm Melvin... Melvin James from Fairhaven. Are you visiting relatives or did you move here?"

"Actually," the guy said as he shuffled around revealing his massive manhood to Melvin, which only made Melvin's heart pound all the more. "I just moved back home from Chicago. I guess you've forgotten me, it's been so long, Melvin."

"Have we met before?" Melvin asked astonished attempting to recollect who this Eric Curbie was. He began to review the channels of his mind for recollection. High School? No? College? Definitely not? The Apartment Club back in the day? Possibly? Where?

"O.K." the guy giggled. "Let me give you a hint, then."

"*Oh, shit, here we go,*" Melvin thought. "*Please, Jesus, don't let this be one of those one night stands from way back when in my drinking days.*"

"I left Tennessee when I was about twelve," Eric said.

"O.K." Melvin said looking as if to say... "And?"

"We both attended Mt. Carmel in Fairhaven years ago," Eric clued again.

Melvin thought hard and a small ray of recollection began to return to him but he needed more information.

"We were both Royal Ambassadors."

"*Hell,*" Melvin thought. "*Everybody was Royal Ambassadors then or get your ass tore up for not participating. Those folk didn't play back then about children not participating in something meaningful to them.*"

"I'm still trying to remember," Melvin confessed. "You know every boy had to be a Royal Ambassador and every girl had to be a Red Circle Girl back in the day or you would get talked about so bad about being a disobedient child or would be alienated because you were the only child at home by yourself when everybody else was at church."

Eric laughed.

"O.K." he said. "Remember the little boy who was sent to the pastor's office for asking was David and Jonathan gay?"

Melvin laughed so hard until his sides began to hurt. He remembered the day very well. He had wanted to ask the same question but dared not to ask the question. The lesson that evening had chronicled the friendship of David and Jonathan and the Scripture was read about the love David had for Jonathan and this little boy asked the famous question that got him put out of the Royal Ambassadors.

"That was you?" Melvin asked as he attempted to gain his composure.

"That was me?" Eric laughed. "So many years ago."

"I often wondered what happened to you."

"We moved to Chicago the following Wednesday but that question burned in my heart that day."

"Oh, I thought you got thrown out," Melvin confessed. "What did Pastor say or do to you?"

"He just explained the nature of friendship and love," Eric said as his eyes seemed to glow in admiration as he thought fondly of the old pastor of Mt. Carmel. The devout Reverend Doctor C. J. Seats.

"And what was that?" Melvin asked genuinely interested in knowing the reply. He had loved Reverend Dr. Seats as well and had many fond memories of him. Dr. Seats had pastored Mt. Carmel for forty years and had died a week before his official retirement.

"Dr. Seats had said that in life I would find friends that I will find are closer to me than my actual siblings and because of this I will love them as genuinely as I do my own siblings," Eric explained. "He went on to say that to describe the relationship of David and Jonathan, I could not think carnally but Spiritually."

"He was indeed a clever man," Melvin laughed. "That was a very good answer to give to a ten year old child rather than getting crazy and upset. Did you find his response to be wise or evading?"

"Both," Eric laughed. "His words were true but I still think that David and Jonathan were knocking the boots."

"Well," Melvin laughed. "I could care less. I wish my boots were knocked every now and then and then I could talk about it more."

"Somebody as fine as you?" Eric said in amazement as he looked Melvin up and down from head to toe. "You mean to tell me you are single?"

This response somewhat caught Melvin off guard. Melvin was also amazed at how freely he was talking to someone that he could barely remember even though Eric did grow up to be a fine specimen of a man.

"Unfortunately," Melvin said sheepishly. "I am."

"Well," Eric beamed. "Maybe we can change that."

"I beg your pardon?"

"Oh excuse me," Eric said. "Maybe I can change that."

Melvin had to shake his head to make certain that he had just heard this man correctly. He became nervous all of a sudden. He did not want to jump head over heels into something but loneliness was a bitch! He looked at the man who was now standing directly in front of him... profiling! *Jesus, Jesus, Jesus,"* Melvin thought quickly. The preacher had always said: "Just say: *"Jesus"* three times when you need eternal help and strength." At this moment, Melvin needed strength, encouragement, guidance, direction, help... help... help! Eric was absolutely gorgeous but he had always been taught that anyone Eric's shade of black was an offense. However, Melvin's vanity began to fade when he looked at the sight before him. Eric did not need to be at anybody's gym He was a solidly built man standing six feet four inches. By observing Eric's physique, Melvin knew from experience that his waistline was a thirty -eight. Melvin imagined Eric's gigantic hands wrapping themselves around his tiny waste in the throes of passion. To make matters worse for Melvin, Eric sported shoulder lengthen dreadlocks. Melvin's eyes traveled below the magnificent torso and chiseled chest resting them on Eric's crotch... *"Jesus, Jesus, Jesus!"*

"Child, child, child," Melvin moaned as his eyes curled in his head. "Don't say that."

"Why?" Eric said somewhat sadly. "Am I too black for you or something? I know how a lot of you folk are..."

"Wait just a minute," Melvin said as his train of thought was interrupted. "First, of all, Eric, I didn't even know that you were gay. Secondly, I just met you. Third, if you have a lot of issues about your complexion then no, we can be nothing more than friends. Shit, I'm sitting here hot as a fourth of July firecracker that's just been lit and you talking shit to me..."

"You mean you don't have a problem with my color," Eric said. "I didn't think you type of people cared much for black folk."

"You type of people?"

"You know, you guys who are successful and children of Fairhaven's elite and all..."

Melvin looked at the hurt in Eric's face and was consumed with compassion. He looked further at Eric and was consumed by passion. Before he realized it, he had placed his arms around Eric's huge neck, grasped his head, and kissed his thick, red lips.

"I will tolerate only a little conversation about your complex," Melvin said as he stared Eric squarely in the eyes. "But I warn you, I am a bitch on some days and sweet as honey on others. I am far from a perfect man and do not wish to be put on that pedestal. I have been in one serious relationship and have fucked off with countless men in an attempt to find love. I will help you sort out your problems if you are willing to help me sort out mine. If you want a relationship, we can work towards one. If you want to fuck, that's negotiable. That's all I can say but I have to get out of here before I lose myself in you."

Melvin slid off of the bench and began to walk hurriedly toward the locker room. He could not believe what he had just said. He could not believe what he had just done. Yet he had. He wanted Eric more than life itself at this moment but as he walked through the corridor all of his demons began to haunt him. So many men wanted to date him because he was the son of a prosperous funeral director. In the rural south, funeral directors were prestigious business people in the African-American community. Few people valued him for being himself... Melvin. Few people, including his own family, knew the real Melvin. Even fewer people knew the intimate Melvin. Julian had won his heart, broke his heart, and returned it to him. The Rev had been his private goal and personal conquest yet The Rev was in a committed relationship with one of his close friends at this point in the history and annals of the life of Melvin James. For the first time in years, there was a man who wanted him. A fine man. A black man. A big dicked man. Judging the man's present countenance... a good man. Personally, he had to admit, he always wanted to date a man as black as the ace of spade. He had grown tired of dating what rural African-America deemed good-looking - this being a man of African-American descent whose skin was so light until he either looked white or could easily pass for white. This same culture, straight, gay, or bi-sexual, all sang the herald of Afro centricity yet so often if a person was darker, had kinkier hair, or larger lips, this person was considered ugly. God forbid if a person wore dreads, braids, or an old-fashioned corn roll. You were then considered unprofessional or trying to be too black or trying to be something or someone you were not. Men wore low cut haircuts and the perpetual fade while women were expected to wear permanents, waves, or freezes. Melvin personally thanked God for the new revolution of the younger generation. No, he did not understand them fully yet they did not mind braiding their hair or twisting it into dreads until they grew into beautiful locks of deep ebony, brown, or sandy shades amidst cocoa brown, deep black, and Carmel colored skin. The nineties began to bring Southern rural hypocrisy to its knees. Melvin could sense a revolution yet nothing drastic enough had occurred within the confines of the rural South to make this course of action occur. And now, this gorgeous man presented himself before Melvin with issues that were unnecessary.

Melvin could not even begin to process it all. Why? Why were so many African-American gay men who had been born in the sixties and seventies living such lives as the one that he himself lived? It was as if the works of Langston Hughes, Wallace Thurman, James Baldwin, Essex Hemphill, Joseph Beam, Larry Duplechan, and so many other great authors and activist of the past had worked in vain. Sadly, Southern rural African-American gay men either refused to read or refused to apply what they had read. As the country approached the twenty-first century, countless publications, novels, and resources of information had finally reached the rural South yet many African-American gay men continued to live and die in silence. As they lived and died in silence, they, in order to fit into the established culture of the traditional African-American rural south, would often participate in the ridicule and malicious evilness of making other African-American gay men who were "out" of the "closet" and free of the lie... miserable. It was nothing for a known gay man to participate in gay bashing with straight women or straight men. No, the bashing was not necessarily to beat another individual yet Melvin often remembered conversations such as:

"Girl, just look at him, twisting and all of that..." says a female.

"Yeah, I know, honey," responds a gay man.

"I wouldn't trust him around my man," she says and giggles. "No, offense to you."

"No offense taken, girl," the gay man responds.

This was always a total and complete sell out in Melvin's mind. For one, whoever said that gay men wanted to be with someone else's problem? Whoever said that this same woman did not feel this same way about the very gay man in whom she discussed another gay man? Why were careless issues of this nature ever mentioned in general conversation?

"Are you all right?" Eric asked as he stepped behind Melvin in the locker room.

"Yeah," Melvin said as he closed the locker door. "I was just in deep thought."

"You were always a thinker," Eric laughed as he reached into his locker and retrieved his duffel bag.

Melvin laughed.

"I never thought that you paid this much attention to me."

"I actually used to have fantasies about you when we were children," Eric admitted. "I was dealing with my sexuality way back then and didn't even know it."

"What are you doing when you leave here?"

"Nothing really, what's up?"

"Would you like to come back to my place for a bite to eat?"

"Depends on what's cooking?"

Melvin laughed.

"I cooked a big pot of soup yesterday and really didn't want to have to be bothered with it for too many days before I freeze it."

"Are you sure that you're up for company?"

"Didn't I invite you?"

Eric revealed those thirty-two beautiful white teeth.

"Child," Melvin laughed. "Don't do that!"

"Do what?" Eric grinned.

"Show me those beautiful teeth," Melvin snickered. "Has anyone ever told you just what a beautiful smile you have?"

"Not until just now," Eric laughed.

"Child, I'm parked right outside," Melvin said as he grabbed his duffel bag and began to march out of the locker room and out of the gym.

Eric followed him into the parking lot, opened his car door for him after Melvin unlocked it, and smiled.

Eric then ran to his low riding Mazda truck, jumped in, started the ignition, and blasted the reggae so loudly until the windows in Melvin's car began to shake from the bass from his system.

"Oh, hell," Melvin thought. *"This has to be one of James Earl Hardy's B-Boys from B-Boy Blues. You go Melvin, guhl!"*

Melvin sped off with Eric trailing quickly behind him. Every now and then, Melvin enjoyed the excitement of a high speed chase and he turned the corner of his small street that lead to his home driving 65 miles per hour with Eric directly on his tail.

Melvin pulled into his drive so fast until Eric passed the turn and continued down the street before he realized that Melvin had pulled into a drive.

Melvin laughed as Eric backed the truck into his driveway with the music blasting at full capacity.

"Boy, you are going to have to turn that noise down or someone will call the police on you," Melvin laughed.

"My bad," Eric said as he turned the ignition of his truck off which immediately turned the music completely off. "Are you sure that you are up to guest this evening?"

"Is he crazy?" Melvin thought. *"Hell yeah I'm up to guest when he is a six foot four fine ass niggah like this!"*

"I invited you, didn't I?" Melvin responded.

"Then let's do it. What's for dinner?" Eric asked as he met Melvin at the front door of Melvin's home.

This felt great to Melvin. He had not been escorted home by someone in whom he wanted to escort him home in so long until it almost felt strange but it certainly felt good.

Eric followed Melvin into the house and gasped at the beauty. African art was strategically placed around the entire great room while in every other corner small gay relics were displayed. Eric loved it.

"Would you like to take a shower while I get dinner on?" Melvin asked as he headed toward his bedroom.

"Sure, I need to run and get my change of clothes though because these are a bit funky."

"Cool, you can use the guest bathroom."

"Is this the house your grandparents used to live in?" Eric asked as he looked about the house attempting to remember how it looked in the past.

"This is it with a hell of a lot of renovation," Melvin laughed. "I could not live in here with it looking like it did when Gramps and Gran lived here. Child all of that antique shit had to get up out of here."

"Cool," Eric said as he ran out to his truck and in record time returned into the house with his duffel bag.

Melvin went into the kitchen and began to prepare a quick evening meal.

"Would you like a drink or something?" he called to Eric as Eric continued to admire the art and relics.

"I'll have a glass of orange juice if you didn't mind."

"No problem. Are you sure you don't want anything stronger? I have beer, wine, wine coolers, and stronger stuff if you'd like?"

"I don't drink alcohol."

"*Thank you, Jesus!*" Melvin said to himself as he threw his hands upward towards heaven in praise.

"You can go on into the bathroom whenever you get ready. The towels are already out and there is plenty of soap in there as well. If you need anything else just holler."

"Bet," Eric said as he slipped into the guest bathroom and closed the door behind him.

Soon, Melvin heard the sound of the water falling from the shower onto flesh. "*Jesus, Jesus, Jesus.*" Melvin said as he walked to his private bathroom and prepared to take a shower himself.

The one thing Melvin prided himself on was his ability to cook a fabulous meal out of little or nothing. Dinner consisted of fresh fruit salad, homemade chicken soup, *Hi-Ho* crackers, and *Hawaiian* punch. There was nothing spectacular by any means but something nourishing to the soul.

As dinner progressed, Melvin finally met and discovered the true Eric as Eric finally met and discovered the true Melvin.

"Why did you all move north anyway?" Melvin asked Eric when it seemed as if the conversation was beginning to die.

"Because my grandmother was a bitch on wheels."

"Mrs. Sadie?"

"Mrs. Sadie!"

"Why do you say that, I always thought she was a sweet little old lady," Melvin said as he thought about the little woman who made it a point to come to Homecoming, Easter Service, Christmas Service, Father's Day Service and Thanksgiving service every year at Mt. Carmel.

"She hated my mother and despised all of us and because of that mom's decided to book," Eric said.

"Why did she hate you guys," Melvin asked bewildered because he could not fathom any grandmother disliking her own grandchildren, especially Mrs. Sadie Curbie.

"She hated us because we were all dark skinned children," Eric said with mixed feelings of hate, hurt, and sadness.

"I don't understand?" Melvin confessed.

"Well, you remember Uncle King Curbie, right?"

"Yeah, wasn't he your uncle?"

"Yes, " Eric replied. "And he was also the apple of my grandmother's eye. My dad could do nothing right in her eye sight and when he married my dark skinned mother she flipped, so I am told."

"Why, your mother is a beautiful lady?"

"Mrs. Sadie didn't think so," Eric recounted. "She always threw my mother's color up in her face. She hated dark skinned people and always told us as children that we would never amount to anything because people wouldn't trust black assed niggah children like us."

"Oh, my God!"

"Yeah, old lady Sadie B. was hell on wheels when she was outside of the church. She even claimed Josh and Jeremy over me and my brothers and sisters because they were all fair skinned even though they were all bastards."

"Wait a minute," Melvin said. "I thought Josh and Jeremy were Mr. King's children."

"Hell, naw, man," Eric said in disgust. "My uncle adopted them before the twins were born. Sadie B. used to give Trish Ann hell too before the twins were born. After Trish assured that Curbie blood would continue on, that old bitch was ready to die."

"Eric!" Melvin said in disbelief as well as respect for the elderly.

"I'm sorry but that's the truth," Eric said. His eyes had a slight gleam in them as if tears would fall any moment in reliving his terrible past with his grandmother. "Even when my brothers and sisters graduated Howard, Yale, and Princeton with Master's and PhD's that bitch didn't in as much as say I'm proud of you."

"Child, you are harboring too much hate," Melvin said softly as he watched the expression on Eric's face turn completely cold as ice.

"That old woman used to beat our ass for the least of things and Josh and Jeremy got away with pure murder. She even beat my ass when she caught Josh trying to screw me. Hell, I was trying to keep the niggah off of me and she beat my ass."

"Josh tried to screw you when you all were growing up?"

"Hell, yeah, and would get mad because I wouldn't let him. I didn't think it was right because we were supposed to be family but he would always say that my daddy and his daddy were not brothers so that made us no kin so what difference did it make."

"Oh," Melvin said as he fanned himself with a dinner napkin. "This is too much for me to process, baby."

"That motherfucker was freaky as hell. He always tried to get in my draws and suck on my dick or play with my ass and if I didn't do it then he would run and tell Sadie that I was messing with him and I would get my as tore up. I hate him at times but feel sorry for his crazy ass at other times."

"Don't hate him," Melvin advised. "Eric, if you hate him it will consume you. It is best to let some things go and you both are fully grown men now."

"Yeah," Eric laughed. "I know. But the only thing that gets me is this. Do you know that bastard had the nerve enough to proposition me last week when he found out that his old piece didn't want his sorry ass anymore?"

Melvin was too shocked at this point. He had almost forgotten that Bradley and Josh used to have a thing going on but did not know

that it was still going on so close to the new millennium. He thought that the Josh and Bradley fling had concluded in high school. This new revelation was too much to bear.

"First, isn't Josh married and second, do I know this person?"

"Yeah, he married that LaKeisha girl to front but he has been Bradley Kelly's pimp for years."

Melvin's heart sank. He could not digest this information.

"Pimp?"

"Yeah, he had that boy come all of the way to Atlanta to ho for him in order that he could live the life of a king while he was in school and finally the boy met this white man and kicked his ass to the curb. Anyway, when he came back a few weeks ago, he paid Bradley a visit and got his feelings hurt because the boy told him to go fuck off."

"Jesus, Jesus, Jesus," Melvin said before he realized he had said it aloud.

"Why you calling on the Lord? It ain't that crucial."

"Bradley is my best friend and I didn't know those were the reasons he went to Atlanta."

"I doubt he went to Atlanta to ho but he obviously turned into a good one cause he ain't doing to bad for himself these days."

"Bradley has not been in a relationship or anything else for years. I can vouch for that."

"Well, all I know is that when Bradley turned the motherfucker down and he found out I was in town he brought his crazy ass by my apartment begging for some ass and I almost went slap ass off on him."

"Thank the Lord for grace and mercy!"

"He better thank some damn body because I ain't going out like that. All the ass whippings I got because of him and his crack head brother, I wouldn't spit on him if he went to hell."

"Child, you are harboring to much hate," Melvin said as he looked at how angry Eric was with Josh and Jeremy. "You never know when those very people will need you and if you refuse them, God will hold you accountable."

"I don't mind helping the crazy fuckers but I ain't got to fuck them or let them fuck me in order to help them."

"No one said that you had to have sex with them to help them. Child, somebody is going to have to help Jeremy because he is so gone on those damned drugs until I wouldn't doubt it if he came up dead or something."

"Now that's the crazy motherfucker of the two of them. He is doing drugs for more than he is letting on and I just can't put my finger on it just yet."

"What do you mean?"

"I came back here last year to work as a journalist for the *Fairhaven Journal* and I did a report on drug abuse and drug attics. Not that my findings tell you anything about Josh but all I know is this, he used to just be a common crack head, now he is stone gone."

"When did you notice his major change?"

"I can't really tell. I didn't get here until winter of last year. I knew that when I came home for Sadie B.'s funeral he was just using them but when I moved back to Fairhaven he had changed dramatically."

Melvin felt as if he had just been given some information that he needed but he could not put his finger on what God was trying to tell him.

"You've been here this long?" Melvin asked as he looked up at Eric in amazement.

"Yeah," Eric laughed. "I see you all the time but you don't see me. I'm a reporter and I like it like that!"

"Have you been casing me out?"

"Maybe, maybe not, who's to say?"

"Well, I'll just be damned," Melvin laughed. "So it was no surprise that you saw me at the gym tonight?"

"No, actually, I usually go close to closing because that's the only time I get to go by there because of my schedule. But I saw you about a month ago and just decided to wait until you decided to grace the place again before I approached you."

"Well, I'll be damned."

"No, baby, you won't be damned," Eric grinned slyly. "Not if I can help it."

"Ooo, boy," Melvin giggled. "Them there is feuding words."

"Depends on the type of feud you looking for," Eric laughed as he gently caressed Melvin's thigh.

"Oh, that feels good, you shouldn't do that," Melvin purred.

"Maybe I want to do that," Eric whispered. "Maybe that's what you need. Maybe that's what I need. Maybe it's time for you to stop running around the world looking for love when I can be your knight in shining armor."

"Ooo," Melvin chuckled. "A black knight at my disposal."

"If you just let me into your heart, into your life, into your world," Eric pleaded gently. "I'll be your Black king, Melvin."

Melvin's heart fluttered.

"But you don't know me, Eric," Melvin said as a tear began to roll down his cheek. "I'm such a difficult person and my standards are extremely grand and I have so very many issues."

"Then let me be your black knight," Eric said as his hand gently began to caress Melvin's inner thighs moving slowly toward his buttocks. "Let me help you unpack your baggage and you help me unpack mine. I've wanted you for years now, Melvin. I've looked for you every since I've been back to Fairhaven. I sit silently in the back pews of Mt. Carmel while you direct the choir and sing the wonderful songs of Zion."

"Over my head, I hear music in the air," Melvin said as his eyes fluttered at the gentle touch of Eric's massive yet sensual hands. They were so huge yet so soft and gentle. They could tear a bear apart yet could rock a disturbed baby to sleep. And these big, black hands of a big black knight massaged Melvin's legs and buttocks with such a sweet sensation until Melvin almost screamed in ecstasy when he had not yet begun to fully embrace the throws of passion this sexy black man could give him.

Chapter Seven

And It's Gone Be Tonight

Melvin's mind told him to stop the madness before he got in too deep. He did not need to experience heartache and pain anymore. He was not up to the challenge of trying to build a new relationship anymore. After all, he was twenty-nine and well into his career. Society said no to this dark skinned brother. This was the first date with this man. He still had unresolved issues with his homosexuality. This man had issues that Melvin was not so sure that he was prepared to help sort through.

All of this was so factual yet absolutely none of this mattered to his lonely heart. It had been so long since a man had embraced him. It had been so long since he had what he desired... a black berry with sweet juice! It had been so long since any one had touched the spots on his body that made his entire soul quiver. It had been so long since anyone had admired him for Melvin. It had been so long since he had engaged in meaningful sex.

He could not fight his burning passions and hot desires as Eric lifted him from his chair and placed his large face with full thick lips onto Melvin's. Melvin melted in his arms and returned the kiss with a hot, wet, passionate kiss that was so fierce until it almost unnerved Eric.

Melvin wrapped his arms around Eric's neck and his legs around Eric's waist and seized this moment. "*Lord, you know my heart!*" he thought as Eric passionately returned his wet, hot, juicy, kisses slowly walking toward Melvin's bedroom.

"Are you sure you are ready to handle this?" Eric whispered between kissed to his lips, cheeks, neck, and shoulders.

"Right now the only thing I want is you man," Melvin whimpered. "Please don't break my heart."

"I date for the long haul, baby," Eric growled. "I want you forever."

Tears gushed down Melvin's cheeks at these words. It had been so long since he had heard them. It had been so long since he had experienced any type of true and real affection. It had been so long since any one had given a damn about him rather than his possessions.

"I'll kill you if you break my heart," Melvin sobbed softly.

"As long as I have waited for this moment, baby," Eric said as he began to slowly kiss Melvin entire face. "I'll commit suicide before I'll hurt you."

At those words, Melvin ripped Eric's shirt completely off of him and plunged forward onto his huge bare chest with tiny bites of passion sinking slightly into Eric's dark skin.

"Ooo," Eric moaned. "A tiger unfolds."

Melvin growled slightly like a tiger as he slowly nibbled on Eric's huge chest slowly making his way to Eric's nipples where he gentle bit them simultaneously followed by a quick lick of his tongue.

Eric sat down on the bed and Melvin fell on top of him kissing his bare chest while Eric managed to maneuver Melvin out of his shirt, pants, and under wear in a single twist of his huge paws.

"Can you love me for me?" Melvin growled.

"Let me show you?" Eric said as he flipped Melvin onto his back and removed his pants and underwear in one motion.

"Damn this man is good!" Melvin thought as his eyes crossed when this huge man slowly began to lick his toes one at a time in circular motions.

"Jesus, Jesus, Jesus," Melvin screamed in his mind.

"I've wanted you for so long, Melvin," Eric whispered between wet, juicy kisses to Melvin's toes, feet, and ankles.

Melvin's entire body shook from passion and excitement.

"Hold on!" Melvin said as he clutched his heart and sat straight up in the bed.

"What's wrong?" Eric asked. "Did I do something wrong?"

"Hell the fuck no!" Melvin thought as his body continued to quiver.

"You've done nothing wrong but I want this night to be magical and I don't ever want it to end. I need to hear Luther, baby."

"Fuck, Luther," Eric said as he grabbed Melvin's legs and began to massage his entire body. "I want you badly, slowly, passionately, and romantically and it's going to be tonight."

"You got it," Melvin said as his eyes rolled up into his head and he fell face forward onto the bed only to feel Eric's sensual tongue begin to slip and slide up his right leg and then his left and back to his right and on to his left and soon on his left cheek and then his right cheek and his big hands began to massage Melvin's tiny body as if it were a piece of clay.

"This feeeeels soooo…." Melvin moaned as his body began to shake and shiver as Eric began to slowly slip his tongue inside, outside, and all around his butt, his cheeks, and every portion of the area that could be licked, caressed, massaged, and manipulated.

If Melvin's bed had been a dance floor, if this episode in Melvin's life had been a dance contest, Eric would have won the contest with flying colors. His moves were so gentle yet so aggressive; so polished yet so rugged; so masculine yet so gently feminine; so honorable yet so raunchy. For the first time in Melvin's entire life, he wanted no one except this deep dark man who was indeed "blacker than a hundred midnights down in a cypress swamp."

Melvin could not resist seeing the prize in which he only glimpsed at the gym. He could not resist feeling the prize in which he only glimpsed at the gym. He could not resist touching the prize in which he only glimpsed at the gym. Eric sensed the longing and twisted his body whereas his massive manhood was neatly exposed to the panting and wanton Melvin.

"Oh, hell yeah, Curbies are blessed." Melvin said as his fingers slowly stroked the entire ten-inch shaft of his knight in shining armor.

Eric moaned as he felt the warm moist lips slowly encase his manhood like a gentle glove.

And like a symphony, Melvin made music with Eric as they slowly began to suck, lick, slurp, taste, and feel one another's bodies.

"I can wait no longer," Eric said as he gently pulled Melvin away from his manhood and onto his back.

Melvin's body was so hot until it seemed as if every pore of his body secreted boiling lava rather than sweat.

Eric looked lovingly into Melvin's eyes. Melvin passionately looked into Eric's eyes.

Melvin's eyes rolled into the back of his head as Eric slowly began to push his organ into Melvin's awaiting body. For the first time in years, someone actually cared enough to be gentle, passionate, and gracious when they entered into Melvin's courts. *"Child, this is enough to shout on right now,"* Melvin thought wickedly when he realized that Eric had been clever enough to slip a condom on without him noticing Eric ever had one in his possession.

And shout he did. Not Spiritually, though. Melvin shouted in ecstasy as Eric manipulated his body as if he were a great master musician composing a ballad to be presented before royalty. Melvin screamed passionately for the first time in his life. Melvin moaned from deep within. Melvin groaned with such intensity until he knew he could not let this end.

Eric glided slowly inward and flowed gently outward causing Melvin to claw gently into his huge back.

"Oh, Eric," Melvin moaned as he realized this big black African-American man who was "blacker than a hundred midnights down in a cypress swamp" was rocking his world. Actually, Eric was more like a 9.5 on the Richter scale.

"I've been waiting all night for you to call my name, baby," Eric whispered.

"I'll.." Melvin moaned.

Eric continued to slowly stroke and work it out.

"I'll call..."

He moved gently like a gentle breeze on the ocean.

"I'll call your..."

Melvin forgot about any other man prior to this African king with dread locks in his bed at this moment.

"I'll call your name..."

Each stroke made him forget whatever it was he was so terribly attempting to remember.

"I'll call your name forever..."

"Oh, baby," Eric moaned.

Melvin could no longer focus. His mind was in turmoil.

"If you let me…"

"I'll let you baby," Eric groaned. "If you'll only promise to love me for me."

And yet this man was the largest Melvin had ever had and he was indeed the best.

"Oh, I will love you, my sweet…"

Melvin wished his body would allow him to respond in words to such sweet repose as his body felt at every thrust Eric provided.

"Oh, Eric…"

"Oh, baby…"

And both Melvin and Eric shivered for what seemed an eternity as each produced the most passionate orgasm they had ever produced in this life.

Melvin looked into Eric's eyes and tears began to stream down his face again. He could not believe that he had fallen in love again in such a crazy manner with someone he really did not know yet he, for some strange reason, trusted with all of his heart, mind, and soul.

Eric could not believe that he had finally managed to sleep with the man of his dreams. He had never felt worthy enough to be loved and thus had fought against loving anyone. He was a master at sabotaging relationships that he did not think would be worth his time or energy. Someone had told him just a year ago to go back to the place that hurt him the most and there he would find love. He never believed it. He never thought it possible. And now, within a four-hour period of time, he had managed to fall deeply and passionately in love with someone who for years had been a mere figment of his imagination.

Eric was afraid.

Melvin was afraid.

"I'm willing to try this," Melvin said as he lay in the huge armpit of Eric. "It has been so long until I really don't know what to do or what to expect except heartache and heartbreak."

"I'm new to the relationship scene in this aspect, Melvin, but if you allow me the chance, I promise I'll love you unconditionally."

"Well, sir," Melvin smiled as he looked into Eric's eyes and twirled his finger into one of Eric's dreadlocks. "You are in for a challenge but I'm mighty afraid that I am too."

"I live for challenges," Eric laughed. "The only thing I expect of you is to be faithful and honest with me about everything."

"I'll be brutally honest," Melvin confessed. "I have no reason not to be faithful to my black knight."

Eric kissed his forehead tenderly.

"What was that for?"

"Being everything I thought you would be."

Melvin kissed Eric's cheek.

"What was that for?"

"Being more than my expectations of you!"

Eric smiled.

Melvin smiled.

Slowly, sleep engulfed the two of them against both of their wills. They both wanted to savor the moments and hold fast to them for as long as life would grant them the opportunity. Yet sleep gently closed Eric's eyes and gently closed Melvin's eyes allowing Melvin the first opportunity to rest in the bosom of **"his"** man.

It was a new sensation for them both yet it was a sweet serenity about it all. At last Melvin had found love. At last Eric had found love.

For the first time ever, Melvin had an overnight guest who was not put out of the house at the crack of dawn.

For the first time ever, Eric did not feel guilty for sleeping with a man.

For the first time ever both Melvin and Eric entrusted their hearts, minds, and souls to another individual.

Chapter Eight

In Times Like These

"You did what?" Bradley yelled over the telephone in excitement.

"Child, I didn't stutter," Melvin giggled.

"God that's a black ass man," Bradley laughed.

"You know my motto, the blacker the berry, the sweeter the juice."

"Yeah, and you know mine as well," Bradley laughed. "The lighter the filling, the sweeter the supreme!"

Melvin laughed. It was the first time he could gossip about his personal life in years and actually feel good about it.

"He says he knows you," Melvin said in an attempt to get more information from Bradley in regards to Eric Curbie.

"Hell," Bradley commented. "He ought to know me. I fucked his cousin for years."

"I thought you and Josh broke up before you went to Atlanta?"

"Child, no," Bradley laughed. "We didn't break up until after I got to Atlanta and he thought that he was going to pimp me, child."

"What in the hell were you doing in Atlanta?"

"The same damn thing you were doing in Tennessee… fucking in both pants legs. Don't come for me this morning, you know I'll roast your ass."

"I'm just trying to get a few things clear in my mind," Melvin admitted as he recounted his conversation with Eric.

"Just what are you trying to get clear?" Bradley asked.

"Well," Melvin mumbled.

"Speak up, I can't hear you!"

"Well, I was told that you were being pimped by Josh in Atlanta and left him for another pimp."

"Well, you got your damned facts wrong," Bradley said slightly agitated. "First of all, I never had a pimp although I was a grand ho, honey! Oh, yes, since you want to hear it, I'll tell you all about it."

"You don't have to do this since we are supposed to be best friends and you didn't do it after all of these years."

"You are still trying to come for me, wench but I'm getting ready to tell you in this manner," Bradley said. "First, the Bible tells us that we are not supposed to let our left hand know what our right hand is doing."

"Oh, so that's how it is, then?"

"No, I just didn't see a need to tell you what I was doing especially since you caught me in the act in Nashville years ago and I thought you would have realized it then."

"Child, I forgot all about that incident."

"Anyway, I was a ho for Bradley and no one else. I paid the cost to be the boss in my crib. Yeah, I let Josh stay with me for a while but he wanted an idiot and I couldn't be his idiot."

"What do you mean?"

"He wanted me to be a ho and sleep with him while he courted and eventually married LaKeisha. I wasn't having it."

"Why did you let my friend marry him and you knew what he was about all along?"

"First of all, she is your friend and if you wanted her to know then you should have told her. Second, she's not as dumb as all of you all seem to think. She knew what the deal was and that is precisely the reason they have been in separate beds for years now."

"How in the hell did you find that out?"

"I have my ways. But anyway, Josh kept bringing all of these strange people to my place and the straw that broke the camel's back with me and was when I found out that he was trying to have his cousin up in my crib."

"Do you mean Eric?"

"Eric's brother, child, Ernest."

Melvin was speechless for a moment.

"Well, I'll be damned," Melvin finally managed to say.

"He didn't have the boy did he?"

"No but the boy beat the shit out of him and then left Atlanta and moved to DC. Last I hear he had married after graduating from Howard."

"Well, what did you do after you found this out?"

"Child, I finally accepted George's offer and did the relationship thing."

"Who in the hell is George?"

"Oh, George was the doctor that I dated in Atlanta. He was very wealthy but too goddamned domineering for my taste."

"Did you love him?"

"I tried to but he smothered the hell out of me."

"What made you leave him?"

"I got tired of spending his money."

Melvin could not help but laugh at his friend. Bradley was honest to the core and would not hold back the truth if you inquired it of him.

"Well, what happened then?"

"Oh, a few stocks and a few bonds later, I met Arthur the fashion merchandiser."

"You bitch, that's who set you up isn't it?"

"Not really but he really taught me the ropes," Bradley laughed. "Child I went everywhere from New York to Paris to London to Naples even to China with that man."

"Was he black?"

"Why do you ask?"

"I haven't heard of any black fashion merchandisers doing all of that," Melvin confessed.

"Hell, you haven't heard of black men doing shit because you just now began to read about all of the accomplishments of our people but Arthur and George was both white. Child, you know I would have had to beat a niggah down."

"Whatever."

"As mean as I was back then, child please."

"Well why did you and Arthur break up?"

"Arthur and I did not break up we only separated."

"What do you mean?"

"Child, Arthur and I did vows and everything," Bradley laughed.

"Did vows?" Melvin asked. "What do you mean did vows?"

"I married Arthur, bitch."

"You are married?"

"I am separated."

"Oh my God!"

"The Lord has nothing to do with this and I would appreciate it if you would keep Him out of this conversation! Thank you very much!"

"Bitch, you are married?"

"Actually, I am widowed."

"You're talking in riddles, Bradley," Melvin said.

"Do you remember when I went to Atlanta about three months ago on urgent business?"

"Yes, but I just thought you had gone to another garment show or something. What happened?"

"Child, I went to Arthur's funeral," Bradley said without any remorse. "He had overdosed on heroin."

"Get outta here!"

"Is that why you left him?"

"Did the sun rise this morning?" Bradley laughed. "Hell, yeah, that's why I left him. He was a sweet man but I gave him every opportunity in the world to go to rehabilitation for his problem and he kept bullshitting. So, I told him I was leaving and taking an insurance policy out ion his ass and he had better leave me everything in the will or I was cremating him and flushing his ass down the toilet."

"Bradley!"

"Child, if you have never lived with a damned drug attic then you will never know. My life was hell towards the end. And I actually liked Arthur."

"Well, what did he leave you?"

"Bitch, I just told you the son-of-a-bitch was a heroin attic. He died penniless."

"So, how was he buried?"

"I kept my damned promise to him," Bradley said wryly.

"You didn't?"

"I wasn't spending a cent on his ass when he didn't have to die that way! Since he wanted to throw his life down the toilet, that's where I threw his remains - down the fucking toilet."

Melvin's legs went weak. He had to sit down.

"Bradley!"

"What did his family say?"

"What family? Those folk disowned him years before he even met me because they knew he was a damned heroin attic."

"His family was like Frederick's family?"

"No, those people weren't religious idiots like Hortence. They had tried everything until they couldn't take anymore. So they washed their hands of him completely."

"Why did you marry him, then?" Melvin asked.

"When I met him, he was actually recovering and doing great," Bradley began as he thought about his adventurous life with Arthur. "We were in love. Damn, I can finally say and admit that. He cherished me but he cherished that shit more than he cherished me and I didn't appreciate that very much at all!"

"So you have been in love," Melvin smiled at the thought of his friend knowing love as he had begun to rediscover it.

"Oh, yeah," Bradley laughed wryly. "I loved him deeply. Against all the odds, I loved him but when you can fuck up a hundred thousand dollar a year job for a goddamned addiction, it's time for Bradley to hit the road."

"How did you find out?"

"When I was sitting at the house one day working my ass off as a designer and all of a sudden the lights, gas and water, everything went off completely. Then, I discovered we were three months behind in rent and all of the credit cards were maxed out."

"Damn, so how did you get out of it?"

"Easily, I cashed in a favor from George and sold a CD and brought my ass back home to Tennessee."

"So what happened to Arthur?"

"Eventually he lost his job and engulfed his entire existence into using that shit."

"That's scary as hell."

"It wasn't scary for me because I knew it was a matter of time so I took out about twelve two hundred thousand dollar burial insurance policies on his ass and made sure I kept them paid up. It was expensive as hell but I outlasted that son-of-a..."

"Bradley!"

"And as sure as my promise, when the Atlanta police department called me to come and identify his body I got on the first thing smoking to Atlanta, looked at how pitiful he had become. Called his folks and they told me to do whatever I wished. So, I did."

"And that was?"

"I fried his ass like I told him I would and then flushed his remains down the toilet exactly like I told him I would do!"

"Why so much hatred, Bradley?"

"It wasn't hatred," Bradley confessed. "I was just pissed off at the fact that he loved heroin, cocaine, and every other drug more than he loved me. I had a very hard time dealing with that. So, since he allowed his life to go down the toilet, so did his remains and I am now a millionaire!"

Melvin could not respond because his mouth was wide open.

"Close your mouth, bitch," Bradley laughed as he envisioned Melvin. "I was the class ho, the low life from RoEllen and finally all of the years of lying on this back has come to fruition and I will never lie on my back again for anyone. Yeah, I know my methods have not been the most honorable ones but I have outlasted the best and I can truly say that I outlasted the test of time. I don't have AIDS. I am still young. I am going to retire when I feel like retiring. And I saved the fucking toilet seat that I flushed that bastard down because if it was not for his stupidity, we could have enjoyed this together."

"You are so damned deep until you are scary," Melvin finally managed to say,

"I'm deep in money, guhl!"

"Will you never date again?"

"What for?" Bradley laughed. "I'm not lonely. Last I recall, you were the lonely one between the two of us. Child, Frederick's death taught me well on allowing sick ass trade in your house and in your life! No, I will never be in a relationship again."

"So what are you going to do now since you are a millionaire?"

"Exactly what I do now, work every day for a living," Bradley laughed. "Hell, I'm not in a rush to spend my hard earned money. It took more sacrifices than you think in order to keep those damned policies up. I sat over in this place of mine plenty of days without food and shit just because I knew that it was only a matter of time."

"You did not have food in the house?"

"There have been plenty of days I went without a whole lot of shit but I don't have to advertise to the world my misfortunes."

"Bradley, you know I would have put groceries in your house regardless of what was going on."

"I know you would have but I didn't ask you to, now did I?"

"No, you didn't"

"Well, just sit tight and watch me bless the children. I can't forget Frederick's last words to the group: when the children just get together."

"If we do, we can take the south by storm," Melvin laughed.

"Child, the south will wake up or be left behind. I'm getting to old to do all of the shit I used to do and I am certainly tired and worn out now."

"Child, you aren't getting ready to die on me are you?"

"Hell naw, not when I just became a millionaire, bitch are you crazy?"

"You just sounded too distant there for a minute and I don't want a repeat of Frederick," Melvin said as he began to remember. "He do you think we know the murderer of Frederick?"

"I bet if we do," Bradley said dryly. "We just haven't invested enough money into finding out who it was but it has to be somebody who knew him."

"I keep feeling as if we are stumbling around on the evidence all of the time."

"Nine times out of ten, the answer is right before us but we just have to figure it out. But, you better believe we will find closure before the end of the year."

"Well, I hope so."

"We will," Bradley said. "Well, anyway, I'm glad you finally got your stuff stirred and I honestly do pray for the success of the relationship. Eric is a good guy and I have always respected him with his big dicked ass."

"And how would you know his dick size?"

"A ho knows all," Bradley laughed.

"Well you ain't never lied, child!" Melvin laughed.

"That man ain't that damned big and tall for nothing."

"Child, child, child," Melvin giggled. "I have never felt this good in my life."

"Beware, guhl," Bradley warned. "Everyday won't be peaches and cream."

"Remember my first love?"

"Say no more, hell, in times like these; I'm just happy that there is somebody for everybody and nobody for me!"

"Oh there is somebody for you if you want to date again."

"You just don't get it do you?"

"Get what?"

"I don't want to date no more," Bradley said wryly. "I flushed my heart down the toilet with the remains of my late husband."

"Can I ask you something?" Melvin asked sincerely from his heart and true boyish self, which warmed Bradley's spirit.

"What, Melvin?"

"What was it like being married and in love?"

"It was the opportunity of a life time," Bradley said as he fondly thought about his relationship with Arthur.

"Was there any difference with him being white?"

"He could have been purple," Bradley said as a tear rolled down his face. "I was the happiest man alive just knowing that he loved Bradley for Bradley not Bradley for sex or money or anything else. Arthur loved me for me. I never saw him as being white. I just saw him as being my soul mate. We flew to Hawaii and exchanged vows. We honeymooned in Paris. He tried to love me more but could not."

"Well, why did you flush him, then?"

"Oh, I flushed some of him but I kept most of him."

"How sweet."

"Yeah, my roses needed fertilizer and since he was being a pain in the ass and wouldn't flush completely down the commode, I thought about how much he loved our rose garden in Atlanta. So, when you come to the house again, you will notice my new rose garden. Just know that Arthur will always be with me through the seasons."

This time it was Melvin who shed a tear.

"Bitch, you are crazy!" Melvin laughed as he wiped a tear from his eye.

"Yeah, but I'm yet a millionaire," Bradley laughed. "It took me all of ten years to do what I told you I would do when we graduated high school."

"Well, you did it," Melvin laughed slightly. "Enjoy!"

"I will to a degree but I find myself in my rose garden a lot more often these days spending time with my husband."

"You'll find love again," Melvin assured.

"No, baby, that is for you. I have a new mission to accomplish. Never again will I watch a human who could love as tenderly as Arthur could love just throw his entire life away on a damned fix."

"You need to heal, my friend."

"I heal when I see just how beautiful my roses bloom now since Arthur is out there with them," Bradley laughed.

"You are crazy, bitch!"

"And I love you too."

"Bye child!"

"Bye!"

Chapter Nine
I'm Working On A Mission

Mt. Carmel Missionary Baptist Church monumentally stood on a hill in Fairhaven providing a rich foundation of African-American history to this small community. Mt. Carmel was the most sacred place on earth to many of its parishioners and it held a warm place in their hearts. Just walking on the grounds gave a person a Spiritually connected feeling knowing that the toil and labor rendered by the founding fathers and mothers provided an illustrious edifice in this present age. The church, like so many churches in the African-American rural south, had been organized and established by former slaves and former slave children. Originally, seven families had come together to worship and praise God for bringing them into freedom. The founder was a former house slave who had learned how to read and was called by God to spread the Word to God's children who suffered throughout slavery. A one-room building erected on top of a hill in the middle of a grove of oak and pine trees became home to the meeting place of these former slaves. Here, they risked life itself learning to read, write, and reason. After emancipation, the land was purchased for $30.00 and the once hidden path that leads to Mt. Carmel was cleared into a dirt road. Strength and determination held the congregation together after the first burning of the church in 1885 by the Ku Klux Klan. After the first church burning, a second building was erected that held more people due to an increasing membership. This building burned down in 1934, which led the building of the present edifice. Seven of the congregation's affluent members organized with the pastor and congregation and hired contractors to build a momentous edifice that would be a sign of hope to African-American persons who would see it. Frederick Perry's great-grandmother, Jewel Temples met with the pastor and head deacons and demanded the right to contribute to the cause. Although it was a very well kept secret for years, no one knew that the church had been funded by the owner of the town brothel along with Obadiah James, the first mortician in Fairhaven who, subsequently, was Melvin James' great-grandfather. Obadiah was a deacon at Mt. Carmel who, like many of the deacons of Mt. Carmel, patronized Jewel's brothel and bar. One night, the head deacons were at the bar discussing the fate of the church when Jewel demanded that she be allowed to help.

"What will our wives say if they ever found out?" Obadiah complained.

"The same damn thang they will say if they find out you here," Jewel yelled as she spit snuff into a nearby spittoon. "Yall need help and I'm willin' to help ya."

"But what about our pastor?" Thomas Fields whined in his weary sounding voice.

"Ain't he about ready to die anyway?" Jewel asked. "Hell, old man Kelly has been around for a long time now. Since as long as I can remember. He ought to be about a hundred this year."

"Yeah, but he is our founder and pastor," Obadiah said wearily. "You know how those folk from Rock Spring can get at times."

"Well, he ain't a Smith," Grimlock Gauldin laughed as he smoked on his long cigar. "Those Smith's from over at Rock Spring would sniff a rat at any time."

Grimlock Gauldin was a heavyset man who owned Fairhaven's only black grocery. He had buried three wives and was now searching for his fourth. He was willing to find her anywhere and Jewel often provided him with the best advice on who to marry.

"Marry some fragile idiot and you'll be all right," she would laugh behind a snuff filled mouth that forever revealed the symbol of her wealth as anyone could note the gold caps on several of her "good" teeth. "Ain't nobody else gonna put up wit yo' shit and if they have a good mind they show ain't gonna want no house full of bad ass runny nose brats dat you got."

"Hell, those Kelly's from over at Rock Sprang ain't all that holy either," Jewel laughed. "Old man Kelly is about the most even tempered out of the bunch"

"Naw, now," Grimlock laughed. "If it weren't for him I think many of 'em would have gone bad. But some of them Smith's are all right with me."

"Yeah, I heard about Effus hitting that white man downtown Dyersburg," Obadiah laughed.

Grimlock shuttered.

"That wasn't wise to me," Grimlock said as he exhaled a cloud of smoke. "You know they hung a man a few years ago down on the square and then he turned around and provoked them folk by hittin' one of 'em."

"Well he should've hit 'em," Jewel said as she rubbed her mouth on the back of the sleeve of her blouse. "I give him credit. He fought in the war and come home and has to be a second-class citizen because he colored. He should've hit that white man if that white man was bothering him. Effus Smith don't bother nobody."

The group remained silent as they thought about the tall yet skinny black man from Rock Spring. They could think of nothing but nice thoughts about him because he was a hard working gentle man who bothered no one.

"Well, they could have burned down his home and all of Rock Sprang," Grimlock said nervously.

"Those Smith's were waiting on the white folk," Obadiah laughed. "They tell me that every thang that could hold a gun including the mules and chickens were waiting on an uprising."

"Well, I heard that Cribbs told the white man that if he went out to Rock Spring bothering those Smiths then he would get whatever he deserved," Obadiah smiled knowing that if John Cribbs, the sheriff and ruler of Dyer County, validated a black man in the 1930s, nothing would happen to him.

"Well, who gone talk to the pastor?" Ennis Nelson, Fairhaven's only black doctor asked softly. Ennis never cheated on his wife but always met with other men for a shot of whiskey and a game of cards in order to settle his nerves from the injustices of the medical profession throughout daily life in the rural south.

"I'll talk to the old bastard," Jewel laughed.

"It would help us out," Grimlock Gauldin laughed.

"So then is it settled?" Ennis asked as a frown appeared on his face.

"You know we can't let a woman go and ask this from our pastor," Obadiah said grimly. "He would kick us all of the deacon board and shame us all."

"We don't talk about shame in hear," Jewel laughed. "This is a ho house and juke joint, you know?"

"Then I'll tell him," Obadiah said as he took a drink of his whiskey.

A week after this conversation, the great pastor and founder of Mt. Carmel died of natural causes at the wonderful age of 106 after serving the congregation for over fifty years. A massive edifice was constructed during the "search" for a new leader. For fifty years the conversation, plan, and action was never discussed.

Melvin sat in his regular pew in Mt. Carmel. He could not help but laugh when he thought about how he had become exactly like many of the elderly women who sat in the "mother board" or "Amen corner." He would almost fight with anyone who sat in "his" seat on the Sundays that he did not sing in the choir.

Services had begun to change at Mt. Carmel as time settled on the rural southern community. None of the choirs marched down the aisle at the opening of the services except on First Sunday which was Communion Sunday or Homecoming Sunday. An old "Dr. Watts" hymn was no longer sung during devotion except on Homecoming Sunday. Unfortunately, there were few members who knew how to lead them in the same manner that the elders of yesteryear could sing them.

The announcement secretary was no longer an elderly lady but now a young, very articulate deacon's wife. Now since the Josh Curbie Family had returned to Fairhaven and reinstated his membership, he had been quickly made a deacon. His wife, and Melvin's friend LaKeisha, was given the responsibility of being the announcement secretary after the passing of the former announcement secretary. Now, every Sunday morning before Etta James welcomed the visitors, LaKeisha Nelson Curbie read the announcements.

On this particular Sunday morning the church was shocked along with Melvin. Mrs. Lilly, who was now a beautiful ninety-year-old diva, had casually slipped a well-typed and well articulated letter of resignation into the hands of the announcement secretary. As the new secretary read the resignation, Mrs. Lilly sat stoically on her front row pew with her head held high. She was dressed to kill in a gorgeous lace chiffon black dress with matching gloves, lace handkerchief, and wide a brimmed hat full of plumes and feathers. The members of the Senior Choir who sat in the audience on that particular Sunday could be heard screaming or breaking down in tears as the announcement secretary pressed through the resignation letter. Pastor Garrison, in distress, publicly asked Mrs. Lilly to reconsider. She, in return, rose from her seat, walked to the podium, and began to speak to a very teary eyed congregation.

"... I am retiring for me not because the church has done anything to upset me," she said. "I thank the Lord for enabling me to see ninety this year. I made up in my mind a long time ago: If the

Lord spared me to see ninety, I would take my seat and give the Music Ministry over to the younger generation. I have served Mt. Carmel since I was a child. I remember Reverend Kelly sending me to the National Baptist Convention in order to keep abreast at what the rest of the world was doing musically. I've played for at least four generations of baptismals, weddings, and funerals. I can even remember when musicians were only paid twenty-five cents for Sunday School and two dollars for Morning Worship Services."

The entire congregation laughed.

"I've served under the pastorate of all of our church's pastors and have been well received by the pastors and the congregation. For this I love you but please, it is time for our Music Ministry to move forward. I only pray that you new musicians will just remember where we have come from. This church has not always been a splendid edifice. As a matter of fact, this particular edifice was built through a determination and collaboration of deacons and a person who I feel God blessed for her efforts. Nevertheless, I will play for the remainder of this month on my two Sundays but after that I am taking my seat on my pew. You all pray my strength in the Lord."

The congregation rose to its feet and gave her a standing ovation as she gracefully walked to her front row seat and gracefully sat down. As a tribute to Mrs. Lilly, Mt. Carmel's award winning Gospel Choir under the direction of Howard Avery began singing "He's Calling Me!"

Now Melvin felt as if he was at church. Very few musicians in the 1990s played the traditional gospel music during the morning worship celebration yet Howard would always manage to keep at least one traditional selection in his music ministry.

Melvin, like other members of the congregation, quickly became absorbed in the rhythmic and Spiritual beat of the music. Melvin again knew he was "at church" when he began to hear the sound of shoe heels tapping in time to the beat of the music as hands began to clap as melodious voices were lifted up in praise to God as the music took the entire congregation back in time for a moment.

"He's calling me," the soloist led as the choir and members of the congregation who sang in various choirs responded with "He's calling me!"

"My God's calling me," she continued. "Every day of my life I can hear God calling me..."

"He's calling me" the choir sang in response.

"Don't you know God's calling," she sang.

"Calling me from labor to a life of eternity"

"Oh, yeah"

"I can hear Jesus calling me, calling me!"

Beyond the shouting, the tears of sadness, and the testimonials of the saints, Melvin was yet proud to be a part of a historic and momentous moment within the history of his church. Even he had to stand up out of his seat when the soloist strutted down the aisles singing as the choir would answer her melodious questions with harmonic responses.

When the joyous and festive moment ended, he like many others sat down and prepared for the sermon for the day.

The sermon began wonderfully. The pastor's delivery was great and totally Spiritually filled. Somehow, the sermon took a turn for the worse and Melvin began to become fueled with rage as he listened.

"... So often people flock to these fraternities trying to be a part of an educated society. But I've come to tell you today that there is no holiness in them. Yeah, I know many of you are members of these organizations but if you study you will discover that these organizations were founded by homosexuals who put logic before God. If you study the Greeks, you would know that most Greek philosophers were homosexuals and were masters of logic and reasoning yet in their reasoning they did not know God..."

Melvin shut down completely. He glanced over the congregation and watched *AKA's, Delta's, Sigmas, Zetas, Ques, Omegans, Alphas, Kappas, Eastern Stars,* and *Masons* all swell up with indignation. Melvin almost laughed as he saw how many backs straighten up and heads position themselves for battle as the "Amens" began to cease and a cloud of anger began to hang over the congregation.

Melvin looked toward the organ into the face of Howard. Howard, the man who perpetually wore a huge smile now wore a stone face. The mother board was filled with Eastern stars as the minister's and deacons' wives, usher board, and choir all held sorority members in the various auxiliaries. The deacons and male members of the church were mostly Masons or affiliated with some fraternal organization. And yet, the pastor continued to preach amidst upturned mouths, folded arms, and statuesque held heads. Even the people who normally slept during church were now attentive to what was being said from across what was considered "their" pulpit!

The sermon came to an end without an "Amen," "Hallelujah," "Thank You, Jesus" - nothing except silence.

Melvin almost became fearful for the pastor. The church had not been this silent in all of his years of membership within it. Yet it was an ice-cold feeling in the sanctuary when just moments prior the church had gone forth in praise.

The final song did nothing to uplift the killing of the Holy Spirit on that Sunday. However, the song that was chosen added salt to injury. Pastor Garrison asked the congregation and choir to sing with him *"The Solid Rock"* Angrily the congregation and choir sang:

"My Hope Is Built On Nothing Less Than Jesus' Blood And Righteousness.
I dare not trust the sweetest frame but wholly lean on Jesus' Name.
On Christ the solid Rock I stand, all other ground is sinking sand!
All other ground is sinking sand."

The sanctuary cleared in ten minutes flat after the benediction. Members quickly greeted one another as well as the pastor but no one tarried long.

Melvin briefly spoke to Eric who had a slight smirk on his face as he looked at the pastor and the attitude of many of the members.

"I didn't know you were here today," Melvin whispered as they shook hands and exchanged pleasantries.

"I told you that I attend every Sunday," Eric laughed. "I'm very happy that I attended this Sunday, though. Man, I have never seen so many pissed off people in my life as I saw today."

"Well, I'm not going to be pissed off because I'm going to go and talk with him."

"Why?"

"Because I pay tithes here and I am a member here and I refuse to go home pissed off because of something that I may have misinterpreted."

"What are you doing later, then?"

"I'm going over to my mom and dad's house for Sunday dinner and then I'm going home, any reason you asked?"

"I was going out to eat and wanted to know if you wanted to join me but I understand."

"You are welcomed to eat with us," Melvin said as he attempted to not lose his cool, calm, and collected head in the presence of his new man.

"I'm not ready for the family thing yet," Eric chuckled. "But I will come by later tonight."

"Cool," Melvin said as he exchanged pleasantries with an elderly AKA member who seemed to be forcing a smile on her face.

"He might not have a church after this Sunday," Eric whispered to Melvin as he noticed a few of the elderly sorority women congregating before exiting the sanctuary.

"Child, you know this church is full of AKAs, Deltas, Zetas, and Eastern Stars and that is just the women. The men make up a whole new aspect of orders."

"Are you a member of anything?"

"Omega Phi Theta."

Eric laughed.

"See you tonight," he said as he squeezed Melvin's hand softly and then walked out of the church.

Melvin took a deep breath and then walked to the front of the church were a few people were congregated exchanging pleasantries with Pastor Garrison.

"Good afternoon, Pastor Garrison," Melvin said as he extended his hand to the young minister. It was amazing that this man was only a few years older than he was but had made a very terrible mistake on this particular Sunday morning.

"Good afternoon, Brother Melvin," he said as he stretched out his hand in an effort to shake Melvin's hand. Melvin offered his hand.

"May I speak with you for a moment in your office?"

"Certainly, give me a few minutes."

Melvin walked toward the pastor's study and waited for Reverend Garrison to complete his greetings. Melvin could hear the finance committee counting money in the finance room as a slight murmur began as always in that room.

"Come on in," Reverend Garrison said to Melvin as he finally broke free from the last congregation member.

Melvin followed him into the pastor study.

Reverend Garrison motioned for Melvin to sit down.

Melvin sat in a chair in front of the pastor's desk as the Rev. Garrison sat down.

"What can I help you with today?"

"I'm going to skip all of the madness and get right to the point, if that is fine with you, Pastor?"

"By all means, please do."

"I did not understand where you were coming from in your sermon and I really need clarity?"

"What part did you not understand, son?"

Melvin looked at him crazily. This man called him son when he was not old enough to even think about being his father. But, he could get over this and hopefully find clarity on what went across the pulpit on this Sunday.

"I'm confused at what you meant by saying that fraternal organizations were founded by homosexuals," Melvin said as he noticed as very perplexed expression form on the pastor's face.

"Is that what you understood me to say?"

"Yes it is and I highly disagree with you."

"First, son," he began. "That is not what I said nor was my intended delivery meant in that manner."

"Then what was your meaning?"

"I simply meant that many of our members do everything to become a part of fraternal organizations and never truly search the histories behind them."

"Well, have you searched the histories behind the fraternal organizations to which many of your members are pledged to?"

"Yes and that is what I said during my sermon. Many of the fraternal organizations were formed because people wanted to be like the Greeks who were very great thinkers indeed. But they were homosexuals and they did not believe in God and often mocked God."

"That is the craziest thing I have ever heard in my life," Melvin said as he looked in disbelief at his pastor.

"Was Socrates not a homosexual?"

"Fraternal organizations have nothing to do with Socrates," Melvin defended. "African-American fraternities definitely have nothing to do with Socrates."

"You still miss my point," Garrison continued. "I'm just saying that so many of our people flock to get into these organizations and do everything in their power to support something that was founded upon the principles of Greek mythology and ideology and those great thinkers were homosexual and did not have a faith in the God that we serve."

"My only complaint is the that you are saying fraternal organizations were founded by people who did not have a faith in God therefore fraternities are no good."

"No, I'm saying that when we place a greater emphasis on the fraternity structure, belief, and system and forget about God then we are as guilty as many of the homosexuals for which they were formed."

"I'm sorry but I have a conflict with everything that you are saying," Melvin said attempting to contain his anger.

"You must be in one of these fraternities?"

"Oh it is much greater than that," Melvin confessed. "First, I feel as if you have insulted me, and then you have insulted my fraternity second."

"I don't understand," Garrison said as he looked into Melvin's eyes for clarity and meaning.

"First, Pastor, I am homosexual but I have never lost my faith, belief, and hope in God. Second, my fraternity was not formed by homosexuals nor has the intent ever been to discredit God in any way. As a matter of fact, over ninety percent of my fraternity brothers are standing members in someone's church."

Garrison sat stunned in his seat for a moment.

"I am so sorry." he said which shocked Melvin. "I did not realize how you felt but I need some understanding now."

"I'm listening," Melvin said knowing where the conversation may or may not go from this point on.

"Did I offend you by saying that fraternity systems were formed by homosexuals?"

"Yes, because that is a racist lie and I cannot respect my pastor or even listen to that type of hate coming from the pulpit and church where I found the Lord."

"The point that I was trying to make…"

"I know…" Melvin said wryly. "If you hate homosexuals enough then people will understand to pledge but to keep focused on God."

"That is totally farfetched," Garrison said. ""My question to you, however, is what do you want me to do? How can I educate the congregation if you cannot educate me?"

"Educate you on what?"

"Well, first of all Melvin, let me repent before you right now," Garrison said which totally shocked Melvin. "I am sorry. I came from a wrong angle and therefore misinformed my congregation. First of all, I have never preached Sodom and Gomorra because there are too many other people preaching it so ridiculously until there is not truth in it. Second, I really don't understand homosexuality enough to really talk about it. I can only go God's way and I know that God can save any and everybody."

Melvin was totally bewildered at this point. He expected something totally different from his pastor and now it seemed as if his pastor was at least attempting to reason with him.

"What exactly are you saying, Pastor?"

"The only thing that I am saying is that nowhere in the Bible does it say that a man cannot go to heaven for being a homosexual, however, all sin of the flesh will be judged."

"I'm confused Pastor."

"What's confusing about it," Garrison said. "All sex outside of marriage is sin. If I have sex before I marry then I am no greater or no less than anyone else. Do you understand where I am coming?"

"Man I am so confused right now until I don't know what to do," Melvin confessed.

"Well, first of all, don't think that I am trying to make a pass at you or anything because I am not but I have been around the world enough to know that there are homosexuals in the church as well as everywhere else. I just thank you for calling my hand on an issue and forcing me to continue to walk in God's statutes."

Melvin was overwhelmed.

"Well how do you plan on rectifying the fraternity situation with the church being that plenty of your members are hot with you right now?"

"Oh, I don't plan on changing anything," he said. "Things will work themselves out. They always do."

"You mean you are going to leave it in the air just like that?"

"Well, yes for many reasons."

"They are?"

"Tell me the last time you visited the AIDS clinic?"

"I haven't. What does that have to do with anything?" Melvin asked.

"How can you chastise me when you have not seen something that is very prevalent in the homosexual world? Can you even say that you know and understand your own plight?"

"So you will leave things as they are?"

"Did the congregation get angry with me today?"

"Ninety percent of the members were mad," Melvin confessed.

"Then I have done my job," Garrison laughed.

Melvin shook his head in disbelief.

"I don't understand," Melvin said as he looked at the genuine grin on his pastor's face.

"Well, out of a congregation of four hundred, only one came to question what I had to say today. Give me about three months. You'll understand it all then," Garrison laughed.

"Are you working on some type of new mission, Pastor?"

"You bet," Garrison laughed. "It's a mission that you will be working on as well in the future. One way or the other you will get up and do something for your community or you will be one of the ones either left behind or to help remove me from this position."

"Why pastor?"

"Mt. Carmel cannot afford to stay behind in the new millennium or the church will cease to exist. Yeah, there will be some sermons that will be challenging to your mind and I hope that they make you angry enough to change otherwise I have not done my job as your pastor. No, I do not understand homosexuality but I understand Spirituality and that is what I want you to come to terms with, Melvin."

"I must admit, I expected you to gay bash," Melvin said earnestly.

"Well, Melvin, if I gay bashed then I would lose key members of my congregation but if I just preach God's word whatever my beliefs are will become null and void and God will do the rest."

"So are you saying that you support homosexuality?"

"No I am not!" Garrison admitted. "I'm saying that I support Spirituality. I support being born again and I do not want you to get the two confused. This community is on the verge of many major events and Spirituality is going to be far more important than sexuality."

"So you don't have a problem with my sexuality?"

"Do *you* have a problem with your sexuality, Melvin?" Garrison said and stood up.

"I don't know," Melvin said in bewilderment.

"Well, Melvin, figure it out. I admire you for at least sharing this with me and I will take it into consideration but if you will excuse me, I have to get out of here to get to Sunday dinner... You have my card; call me if you need me."

"Yes sir," Melvin said as he stood, shook his pastor's hand and left.

Chapter Ten

Where The Table Is Spread

Melvin turned onto Chestnut Street and into the drive of his parents. The two-story house had not changed much in twenty-five years with the exception of the children continuously leaving it. Melvin always enjoyed Sunday dinner and it was always served at the same time as it had been in previous years - one thirty or immediately after church.. Although not as festive as eating holiday meals at his grandparent's home, it was still home.

"What in the world was Mrs. Lilly talking about today?" Melvin asked his mother as he helped her set the dining room table.

"When she resigned or what?" Etta asked as she busied herself about the kitchen in preparation for her family to enter the dining room for Sunday dinner.

"When she said something about the present edifice was built by special people or something," Melvin asked.

"Oh, she was just talking about Mrs. Jewel, the Madame of the one and only brothel slash bar slash café in Fairhaven."

"Who was Mrs. Jewel?" Melvin asked as he wandered about the kitchen and dining room placing covered dishes strategically about the eating table before the family came in from the den or various bedrooms.

"I think she was your friend, Frederick's great-grandmother," Etta said softly. "That was one of the reasons there was no big fuss made over burying him in the church cemetery."

"I don't understand, mother," Melvin said. "What happened way back when that was so important to the church history?"

"The church was built by the professional African-American people of Fairhaven but Mrs. Jewel was one of the chief financial backers. Certainly black people didn't have that much money back in those days but she did and it was considered tainted money."

"Frederick's grandmother was the owner of a brothel?" Melvin said in amazement.

"Child, your great-grandfather was one of the deacons who help to secure the money from her to get the church built as magnificently as it is," Etta laughed as she thought about Obadiah James. "He and a few other older men. They said Reverend Kelly died a week after they had made plans to ask Mrs. Jewel for the money."

"Black people really like to live a lie," Melvin said. "So they built the church with her money?"

"Not fully but she was responsible for the church being as large and as magnificent as this one is. She hired a white architect and told him that she wanted a brick cathedral built. So the church raised money and she raised money and whatever the church raised she matched it and the very sanctuary you sit in today was funded by the owner of a brothel, a doctor, a mortician, a grocer, about eight or nine teachers, and the rest were maids and farmers and you know that black farmers certainly did not have *that* type of money back then."

"Well, I'll say," Melvin laughed. "Me and the pastor had a talk about that ridiculous sermon he preached today."

"I'd rather not discuss Pastor Garrison right now because so many of my sorors called me this afternoon until I could scream," Etta laughed as she walked into the dining room, made one last inspection and then yelled for the family to come to diner.

The dining room was full of people within three minutes. Melvin's sisters: Clarice, Elaine, and Dawn came from various parts of the house with husbands and children at foot. Clarice was now the Vice-President of the family funeral home. Her husband, Gregory Nolan was now a licensed embalmer and worked with Clarence as well at the funeral home. They had two sons: Clarence James Nolan and Edward Charles Nolan. Elaine did not have a husband but had five children: Clarence James, II, Jeremiah Hanks- James, Ethan James, Elizabeth James, and Robert James. Elaine was a C.N.A. at the local nursing home. Clarence was not at all pleased with this daughter and forever made it known although he loved all of his grandchildren dearly. Dawn lived at home and refused to move, work, or go to school. Clarence gave her an ultimatum of doing some type of work or leaving his house. Hence, she sells burial insurance at her leisure for James Funeral Home. She had no children yet every three month she brought a new boy friend to Sunday dinner. Clarence was definitely not pleased with Dawn yet in his tirade this was the daughter who didn't mind cursing him out and refusing to leave his house.

"*What a family,*" Melvin thought. "*But I love them dearly.*"

Clarence sat at the head of the table, said grace, and dinner was served. Being it was a new quarter, Dawn presented a new face at the dinner table. Chaos resumed as always on Sundays at the James house for Sunday dinner but it was the one time that everyone could see one another during the week.

"Well, son," Clarence said as dinner began. "Since two of my daughters seem to have brought home a man, when are you going to bring someone home for Sunday dinner?"

"Dad," Melvin said as he began to somewhat loose his appetite. "I don't know if you would want me to bring anyone to Sunday dinner."

"Well, I don't see why not," Clarence laughed and looked at the new man who sat next to Dawn. "I can never keep up with who Dawn is going to bring to my dinner table next."

"Well, it won't be a baby," Dawn said. "And I don't have to eat Sunday dinner here you know."

"You are talking to your father," Etta said sharply as her eyes glared onto Dawn. "And you are still at **my** dinner table, young lady."

"Sorry, mom," Dawn said quickly and bowed her head.

"You don't have to say nothing, I'll charge her rent next month and she'll shut up the noise," Clarence laughed as he winked at Dawn.

Dawn stuck her tongue out at her father. Melvin found them to be strangely weird. They would fuss and cuss at one another one moment and the next moment they seemed to be eternal friends. It was a father-daughter relationship like none other. It seemed as if Clarence would have had a better camaraderie with Clarice being that Clarice and her husband were in the same business but Clarence only warmed to her when they discussed business. Etta forbade funeral home business to be discussed at her dinner table for any reason. So, that alleviated conversation between Clarice and her father at the dinner table. Elaine only came to Sunday dinner. She could care less what the family discussed, thought, or planned. As long as her children were included in the industry when they came of age, nothing mattered to her.

"When have you heard from Uncle Claiborne, Melvin?" Dawn asked coyly.

"The other day, why?"

"Oh, I imagined he could give you some tips on how to invite someone to Sunday dinner without causing suspicion."

Etta's mouth flew open.

Clarence fell backward in his chair and dropped his fork onto the floor.

"If I come over there and kick you're..." Melvin said as he shoved his fork into his plate and rose out of his seat.

"Just what the hell are you trying to say?" Clarence asked as he regained his composure but noticed how Melvin had reached Dawn and was about to reach for her neck.

"Melvin, sit down," Etta said firmly.

"Why are you just sitting there, Elaine?" Clarice whispered to Elaine as she watched Elaine continue to eat as if nothing had even happened.

"Hell, I could care less," Elaine said as she continued to eat. "Melvin can kill the tramp for all I care as long as nobody touches my children, I don't give a damn."

"I asked a question and I want an answer," Clarence roared.

"Dawn is trying to be funny," Melvin said as he sat back down in his seat.

"I'm not amused," Clarence grumbled. "What's this about Claiborne?"

Melvin took a deep breath. *"Well, there will be no better time than now, I don't guess."*

"Dawn calls herself telling something for me," Melvin said casually.

Clarence's shoulders dropped as reality struck him like a ton of bricks. ***His only son was a homosexual!***

"How have I gone wrong?" Clarence said as tears began to roll down his cheeks. "What did I do?"

"Dad," Melvin said as he gave Dawn an *"I'm going to kick your ass look."* "You did nothing wrong. I'm just me and that is all it is to it."

"I had no idea," Clarence said as his hands began to shake.

"Dad, there is no need for you to get yourself in an uproar," Melvin said. "It's my life."

"I didn't raise no goddamned faggots," Clarence yelled.

"Clarence Benjamin James!" Etta yelled as her eyes widened in disbelief at her husband. This time it was she who could strangle the entire lot that sat at her dinner table.

"Well you sure as hell don't mind burying them, now do you?" Melvin asked.

"Don't you get smart with me boy," Clarence yelled as he stood up. "You're not too old to get your ass whipped!"

"Old man," Melvin said as he stood up. "I have never disrespected you but if you jump this way I'm going to tear *your* ass up!"

"Child, this is better than *Jerry Springer*," Elaine whispered to Dawn's new boyfriend as she continued to eat or make certain her children ate what was on their plates. Etta stood up in a rage as well.

"You niggahs are gonna sit down right now or I'm gonna be the one fighting up in this damn camp!" Etta roared as she balled her fist tightly and placed them on her tiny hips.

Melvin sat down.

Clarence rolled his eyes and sat down.

Etta twisted her lips, patted her foot and then began to pace the floor in a rage. No one dared say a word for fear of what she might do or say. The only person that seemed comfortable was Elaine who continued to eat and occasionally would interrupt the silence by asking someone to pass her this or pass her that.

"First of all," she finally began after pacing the room for a solid ten minutes. "Dawn, I don't appreciate you attempting to be sly and malicious…"

"I wasn't..."

Boom!

Everyone jumped.

Dawn began to cry.

"When I am talking I don't particularly care to be interrupted," Etta said a she dropped her left shoe back down onto the floor and began to pace again as she spoke. Melvin was yet amazed at how quickly his mother could hit you with a shoe and continues to talk as if you were as obsolete as an old tin can. "Second of all, that ain't none of your damned business! Melvin, I told you to talk with your father after we had our conversation in order to avoid some silly mess like this. You chose not to talk with your father and I *will not* do it for you. Clarence, Melvin is and always will be your son and all hell will break loose up in this camp if you ever refer to my baby as a faggot again in my presence."

"Woman, this is still my house too," Clarence grumbled.

"This will be a lonely house without me in it, Mr. James," Etta said with enough venom to kill a rattlesnake.

"You talking crazy, Etta," Clarence said. "Sit down and let's finish our dinner."

"I ain't sittin nowhere until I get ready to," Etta said.

"I said sit down," Clarence roared.

Etta sat down.

"I've gotten over worse," Clarence grumbled and then looked directly at Melvin. "All I have to say is this; if I ever catch you in dresses I will disown you."

"Whatever," Melvin said as he rolled his eyes at Clarence and then began to continue to attempt to eat his meal. He looked up at Elaine and began to laugh.

"Share the joke," Clarence said with a slight hint of disgust in his voice as he looked at his son.

"We could kill ourselves in here and Elaine would keep on eating and feeding the children."

"Child, please," Elaine said as she wiped one of her children's mouth. "I don't even care. So my brother is gay. And? That ain't gonna put one crumb of bread on my table or pay one bill or buy one diaper! Why should I give a crap?"

Clarence for the first time ever looked at his second born child and laughed. A tear once again surfaced to his eyes as he realized just how little he knew any of his children with the exception of Dawn who always presented him with some type of new dilemma. The reality of the independence of his children settled on his heart as he looked around his dining room table. He and his wife had raised an exceptional group. None of them entered the occupation he thought they should or would want to but none of them except Dawn asked him for anything. Clarice and Gregory had turned the family funeral home into a multi-million dollar company by renovating it and then expanding it to several different locations. Although Elaine was a C.N.A. all of her children were honor roll children and were constantly in the newspaper receiving some type of recognition or award. Best of all, Elaine thought well enough of him to name a child after him. His son, his little boy, the child he never had time for was a very accomplished branch manager of a bank.

"Why the tears, pop?" Gregory asked.

"Oh, when I look at all of you all, if I die tomorrow, I can truly say that I am proud of all of you all," he said as he wiped the rolling tears from his eyes.

"Oh, baby," Etta said as she ran to his side and cupped his head in her bosom.

"Oh, Lord, elderly sex," Dawn jested.

"Ugh!" Melvin, Clarice, and Elaine all said simultaneously.

Everyone laughed.

"It's all jood," Etta laughed.

"Momma, where'd you learn that word?" Melvin laughed.

"Child, I read *B-Boy Blues*," she laughed.

"What's Bee Boy Blues?" Clarice asked.

"A hot novel by this young man from New York," Etta laughed as she returned to her seat only after kissing Clarence on the forehead.

Melvin was totally shocked. *Lord, his mother had read B-Boy Blues! What was the world coming to?*

"Well, I hope you've read it, Melvin," Etta said as she looked at him out of the corner of her eyes and grinned.

"And you know it," Melvin laughed.

"It was the bomb," Elaine joined.

"Why haven't I heard about it?" Clarice asked.

"Why haven't I heard about it if it is so hot?" Dawn asked jealously, she hated to be left out on something that might be "juicy."

"You have to learn to read first," Elaine teased.

"Well you seem to have learned to have sex," Dawn retorted.

"I sure did and by the stream of men that you invite to Sunday dinners you seem to know how to have it as well," Elaine responded evenly.

"*My people, Lord. My people,*" Melvin thought.

"Could you all please," Etta laughed. "The novel is a very good novel. I was pleased with it. I read it after I read E. Lynn Harris's trilogy. Recently I've discovered a southern author named R. Bryant Smith. He has a kindred spirit for sure. Anyway, *B-boy Blues* is good reading most definitely."

"Well, Hardy is very descriptive, that's for sure," Elaine laughed. "What do you think, Melvin?"

"I read the novel three times," Melvin laughed.

"My family," Clarence laughed. "Angry one minute and happy the next."

"Well, that's what a family is about," Elaine laughed. "Now could you please pass the greens?"

Everyone laughed.

Chapter Eleven
Why?

The small house was dark simply because there was no electricity in it. The inhabitants forgot to do the monthly stealing method in order to obtain it but no one seemed to care. There was no running water of any kind in the house either. The foul musty smell of dirty humans hung in the air like a grueling poisonous gas. No sunlight eased its way into the windows. They were all nailed tightly shut with boards. An old mattress was thrown on the floor of what was once a bedroom. An old sofa that had no legs, no arms, and holes throughout it sat in the corner of what was once a living room. An old crate sat I the kitchen where an eating table one sat. There was no stove for cooking yet plenty of cooking took place in the house in an old pot bellied stove that was originally intended for cooking. It was nothing, however, for the crack heads that lived in the house to use any means necessary to cook a new batch of crack if the supply was short during the week and they were forced to share a "rock" between all twelve of them.

In this crack house that sat at the end of Cricket Road behind a small shallow path. The little house was surrounded by tall weeds, thickets, and wild growing trees that camouflaged it from sight rather well. The house had been abandoned years before by the Nelson family in Fairhaven. It had belonged to Wilson Nelson, the bootlegger. He died and the family removed the furniture and boarded the house up, completely forgetting about it.

The crack heads of Fairhaven didn't forget about it, however. It provided them with shelter from the storm and rain, the light of day, and pursuing police if they were being pursued. Because the house sat so far back from the main road, the neighbors who lived on Cricket Road never thought about the house. The only thing they knew was that occasionally a strange looking man or woman would walk down the trail at the end of the dead end street. Everyone seemed to have forgotten the fact that even though there was a trail that lead to Mt. Carmel Baptist Church Cemetery behind Cherry Street. No one seemed to have remembered that there was an abandoned house at the end of a dirt alley that adjoined the cemetery and Cherry Street.

Doubting the powers of the crack head, no one ever felt that a crack head would use the church cemetery as safe passage to a crack house. No one ever suspected that the crack head would have sense to build an added pipe onto the top of the roof where the potbelly stove produced smoke. The pipe extended into a nearby ditch that was connected to a sewer line. Everyone assumed that the smoke they saw that came from the ditch was merely the stench from the sewer. Again, it is unwise to underestimate the powers of a crack head.

The drug dealers were afraid of the house. The few who did know about it would sometimes use it as a refuge when hiding from the police. The entire order changed, however, when Psycho showed up to the crack house and decided since he was the oldest, the meanest, the baddest, and the ugliest crack head, he should rule the house the way he wanted to rule it. And rule it he did.

No one was allowed to sleep in the crack house unless they brought some form of drugs back to the house. A simple rule, yet sometimes difficult when the federal agents decided to make a drug bust on the local drug dealers. Another rule was everybody had to get out during the day at some point and make some form of money in order to support his/her own drug habit. Many cars in Fairhaven missed hubcaps due to the crack heads stealing them in order to sell them to the salvage yard along with their daily aluminum can collection. One of the men who lived in the house actually had a respectable job. He was a professional thief, liar, and gambler. Even Psycho could not outwit Ace. So, Psycho relied heavily on Ace when the issue arose on: "How will the group eat or get drugs when there was three feet of snow on the ground?" "Was Tender, Puss, or Easy the best oral sex ho's in the group or could Ben, Mack, or Tiger use their sex appeal on some lonely faggot or some ugly and lonely woman to get enough money for everybody to get a fix?" Psycho could not be trusted to try sex on anyone anymore because he claimed he could no longer get a hard on. The fact of the matter was that Frederick so often from the grave haunted Psycho.

Often Psycho would become outraged if one of the group came into the house wearing a certain smell. Ben, Mack, or Tiger could never tell the group they had slept with a man in order to obtain money to buy crack. Mack once bragged about the fact that he had slept with a lonely and pathetic "faggot" who paid him $30.00 for oral sex.

"Dat's two rocks, man," Mack laughed as he told his story. "Yeah, that faggot wanted to suck my dick and pay me for it so why not?"

Psycho laughed with Mack and the others. Later, after smoking up the two rocks, Psycho beat Mack merciless.

"What the hell is yo problem?" Ace asked Psycho as he, Ben, and Tiger pulled Psycho off of Mack.

"I don't want to hear about no fuckin', got it?" Psycho growled as he looked at a wretched looking Mack curled up onto the floor. Psycho kicked him just because he looked weak as blood oozed out of the corner of his mouth and bruises covered his entire face.

"Fuck you, man," Mack said as he slithered into a corner and drifted off into a weary form of sleep.

Psycho sat in a corner and smoked round after round after round of marijuana and crack. The rounds of smoking were mixed with drinking 40 ounces of beer or fifths of cheap whiskey or wine that had managed to come into the house at some point during the night.

In the wee hours of the morning when everyone else had passed out and drifted to sleep, Psycho began to become tormented by his thoughts.

The wind would softly begin to blow causing the house to creek. This was no wind to Psycho. It was a voice; a voice that he constantly heard; forever ringing in his ears. A feeble, sad voice nightly asked the same question over and over again…"Why?"

"I don't know why?" Psycho would yell as he would hit the side of the wall causing the sleeping inhabitants to snore louder or stir and turn the opposite direction in which they were sleeping.

"I didn't have any money…" the voice would cry out as a small shadow would appear just above the crack of the window that allowed a ray of light to shine into the room.

"Yeah, you had the money, bitch," Psycho grumbled as he took a long drag off of the makeshift "pipe" that he held in his hand. His "pipe" was his last safe haven to sanity… his last hope.

"Why?" the wind roared sounding like a scream as the house began to shake, the thunder began to roll, and the wind began to scream out into the early hours of the morning just before daybreak

"I didn't mean to," Psycho said as he began to cry. "I just wanted to get a fix. You were the only person who cared. The only person who ever talked to me about my problems? I should have gone pro and I didn't and you never complained once."

"Why?" the wind screamed as the boards on the windows began to shake the tiny house.

"I had to get the money that night," Psycho screamed. "I had to or else I would have trashed somebody else's house. I even trashed my own momma's house for money and you still let me come to your place and take a bath and eat…"

Suddenly the strong wind flung the front door of the tiny house open. The lightening began to flash. The thunder began to roar.

Psycho panicked. He jumped up from his corner and from off of the mattress in which he lay and began to run out of the old house. He thought quickly enough, however, to close the door behind him and throw a latch onto the door entrance to keep anyone from exiting.

In his panic, he accidentally dropped a burning cigarette onto the old mattress that he was sleeping on. The mattress quickly caught fire and the house instantly went up in a blaze.

Psycho ran until he reached Frederick's grave in the cemetery. He never looked back. He never heard the screams of the inhabitants of the old house due to the constant roar of thunder and flicker of lightening.

"Why?" the wind screamed as Psycho reached the tombstone marked PERRY.

"Because nobody gave a damn whether or not I killed you," Psycho screamed loudly and began to beat his fist on the top of the tombstone.

"Why?" the wind continued to scream in his ears.

"Because I was a failure and a fuck up," Psycho cried as the lightning flashed all around him. "I didn't mean to kill you."

"Why" the wind howled.

"What do I have to do to make it up to you?" Psycho cried over the tombstone. "I loved you and I could not understand how I could love another man. I felt that I had to get rid of you because you had begun to love me as well. I knew you didn't deserve a crack head but I didn't want to see you with nobody else."

Psycho cried as the rain began to beat down onto the church that stoically stood nearby. The rain poured down onto his head. The rain poured down onto the flowers that sat atop of the tombstone marked

Frederick Perry
1970 - 1997
Rest In Peace

Suddenly, Psycho felt a fist hit him from behind. He turned around swinging with everything that he had in his soul.

"You son of a bitch," Ace yelled as he punched Psycho.

"What the hell is yo fuckin' problem, man," Psycho growled as he matched Ace's punches pound for pound.

"You burned up those innocent people in the house," Ace said as he punched Psycho one last time in the face and passed out onto the ground.

Psycho turned to look at where the house once stood. A flaming red ball of fire licked the sky as if souls were attempting to travel upward, downward -anywhere except where they were.

Psycho began to run toward the house. Ace stood up from the ground and ran the opposite way.

By the time Psycho reached the house, the roof fell to the ground crushing everything below it.

"Damn, you, Frederick," Psycho screamed as tears rolled down his face.

Soon, sirens began to roar in a distance. He had traveled too far to be caught now. He began to run again through thick trees and tall grass. Dogs barked at him on his move, he barked back at dogs in return forcing the dogs to retreat. He had to get away... far away from this new mess he had gotten himself into.

"Why?" the winds began to scream again as the rain began to pour down heavily upon his head.

"I don't know the fuck why, damn it," he yelled as he ran.

"Why?" the winds raged.

"Fuck you," he yelled as he ran.

Chapter Twelve

When I Rose This Morning

Melvin twisted and turned as his dreams began to torment him during the night. When finally his eyes opened, he was in the arms of a very comforting Eric. Although his heart raced from the dreams in which he could not interpret or understand he was happy to wake in the arms of the man who held the key to his heart.

"Are you all right, baby," Eric asked as he gently rocked a sweaty Melvin back and forth in the massive king sized bed.

"Something keeps chasing me, baby," Melvin said attempting to gain his composure as he sorted through remnants of the dream.

"What is going on?"

"I don't know," Melvin confessed. "The only thing that I know is that someone is chasing me in my dream and has been for years. The dream begins in this house in the living room and that's all that I remember except someone chases me."

"No one will chase you as long as I'm in your life, baby," Eric said as he kissed the top of Melvin's head.

"If I only knew who killed Frederick…"

"Do you think your dream has some type of link to Frederick's death?"

"I don't know but I have had it since the day he died."

"I wasn't here for the funeral and all tell me what happened," Eric said as he held Melvin closely. "If it's not too painful."

"Someone killed him is the only thing that I know," Melvin said as he began to twist slightly out of Eric's grasp. "They put shoe strings on his neck and choked him to death and left him in his apartment dead. But whoever it was raped him as well."

"How do you know?"

"The stench and smell of sex and the blood," Melvin said as he stretched and stood up from the bed. "Bradley, Howard and I found him."

"Well, you mean to tell me that the police have not found the person who murdered him yet?"

"Did Emmett Till get a fair trial down South?"

"Touché," Eric laughed.

Melvin yawned, stretched, and shook his head in order to fully awake and begin to prepare for the day. He walked into the kitchen, looked out of the window at the gloominess of the November morning. The rain beat down heavily onto his emerald green *1997 Honda Accord* as well as Eric's *1980 Chevrolet 4 door Impala* that had been painted white with gold metal flakes.

"He is so ghetto," Melvin chuckled silently to himself as he looked at Eric's car. It was definitely the symbol of the Southern drug dealer's car. The car was fully loaded with a loud sound system, gold rims, tinted windows, a cell phone, and chrome that sparkled beyond the imagination even in the rain. Melvin was almost amazed at just how different this man was from his original vision of the man he would fall in love with. The only time anyone could catch Eric in a suit was for church or a funeral. He had recently begun to attend church when he discovered that Melvin attended, hence, he had to buy an entire new wardrobe of suits. Fortunately, he chose basic suit cuts of double breast or single breast rather than the rainbow assortment of colors, styles, shapes, and shades. Eric owned two vehicles but anyone who knew him knew that he loved his *Impala*. It often amazed Melvin that this 32-year-old man held so dearly to a youth that was definitely gone. Perhaps it was his Chicago south side heritage obtained when he moved north. Perhaps he just enjoyed the new culture that had taken America by storm. Eric could be buck wild but only at his own terms. He religiously worked ten to twelve hours five days per week. His weekends were his. And on the weekend, his entire appearance changed. Baggy clothes, pager, loud car - the works. Melvin was amazed at his transformation yet he had begun to love it all the more.

In all reality, however, Eric lived the life that Melvin so dearly wanted to live- a life of freedom; a life where a person could be whom they wished to be when they wished. Melvin had for so long become trapped in the cultural structure of the old African-American rural South until he had forgotten just what it meant to live. He, like so many of his friends, lived life according to the rules and regulations of the old African-American rural South. This life was one filled with hypocrisy, deceit, and deception - a life where a person had to play the rules according to the unspoken script of conformity. If these rules were broken, life could be made a living hell for the person who chose to step out on faith and go against the grain.

"These young folk are so disrespectful," many of the old dowagers would often complain yet these same people who complained so vehemently against the youth of today were no angels themselves. When the hand of time turned back to youth of the 1920s, 1930s, 1940s, 1950s, and 1960s many of these same people who complained against the youth of the present were some of the most vivacious people on earth. When the truth was revealed, many women had children out of wedlock or by other women's husbands. Many men cheated on their wives. The men did provided for their families however often at funerals in the rural South, bastard children would sit with children of the wives of the husband that had died. What could be said? What happened happened! Yet no one was supposed to mention it even if the wife had been faithful unto death.

Melvin cooked Eric the normal Saturday breakfast which consisted of a pound of bacon, ten slices of country ham, a dozen eggs, a pot of grits, two dozen homemade biscuits, a jar of Etta's peach preserves, a piping hot pot of coffee, and a gallon of orange juice.

"Ooo, baby, this sho smells good," Eric laughed as he entered the kitchen as Melvin maneuvered around like a great master chef.

"Are you sure this is enough?" Melvin asked sarcastically.

"You know I love to eat you and your cooking, baby," Eric laughed as he gently hugged Melvin and then poured himself a cup of coffee as Melvin put the finishing touches on breakfast.

"Boy, I'm gonna have to add you to my income taxes as much as you eat," Melvin laughed.

"Well, you know they say the way to a man's heart is through his stomach," Eric teased.

"Oh, was that the way to yours?" Melvin chuckled as he stroked the top of Eric's head.

Eric sat in thought for a moment and then looked directly at Melvin.

"Well, yeah and no."

"Do tell."

"You are the first person I know who knows how to cook the food I like to eat but I wanted more than your cooking."

"Say that again, boy," Melvin laughed.

"You buggin," Eric laughed as Melvin placed the feast onto the table to serve.

Melvin smiled as he sat down adjacent "his" man!

"Gracious Lord, we humbly thank You for the food we are about to receive for the nourishment of our bodies. And Lord, please bless the hands of the one that prepared it and please Lord, make every day with Melvin a new adventure and experience as I continue to fall deeper in love with him. Amen!"

"Amen!" Melvin said unsure if he had just said Amen to the request for the blessing of food or a consummation of a relationship.

Melvin watched as Eric ate everything that was placed before him. The picture was like watching a child eating ice cream. Eric spared nothing. He was happy to be back in the rural South where people actually cooked good soul food. He was ecstatic that the man he was falling deeply in love with was one of the great cooks of the south.

Before either could fully become absorbed in the moment, the telephone rang.

"Can we ever get a Saturday alone?" Eric grumbled as he continued to pay homage to his Southern feast presented before him.

"It's just Bradley, you know he always calls on Saturday before he goes to work," Melvin laughed as he picked up a phone that was located on the wall near the dining room table.

"Hello."

"Child did you know somebody burned down the old Nelson house that used to sit behind the church?"

"When?"

"Last night," Bradley said in excitement. "Child, six people were found dead inside the house."

"I thought the house had been condemned," Melvin said as he thought about the eye sore at the extreme far end of the church property. Although trees and brush hid the house rather well, every now and then the dilapidated roof would peak its ugly head through.

"Child, it had," Bradley laughed. "But the crack heads got to it and somehow, they all got burnt up in it last night."

"Well, I'll say," Melvin said. "Are you going to the fraternity meeting tonight?"

"Yeah, I guess I'm going to go on and see what they are talking about tonight. Are you going?"

"No, Eric and I have plans for the night," Melvin said with such pride at finally being able to actually say the words again.

"I'll take your dues if you bring them by the store," Bradley chuckled. "How is the basketball player doing anyway?"

"Fine, he's eating right now."

"You got that much food in your house, guhl?" Bradley laughed. "Eric Curbie has always been able to choke down a huge consumption of thangs."

"Shut up, bitch, I hear where you are trying to go," Melvin laughed. "And all cooks keep food in the house, Hell, these aren't my college days anymore and all of my student loans are paid off now. I can splurge a little bit."

"I feel ya," Bradley laughed. "Anyway, where are you all headed tonight?"

"Well, we are going to run down to Beale Street for a while and then we are going to go and check out the new club."

"What new club? Child, what happened to *The Apartment Club?*"

"Guhl, it has been a long time since you've been out! *The Apartment Club* has been closed for a year or two now. The new club is *N-Cognito* on the corner of Front and Vance."

"Child, child, child," Bradley said solemnly. "An era has gone by now. That used to be the only place in West Tennessee that a gay black man could dare to be gay."

"I feel you," Melvin said as he thought about his years of partying at the *Apartment Club.* Briefly he thought about the truth of the reality in Bradley's words. For a full decade or longer, *The Apartment Club* was the only place that gay African-American men could be themselves without penalty or punishment. It was the age before AIDS; the age before insurmountable funerals of friends who had succumb to the deadly disease; and it was the age when people would pile into cars in their finest to party, express their gayness, explore their homosexuality, and be accepted by people who were exactly like them. Yes, everyone in the day had to wear the best clothes, sport the best physics, and throw "shade" to whoever the immortal competition was. But when the party was over everyone had to go back to the darkness from whence they all had come. They had to go back to hiding from the world and the true self - the true identity; back to living life "as is"; and conform or be made to conform. And now, the splendor of life at the *Apartment Club* had finally come to an end. No more free dishwater beer before midnight. No more two-hour drag shows performed by the famous Patty Cakes, Tamika St. John, Tamika St. James, Paula Poindexter, Tanisha Cassidine, and the other great legendary drag queens of the turn of the decade. No more cruising the entire city block that encompassed Madison Avenue and Monroe Avenue, which housed the club, *Wonder Bread,* and *Greyhound* Bus Station. No more smell of freshly baked *Wonder Bread* after the club closed causing everyone to rush to *McDonalds* or *CK's Coffee House.* An era had truly come to an end.

"Well, let me know how this new club is," Bradley laughed. "It has been a long time since I've twirled but, shit, I don't have the time anymore."

"I will," Melvin laughed as he thought about the years when the old group would go to Memphis and dance the night away. Always leaving Memphis around 6 o'clock or 7 o'clock in the morning. They would take 51 North heading to Dyer County or 240 East heading to Jackson. Those were the days. "Hey, I'm supposed to drop by and see Xavier as well while I'm down."

"Tell that hooker to call me."

"I will."

"Bye, child. You love birds have a good time."

"We will. Thanks, Bradley."

"Yeah, yeah, yeah," Bradley said as he hung the telephone up.

Immediately after Melvin hung the telephone up it rang again. Melvin actually thought that it was Bradley but was somewhat taken aback when hearing the different voice.

"Melvin, where's Eric?"

"He's right here, who am I speaking to?"

"This is Josh. May I speak with him? Its urgent."

"Sure," Melvin said as he passed the telephone to Eric who continued to devour the meal sitting in front of him.

"Yeah," Eric said as he answered the telephone.

"Yo, Eric, this is Josh, I need to talk with you, man."

"I'm listening."

"Can we meet somewhere?"

"Hell naw, I got plans for the day, what's up?" Eric said becoming irritated with the entire conversation. He did not like Josh although they were first cousins. He certainly did not appreciate Josh disturbing his Saturday even although it was a gloomy rainy day.

"I think Jeremy is in trouble," Josh said softly.

"So what's new," Eric grumbled as he ran his long fingers slowly through his thick dreads. Melvin sensed his constraint.

"Please, Eric," Josh pleaded. "I don't know who else to turn to."

"Where do you want to meet," Eric grumbled.

"Can you meet me in Dyersburg at Ann's House of Wings?"

"As long as it won't take all day long, I'm headed to Memphis today."

"I hope it won't take too long."

"It better not or you are on your own," Eric said as he slammed the telephone down into its receiver.

"Is everything all right?" Melvin asked as he looked as the unhappiness on Eric's face.

"Josh wants me to meet him in Dyersburg at your frat brother's restaurant."

"Oh, *Ann's House of Wings*?" Melvin laughed as he thought about Grimlock's small but quaint restaurant. Set in the heart of the Bruce Community on Dyersburg's East Side, *Ann's House of Wings* had become a very profitable franchise for Grimlock. Located on the corner of Grant and Southern Street, *Ann's House of Wings* soon became one of the great eateries of rural West Tennessee. Grimlock chose to keep his restaurant open 24 hours per day on weekends in order to accommodate the crowd that normally developed when The American Legion, The Field, The Hill, The Ebony Club, Willie Tole's, Bundy's, or Tamps (Dyersburg's taverns and bars proudly dedicated to serving African-Americans) closed. There was a small billboard that hung in the homey atmosphere of the restaurant that read:

House Rules

Eat as much as you want! Drink as much as you want!
Say what you want!
Tear up anything,
Pay for it one way or the other!

No one dared face the wrath of Grimlock scorned especially being this restaurant, his dream and dedication to his grandmother was more valuable to him than the tons of revenue that he received from its operation.

"Are you going to eat while you are there?" Melvin asked knowing that Eric could not resist the special sauce Grimlock used on the hot and spicy chicken wing platter that people from eight counties came from miles around to eat.

"Did Christ die for the remission of our sin?" Eric teased.

"Leave my Lord out of your bottomless pit called a stomach," Melvin laughed as he gently rubbed Eric's stomach. Amazingly, however, as much as Eric ate, he did not have any sign of pudginess on his massive physiology. Pure and solid country muscle maintained even through life in the North.

"Don't do that or I might be late for my meeting," Eric laughed as he ate the last piece of bacon and then drank a huge glass of orange juice.

"My man," Melvin laughed as he watched Eric in pure amazement.

Eric washed his meal down with a huge glass of orange juice. Melvin began to take the empty dishes off of the dining room table and take them to place them in the dishwasher. An uneasy feeling began to settle over Melvin as he began to think about just who had recently telephoned his home. First, he and Josh were not the best of friends. Yes, they knew one another but they never telephoned one another. Even when Josh and Keisha returned to Fairhaven and joined Mt. Carmel, they only spoke politely to one another in church and that was it. Now, out of the clear blue sky he decides to call and then ask to speak to Eric as if Eric did not have an apartment. Obviously, the news was extremely important. But Melvin did not trust Josh's motives. Melvin knew that Eric did not particularly care for his Curbie kin in Fairhaven because he never hid the fact that he despised Josh and Jeremy. None of it made sense to him.

Melvin watched as Eric stood up, untied his dreads allowing them to flow loosely across his huge shoulders. Eric's huge muscles bulged from underneath his mustard turtleneck sweater revealing even his tiny nipples that Melvin so graciously tickled with his tongue causing a desired arousal in Eric. Melvin could not help but shiver when he observed Eric's huge thighs when Eric stood up to walk into the bedroom to finish dressing for the day's event. Melvin loved to watch this bow legged man strut across the room wearing nothing more than a long mustard turtleneck sweater and navy blue silk boxers. "Jesus, Jesus, Jesus," Melvin thought to himself as a wide grin appeared upon his face. "The preacher said just call Jesus and everything will be all right."

The telephone rang again which interrupted his lustful thoughts.

"Hello," Melvin said as he cleared his throat.

"Hey, child, whassup?"

"Hey, what's going on, Douglas?"

"Notta," Douglas said in his normal unconcerned tone. "I was just calling to see if you were still going to Xavier's party tonight in Memphis?"

"Child, I had completely forgot," Melvin giggled. "Eric and I were planning on going to Memphis today anyway."

"Cool," Douglas said. "Then we'll meet you all there you know it's his thirtieth birthday and he wants the old crew there."

"Yeah, I know," Melvin said thoughtfully as he thought about one of his best friends.

"Well, the party starts at seven," Douglas said. "Y'all do whatever you gonna do by then and we'll see you at Xavier's."

"Yes, sir, Uncle Doug," Melvin laughed. "I'll ask Eric."

"Ask me what?" Eric said as he took Melvin's breath away in one glance. He wore black slacks, the mustard turtleneck, and a leather coat that hung just below his waist.

"If we could stop by one of my class mate's house to celebrate his thirtieth birthday tonight..." Melvin said softly praying Eric would not be disagreeable.

"Sure," Eric said. "Who is that on the phone anyway?"

Melvin forgot that Eric had never met Douglas. Douglas had, in the past, always been too preoccupied with work. When Melvin entertained a few friends, Douglas was never there.

"Oh, this is just Douglas," Melvin said as he noticed a slight arch in Eric's eyebrow. "Desmond's beaux."

"Oh, Eric said."Tell him hey and I look forward to meeting him tonight."

"Douglas, Eric said hey and he looks forward to meeting you tonight."

"You finally got a man?" Douglas laughed for the first time during the entire conversation.

"Yeah, Doug, I finally got a man," Melvin laughed as Eric stood beside the door fumbling in his wallet attempting to look preoccupied.

"Yeah, he sounds like a man too, I bet he is standing there watching you like a hawk to make sure you don't make no pass," Douglas laughed. "Tell him I can't wait to meet him and I hope he drinks a few forty ounces."

"Eric, Douglas says he can't wait to meet you and he hopes you drinks a few forty ounces."

"Tell him, bet," Eric said attempting to look uninterested.

"Bye," Douglas said.

"See you tonight, Douglas," Melvin laughed as he hung up the telephone.

"Gimme a kiss," Eric said as he stood beside the door.

Melvin walked to the door and tip toed forward as Eric knelt downward and placed a juicy passionate kiss on Melvin. Melvin's head began to swim and he had to hold onto Eric in order to maintain his balance. "*Jesus, Jesus, Jesus,*" Melvin thought. "*And what a man indeed.*"

Eric released Melvin slowly and whispered for the first time...

"*I love you, baby.*"

Melvin almost sank to his knees but this time Divine intervention occurred and he managed to stand tall as he gazed into this ebony king's eyes.

"I love you, too," Melvin said boldly.

Eric opened the door and walked of his *Impala.* Melvin stood at the door and watched this man in amazement again. Eric was totally different from Melvin in every sense yet Melvin was heavily attracted to this man. He was everything that Melvin was not. Although Melvin considered himself to be openly gay, he knew that he conformed to society. Eric simply did not give a damn. He was one of the best journalists for *The Fairhaven Journal* and after hours, he was himself. He did not advertise his personal business because this was "*tired and sissyish*" *in* Eric's own words. He was a free spirit and this alone drove Melvin wild with passion.

Eric opened his car door, blew Melvin a kiss and then blasted his music.

"God, he is so ghetto," Melvin laughed. "But I love him."

Melvin recognized the lyrics to the song that boomed through Eric's window providing all of the community with the sultry bards to the new Chicago artist *Lil'Him's Rapp song* entitled *Prince Bitch.*

Eric pulled out of the driveway as Lil'Him's word roared in the air.

Melvin had become accustomed to hearing this particular song because Eric played it so much. It was a bit vulgar for his taste yet it was uniquely fascinating and appealing to Melvin's inner self. He refused to agree with all of the lyrics for the very message in which it was sending but the beat and the rhythm was unique in itself.

Melvin watched in awe and strained to listen to the entire song as Eric sped down the street.

Here I go

About to let you ho's know

You wanna battle me?

Oh my please come back to reality!

Let's not forget you gotta bring security

Like Michael Jackson "Who's Bad"

Shorty don't be mad

Nor sad

Cause I got that Viagra Tongue

and Tight ass you man wish you had.

See I'm his best Bitch

Not his ex Bitch

What's my name?

Prince Bitch!

I got those Viagra lips

Thick and lickable hips

So be ready to unzip

Cause I got that Viagra tongue

That'll keep the niggas sprung

But they gotta be hung

That's right I thought you knew

My shit so tight no need to practice voodoo.

You fake niggah wanna be this bitch

Cause I'm rocking Prada, Iceberg & all that good shit

Prince Bitch

I know you hating cause yo man saw me

And decided to switch

Prince Bitch

My mouth like a dick nest
Fuck the rest
I'm the best
That's right I know I'm tight
5'7 is my height
But as always I must be the shit of the night!

You fake ho's wanna be all up in my shit
But just remember I'm da Baddest Bitch
Prince Bitch

Words from the Prince Bitch:
Always staying on top of my shit!
Not the type of faggot that switch,
So no I'm not a punk bitch!
So can she suck it like me?
Fuck it like me?
Make it skeet like me?
Hell naw cause the bitch ain't tight like me!
Do I make myself clear,
My dear?
No need to fear!
U can't come near!
Put on yo best gear
But remember I'm the hottest thing this year!

So Niggah come wit the real shit
Only if you can top my shit!
That's right I'm that bitch
Yo man wanna stick!

That's right, I said it!

Yo man wanna stick

His dick

In my shit!

Now top that, bitch!

You can't fuck wit the Prince Bitch!

Straight keeping you ho's in check

Wit my dope flows

No time for you fake ho's

Wit no doe

No style

And weak flows

But next time if you wanna top my shit

Come wit the real shit

Or just continue to wish

You was The Prince Bitch!

"All right," Melvin laughed as he closed the door only for the telephone to ring again.

"Hello," he answered on the second ring.

"Hey, queen, whazzup?"

"Hey, Howard, nothing much, what's up with you?"

"Just calling to see if you all are going to Memphis tonight to Xavier's and William's party?"

"Yeah, we plan on going do you wanna ride with us or have you got your car fixed?"

"Oh, I'll need a ride," Howard said.

"O.K., then you **needs** to be ready in about an hour because we'll be ready to go in an hour."

"Child, are you all going out tonight too?" Howard asked.

"We are supposed to go to *N-Cognito*," Melvin said as he looked through his closet for a mustard turtleneck or mustard shirt.

"You'll love it," Howard laughed.

"Child, why are you so damned happy?" Melvin asked almost annoyed.

"Step out your front door and you'll see, bitch," Howard laughed and hung up the telephone.

Melvin walked to the front door and opened it up only to see Howard standing beside a brand new *1999 teal green Ford Contour.*

"You are too twisted, child," Melvin laughed. "When did you get it?"

"Child, I got it today," Howard laughed as Melvin walked toward the car to inspect it. "I got so damned tired of that other car breaking down every week until I could scream."

"Yeah," Melvin laughed. "I must admit. Betsy had seen her last days but I wasn't the one to tell you."

"Child, I just got tired of spending a hundred dollars here to fix this or fifty dollars there to fix that or seventy-five dollars to fix that. After that old bitch broke down on me last week, I prayed and asked the Lord to let it crank just one more time and run just one more time until I could get it to the dealer."

"Weren't you afraid that it wouldn't crank at the dealers?"

"Child, I also prayed that it would crank one more time for the dealer."

"I assume it did," Melvin grinned.

"And you know it," Howard chuckled. "He gave me five hundred for it and I put fifteen hundred down on this thang."

"Well, that wasn't bad considering 1979 Thunderbirds are pretty much out of date."

"I just didn't want a damned car note but when I thought about how much I had to spend to fix that old car, I figured I could pay a note."

"I would have gotten tired of it breaking down on me," Melvin confessed earnestly as he peeked inside of the car at its interior.

"That's why I prayed so hard, child," Howard laughed. "I know that I didn't want to just give those people my car after all of the money I have sunk into it."

"Hell, you had the car since we were in high school Howard."

"And I got my money's worth out of it."

"Considering the car is almost twenty years old, you should have kept it another year and made it a collector's item."

"Collector's item my ass," Howard laughed. "That thang sputtered and spitted all of the way to the dealers and purred like a kitten when I cranked it for him."

"You are too much," Melvin laughed. "Well, are you going to ride with us or are you going to show off your new car tonight?"

"You know I'm going to show off my new car tonight," Howard smiled. "I just wanted to know if you wanted to ride with me or will your man let you?"

"We are going together as I stated earlier," Melvin stated coyly.

"I wonder if Bradley wants to go then. Somebody needs to get that grieving queen out of Dyer County for a while."

"He is supposed to be going to frat meeting tonight but I just didn't feel it tonight."

"Well, I don't feel those old farts tonight either," Howard laughed. "The older we get the more they get set in their ways. And none of us have reached forty yet and you would think we were ancient relics or something."

"Well, the organization can be no better than what you make it," Melvin stated firmly. "There ain't no used in complaining if you never attend a meeting to voice your opinion. And you certainly shouldn't complain if you voice your opinion and someone asks you to do something and then you give them a million excuses on why you can't do what you were asked."

"Well, I feel you, child," Howard said. "I have to go now. I'm going to run and see if Bradley wants to go to Memphis tonight. I don't want to go early."

"I feel you," Melvin laughed as he noticed how Howard had basically run completely from the truth that was just stated. Howard was one of the people who constantly complained about what the fraternity never did but you could seldom find Howard at a meeting. Melvin spearheaded an event and asked Howard to be on his committee and Howard found a million reasons why he could not. Now, he could not face truth. Instead, he like so many other members of various organizations chose to run from truth and fly from work.

"Well, I'll see you tonight, then," Howard said as he jumped into his car and pulled off.

Chapter Thirteen

Here I Come, Here I Go

Eric drove to Dyersburg's East Side normally known as the Bruce Community. He gently laughed to himself when he thought about how full the barber shop would be on a Saturday and how pissed he would be at this particular time if he had short hair still. He remembered how long the lines would be at the two barbershops in town on a Saturday morning. He also remembered, as he turned off of Fair Street and onto Southern Street, just how large a crowd there would be at *Ann's House of Wings* on a Saturday afternoon. Saturdays at *Ann's House of Wings* was chitterling day. Grimlock served a huge plate of chitterlings - boiled or fried, with spaghetti, slaw, white beans, a huge slice of cornbread and a large glass of iced tea served in a *Mason* jar. As Eric pulled into the gravel parking lot, he barely found a parking space as the restaurant was filled with Grimlock's loyal Saturday customers.

Grimlock thought strategically when he opened *Ann's House of Wings*. He made certain that he obtained a liquor license whereas he could serve beer alongside his meals for stragglers and the normal alcoholics that needed to get a quick fix but didn't have the transportation to downtown Dyersburg. *Ann's House of Wings* was a readily availability when the urge crept upon them to get a mid day "drank." The interior of *Ann's house of Wings* provided a rather homey atmosphere. There were plastic red and white checkered table clothes on each table, one laminated menu, a napkin holder, salt and peppershakers, a sugar dispenser, and hot sauce, ketchup, and steak sauce. In the middle of all of these items were a small floral arrangement and an ashtray. There was a wide screened television set up at the bar and a juke box toward the back of the restaurant that played all of the great hits of the 1960s and 1970s.

Eric could never resist playing "*Misty Blue*" and Clarence Thomas' "*Stroking*" whenever he entered the establishment. It just didn't seem right not to do this.

Because Grimlock knew people, he knew what items to keep on his menu on what days. Through the week there was no set menu but on Fridays everyone could expect fried catfish, buffalo fish, crappie and anything that could be fried. On Saturdays everyone knew

to expect boiled or fried chitterlings. Contrary to the complaints of the staff (no one liked to clean chitterlings), the restaurant remained full into the wee hours of the night every weekend. Grimlock certainly did not complain. Between him, Doe, Tessie, and occasionally Miss Ann, herself, *Ann's House of Wings* became a booming success in no time at all.

As Eric walked into the restaurant, his heart warmed to see the old familiar faces seated at the bar watching a game. Jaws, The Shaw, T.A., Bear, Smurf, The Skull - the normal Saturday crew were fussing, cussing, laughing, betting, arguing, agreeing, and/or disagreeing or all of the above on the afternoon game, the latest gossip, or the latest headliner in the news paper. Grimlock always seemed to be in his element when the restaurant was full, sounds of laughter could be heard around the room, and paying customers were filling their stomachs on some of the best food served in the rural West Tennessee area.

"Whazzup, Dreads?" Grimlock greeted Eric as he walked through the door. "I know you want the special today?"

"Hey, Grimlock," Eric laughed. "You know I can't come in here on a Saturday and not get a plate of fried chittlins. Go ahead and fix me up a plate."

"Aight, bet," Grimlock said as he hollered into the kitchen area. "Hey, Doe, fix me up another plate of fried chittlins with a helping of spaghetti."

"You have to wait a minute," the lady yelled back. "WE can only fry so many at a time. I'll bring it out in a minute."

"Aight," Grimlock yelled. "We'll bring it to you. Do you want a hot pepper with that or some white beans and slaw?"

"I'll take the works," Eric laughed as he listened to Grimlock's sales pitch. "Hey, have you seen Josh? I was supposed to meet him here today."

"Yeah, he in the back at a table by himself," Grimlock said. "Go on back there, you'll see him. Is that where you want us to bring the food?"

"That'll be cool," Eric said as he walked through a small corridor that lead to a larger room filled with tables, chairs, and people. The rank smell of pork mixed with cigarette and cigar smoke hung heavily in the air. To hide the smell, a sweet smelling air freshener was constantly sprayed in the room which made the smell worse. The jukebox played Denise LaSalle's *"I Forget To Remember To Forget About You."* As strange as it was to watch the people stuff their bodies full between much talk filled with gossip and the latest news Eric felt a peaceful tranquility that made him appreciative of the rural South. He knew that he was truly at home. Some traditions were new but getting together to eat, laugh, lie, and tell the latest news was an age-old tradition that never changed.

He spotted Josh sitting in at a corner table that was barely visible to the public eye without a second glance. Immediately he knew that Josh was up to no good. His first mind told him to leave but Josh recognized him and waved him to the table.

"Whassup?" Eric said as he slid down into a chair adjacent Josh.

"Nothing much man, how you doing?" Josh said.

"Man, skip the bullshit, what do you want?"

"It's Jeremy," Josh explained. "He's in trouble and I need your help."

Eric stared at Josh in utter amazement. He could not believe that Josh would have the gall to even ask him for a favor especially one in regards to Jeremy. Both he and Josh knew that Jeremy was a hopeless cause and Eric did not have the energy to ascertain even the thought of helping a person who obviously did not want help.

"I know you didn't waste my damn time over Jeremy," Eric said calmly. "He's a fuck up and you know it."

"Just hear me out," Josh pleaded.

"I'm listening," Eric said as a waitress brought him a humongous plate of fried chitterlings with an enormous amount of spaghetti, slaw, white beans, and the thickest slice of cornbread that could ever be imagined. After she placed his plate on the table she motioned to a second waitress who brought him a *Mason* jar filled with tea. Eric grabbed a bottle of hot sauce from the table and shook it gently in his hand, removed the top, and shook it gently over his chitterlings.

Josh waited until Eric finished his preparation to eat before he began.

"I think Jeremy was involved in that house fire last night," Josh said.

"And?" Eric said as he chewed his food praying that Josh said nothing to deter his appetite for this delicacy.

"Well, I know that you work for the paper and I would appreciate it if you could help me keep it out of the paper."

Eric lost his appetite completely.

"If they ask me to do a write up, I'm doing it."

"But he's family, man," Josh said sadly.

"Fuck that mothafucka," Eric said before he thought about what he was saying and how loud he was getting. "You mothafuckas ain't never gave a damn about me so why the fuck should I give a damn about what happens to him?"

"You a gotdamn lie," Josh yelled. "You still pissed off with us because Sadie B. didn't like your ugly black ass. We didn't ever do nothing to you."

"Yeah, whatever," Eric said attempting to control his tongue and temper. "The answer is hell no. What else did you want?"

"Oh, nothing just to tell you that I'm about to be a daddy twice over," Josh smiled.

"Oh, Keisha's having twins?"

"No, Keisha's pregnant and Adrienne's pregnant."

Eric just stared at him.

"Well ain't you gonna congratulate me?"

"On what? Getting your wife and your ho pregnant at the same time? For running up to that church every Sunday playing Mr. Deacon and knowing full well that you fuck off on your wife with anything that allows you to stick your pitiful dick up in them?"

"You just mad cause you can't have kids, that all."

"You got me fucked up, mothafucka," Eric growled attempting vehemently to control his anger and his tongue. Praying to God that he would not strike Josh in this public facility.

"Ah, punk ass niggah," Josh laughed. "You just mad cause you can't get the pussy that I can get."

"The last I heard pussy wasn't the only thing you were chasing."

Josh's face turned red as a beet at this statement

"You black ass mothafucka, I oughtta kick you mothafuckin ass right now," Josh said as he stood up from the table.

"Aight, niggahs," Grimlock yelled. "Take that shit outside."

"He flogging, Grimlock," Eric said as he stared at Josh and then slowly rose from his seat. "I'll pay you for that somebitch to hit me."

"You sell out, mothafucka," Josh growled.

"Yeah, yeah, yeah," Eric said as he motioned the waitress. "Put this in a to-go-box for me, sweetie, this niggah illin' and about to get fucked up!"

"I done told you mothafuckas to take that shit outside before I have to jump in the shit," Grimlock warned.

The waitress quickly brought a Styrofoam sectional plate to the table, emptied the contents of Eric's food into the Styrofoam plate, and gave Eric a bill and the plate.

"Oh, it ain't gone be none of that, Grimlock," Eric said as he quickly passed the waitress a five-dollar bill. "This niggah ain't gonna come for me. He'd rather come for your momma before he'll come for me."

"Mothafucka, you got me fucked up," Josh yelled as he took a swing at Eric and missed.

"Eric laughed at him and walked to the front of the restaurant to pay for his meal."How much do I owe you, Grimlock? Let me hurry up and pay for this and get outside before I get in your debt for crackin a niggah's skull up in hear."

"That'll be seven dollars and seventy-nine cents," Grimlock said as Eric passed him a ten-dollar bill.

"Keep the change, man," Eric said as he stormed out of the door.

Josh quickly followed behind him.

"You need to let that man alone," Grimlock warned Josh. "When you get outside of that door, I don't give a damn what happens as long as yall don't tear up my parking lot and nobody's car out there."

Josh threw a twenty-dollar bill at Grimlock.

"Keep the change, man," he said as he marched outside the door behind Eric.

"Yo, man," Josh said as Eric sat down in his car. "It's like that now?"

"Josh," Eric said as he stood up and faced Josh directly. Josh could feel Eric's breath on his collar. "You are about a second away from an ass whippin that Sadie B. or Trish Ann never gave you in your life. I said hell no, now keep fuckin with me."

"But we are family, Eric," Josh pleaded attempting to rationalize with Eric.

"What the fuck do you want me to do? If they give me the fuckin assignment then I have to write it up. But if your punk ass ever took the time out to read the damned newspaper you would see that I have an editorial that comes out once a week and the other shit I do is the sports section. In other words, I'm the fuckin sports journalist. OK? If they put the shit in the paper and Josh is involved then I can't help you. Got that?"

"Well, why haven't you interviewed me since I'm back and all?"

"You are so trifflin," Eric said as he looked at the seriousness of Josh. He could not help but laugh at Josh. "First, you don't want Jeremy in the paper but you want me to do a write up on you?"

"Well I did play a few years of pro ball and I am assistant principal at Fairhaven Elementary."

"You are so full of it," Eric laughed. "Even when I want to kick your mothafuckin ass you make it impossible."

"You know you love me," Josh teased.

"I'm a Christian," Eric returned. "I'm supposed to love everybody."

Josh laughed this time.

"Well, are you at least proud of me on becoming a daddy?"

"Why would you sleep with two women at the same time? Does your wife know about this other woman?"

"Hell naw, man, you think I'm crazy?"

"Hell yes."

"I couldn't resist. Adrienne used to go out with Bradley years ago and now baby got back," Josh said as his eyes drifted in thought of his new conquest." That big round ass that looks like an apple when you tap it and those luscious tiddies that look like those chocolate drops that you buy at Christmas time. I just had to have a bite."

"Have you ended your fetish for men yet?"

"Oh, not really," Josh admitted. "I got my eye on that Maxwell Quest at the school."

"He's taken."

"So, what does that got to do with anythang?"

"If you want to get them Omega boys on your ass, fuck up and try to mess with The Rev's piece."

"Mr. Quest is fuckin The Rev?"

"Ask him," Eric said. "But if he cusses your ass out then don't feel disappointed. Aren't you afraid of catching AIDS?"

"Hell no, I use protection when I fuck faggots," Josh said earnestly.

"Oh, so Mr. Big Dick has changed his way of life," Eric commented wryly. "You better keep your dick in your pants, boy. I'm told that African-American female cases of HIV/AIDS are on the on rise here in rural West Tennessee."

"I ain't gonna catch shit," Josh grumbled. "Hell, I only fuck with clean women anyway."

"You need to fuck only your wife but that really ain't none of my business, though."

"How are thangs in your life? You don't come to see us no mo. You act like we the plague or something."

"I ain't got time no more," Eric laughed as he jumped into his car. "But, I'm fine."

"Well, what do you think we need to do about Jeremy?"

"That's not my problem," Eric said. "That's yours and Trish Ann's problem."

"He came over to her house this morning with all kind of mud on his clothes and shit and she wouldn't let him in the house after he stole her colored television set last year. So then he came by my house and you know he can't come in my house around my wife and family doin the shit he be doin."

"Well, that is **your** brother," Eric said as he cranked his car up and turned his music up loudly in order to terminate the conversation.

"Bye, Eric," Josh said as he grabbed Eric's hand to shake it. Eric shook his hand and sped away.

Josh was happy but sad. He loved Eric but really didn't understand Eric. Why would he want to ruin his life by being tied down to one person when everybody wanted to give it up for nothing? The only person Josh worried about was his wife. He loved LaKeisha but he just didn't know how to control his fetish for sexual pleasure.

Josh walked toward his car when he recognized an obvious crack head standing beside it.

"You touch my car, mothafucka, and I'm gonna bash your gotdamn head in," Josh growled.

"If you bash my head in, somebitch, then you won't know what I got to tell you," the man said.

"What the hell do *you* have to tell *me*, Ace?" Josh asked suspiciously.

"What's it worth to you?"

"Not a gotdamn thang, mothafucka, but I'm gonna put some whoop ass on you if anythang is stolen out of my ride."

"Man fuck yo ride," Ace said. "But if you don't wanna know about you brother then fuck you!"

Josh looked sternly at Ace.

"What you know?"

"Depends on how much it's worth to you," Ace replied.

"Get in," Josh said as he opened his car door, sat down, and then unlocked the door for Ace to get into the car with him. Ace looked around attempting to scope out the area and then he sat down.

"Well, how murch is it worth to you?"

"Here's twenty dollars, Ace," Josh said as he reached into his wallet and flung a twenty dollar bill at Ace.

"Drive the car," Ace directed.

"Where to?"

"Anywhere just away from here."

Josh cranked the car up and began to drive the wide circle around The Bruce Community as Ace slowly told him the information that he really did not desire to hear.

"Yo brother killed all them folks last night," Ace said.

"How the hell would you know?" Josh asked suspiciously.

"Because I was there, mothafucka," Ace said gruffly.

"Then that makes you an accomplice, right?"

"Naw, mothafucka, yall ain't plantin this shit on me," Ace said.

Josh hit a button on the side of his car that rolled down all of the windows. Ace was as funky as ten skunks in a horse manure pile and Josh couldn't tolerate the smell without a sudden urge to gag..

"Then what the hell is up," Josh asked.

"Last night when that big storm came Psycho was havin some type of night mare. He was so fuckin' loud until I couldn't sleep. So I got up and left out the house. Well, a few minutes later he must have woke up cause he ran out the house and threw the latch down on the door. Well, I was wonderin what was wrong with this mothafucka so I decided to follow him. He went out to the graveyard to that grave of that boy who was murdered a year or so ago. He kept hollerin: "*I done know why I kilt you. Please lemme alone.*" And when I looked up that gotdamn house was on fire. By the time I could make it to the house the whole damned roof was on fire and the last thing I heard was all dem people screamin before the roof fell down on dem killin dem automatically."

"I don't believe you," Josh lied.

"You need to believe somebody," Ace said. "Why you think he would sleep in an abandoned house by a graveyard if something ain't haunting him and makin him stay close to it?"

"Where you wanna go, Ace?" Josh said as he began to speed down Roberts Street towards the railroad track that leads out of The Bruce Community.

"Just gimme ten mo dollahs and den drop me off at de liquor sto'," Ace grinned.

Josh felt the information was worth it. He did not have any tens on him "Damn," he said as he flung another twenty-dollar bill at Ace as he pulled up to a liquor store.

"Get out," Josh said. Ace quickly got out of the car and realized that it was now dark. Josh didn't care as long as he got out of the car where he could spray air freshener to kill the foul odor that Ace left behind in the car. Josh sped off into the night.

Ace walked into the liquor store, bought a bottle of cheap wine and a bottle of cheap vodka. He felt accomplished and exonerated. Now the secret was out and he didn't have to go to the authorities on Psycho for the death of his girlfriend who was one of the victims in the fatal fire.

Ace took a huge gulp of the vodka and began to slowly walk down a dark alley that led away from the liquor store.

The last face Ace saw was the face of Psycho.

The last voice he heard was that of Psycho.

"Tell this, mothafucka," Psycho said as he plunged a knife deep into Ace's heart and twisted it around several times before pulling it out of the man. Ace dropped his wine. He was too surprised to scream for help.

Ace fell to the ground. A pool of blood began to encompass his body. Psycho reached down and wiped the knife clean on Ace's dirty coat. He quickly searched Ace's pockets and retrieved the money, a small piece of crack and the bottle of vodka.

"Snitch ass mothafucka," Psycho said as he spit on Ace's corpse and walked quickly out of the alley.

It was cold and Psycho's coat was thin. He decided that he needed to get rid of the murder weapon but he did not know where to go. He began to walk hurriedly until he reached Easthaven Apartment's in Dyersburg's Future City Community located on the West Side of town. He seized the opportunity of getting rid of the murder weapon when he noticed a huge green garbage dumpster in front of the *Easthaven Apartments* sign.

He walked to the dumpster and slipped when he opened it. This caused a loud disturbance that did not go unnoticed.

"You need to get the hell out of here if you don't live here," the voice rang out in the night like an Angelic announcement of a Saint's arrival.

"Who the fuck is you, you fat bitch," Psycho yelled in fear. The voice had startled him.

"Don't you worry about who I am, you get the hell out of here fumbling around in the damned garbage can like a maniac," Precious said as she looked over the rail in an attempt to see what Psycho was doing.

She did not notice when Psycho slipped the knife into the dumpster between the trash that was already piled high in it.

"You mind your own gotdamn business, bitch," Psycho said as he walked across the lawn.

"Get the hell off of my grass," Precious yelled. "Who are you anyway?"

"None of your business, bitch," Psycho yelled as he walked off of the grass and toward the street. "You need to mind your own gotdamn business and leave mine alone, you fat bitch!"

"I am minding my business," Precious returned as she began to dial a number on her cell phone. "But you need to stay out from over here if you don't live here."

"Fuck you," Psycho said as he walked completely out of the complex and towards a nearby gambling hole.

"Fuck with me, you get a better feeling, you tired bastard," Precious said as she marched back into her office.

Chapter Fourteen

Thieves In The Temple

Melvin borrowed his mother's 1998 *Lincoln Town car* to drive to Memphis for Xavier's thirtieth birthday gala. Although Eric cussed and fussed when Melvin announced they would not drive Eric's *Impala* or Melvin's *Honda Accord,* his note quickly changed when he got behind the steering wheel of the huge car. The car was spacious and comfortable. Eric had to admit, he had not driven a specious or comfortable car since the eighties when he owned his first car, a *Buick LeSabre.* He had legroom for the first time in ages and this he liked. Melvin actually sank down in the seat and could almost make a bed in the car because of its room.

"He was right," Eric thought. *"This is nice and comfortable."*

When Eric pulled the car up to the parsonage of The Universal Morning Star Nondenominational Church he was completely amazed at the splendor. Personally he thanked God that Melvin had decided to borrow the *Lincoln Town Car.* The two story Italianate home that served as the parsonage was strategically set amidst a grove of oak trees and provided a swimming pool and tennis court for those who desired to play while visiting the pastor and his companion.

"Are you sure this is the right place?" Eric asked as he pulled the car in front of the U shaped drive behind the line of other cars that awaited the valet.

"Yeah," Melvin chuckled. "This is Xavier and William's humble abode."

"And what are the occupations of these two people?"

"William pastor's the congregation of the church that furnishes this monstrosity while Xavier is a gospel recording artist."

"So the church is paying for this?"

"Just the house, utilities, his car, and salary," Melvin chuckled.

"I need to change occupations," Eric laughed.

"I'm not first lady material," Melvin laughed.

"But whoever that person is right there could be a first lady," Eric said as he pointed to a man bedecked in fur from head to toe.

"That's actually his title," Melvin laughed. "First Lady Hardaway."

"Now what is his occupation?" Eric asked curiously as he watched the man shake hands with and or hugged several people on the front portico as other people began to arrive at the party.

The valet was about to open Melvin's door when Eric stopped him and ushered him around to his side of the car. As Eric stepped out of the town car, the keys promptly went into the hands of the valet as he walked around the car and opened the door for Melvin himself. Melvin placed both feet out of the car at once slowly extending his hand into Eric's as he gracefully stood up. Eric immediately closed the door behind him. The valet smiled.

"You better work it out, guhl!" Hardaway yelled. "All right for missionary points."

The small crowd on the porch laughed as Hardaway approached Eric and Melvin.

"I'm in your jurisdiction this week, First Lady," Melvin teased as he hugged Hardaway with the famous "*Holy hug.*" The holy hug was a hug of friendship, care, and concern where a person leaned forward the top portion of his/herself toward the person being greeted. Cheeks vaguely rubbed yet the person's body parts were never exposed. Thus, the hug was considered holy because nothing sexual could be gained from the hug yet each person maintained a degree of dignity and respect for the other person.

"Well all right, Saint of the Lord," Hardaway laughed. "And who is this tall fine basketball player looking man you are with this evening, if I may ask?"

Eric grinned.

"First Lady Hardaway, this is my beaux, Eric," Melvin said as Hardaway gave Eric a hug. "Eric this is the Famous First Lady Hardaway of Memphis, Tennessee."

"Ooo," Hardaway squealed as he had to literally tip toe in order to hug Eric. "Child, you certainly can wear your pumps with this man."

"Nice to meet you, ah, ah," Eric stammered in attempting to figure out what to call Hardaway.

"Just call me Hardaway, child," Hardaway laughed.

The three of them walked up the portico. Melvin noticed Douglas and Desmond as he stepped onto the last step.

"Hey, children," Desmond laughed as he hugged Melvin, Eric, and Hardaway simultaneously.

"Hey my Saints of the Lord," Hardaway laughed as he hugged both Douglas and Desmond. "Every time I look at you two I receive inspiration. I'm so proud that you two are yet holding on."

"Child," Douglas laughed with a slight bounce. "My bookie ain't going nowhere!"

"Douglas," Melvin called. "This is my beaux, Eric. Eric this is Douglas who called me this morning."

"Hey whazzup," Eric said as he shook Douglas' hand.

"Slow motion," Douglas returned.

"How long we got to wait to get up in this joint," Eric asked.

Hardaway could not help but laugh as he listened to Eric's lingo.

"This is Xavier," Desmond laughed. "He'll make you wait an hour until he has personally greeted everyone as they come into his home."

"Yeah," Hardaway laughed. "That guhl is about one of the last people in the South who still believe in long receiving lines for a party. But I give him his props though, it will be worth the wait and you should see the guhls here in Memphis scrambling to get on the invitation list to his parties."

"That's Xavier," Douglas laughed.

"Isn't that a bit pretentious?" Eric asked attempting to understand this "receiving line" concept.

"No," Hardaway laughed. "Xavier just refuses to throw a party where he does not personally greet every person that comes through his front door. The invitation list is normally so lengthy until this line could last for hours."

"It's best to get here thirty minutes before the hour the invitation says or you could wait for a long time," Desmond laughed as he noticed Howard and Bradley walking up the front lawn.

"Hey," Desmond called out to them as they passed through the small crowd that gathered on the portico.

"Whew, hey," Bradley laughed as he reached the group. "Child this line gets longer every year."

"Yall know Miss Xavier," Hardaway laughed. "But you all probably don't know these guhls in Memphis. Everybody has been talking about this party for weeks."

"I'm cussing that queen's ass out whenever I get through these doors," Bradley laughed. "It ain't like it ain't cold out here you know."

"You see I have my fur on," Hardaway laughed. "I'm rather warm myself."

"What is that mink or fox?" Eric asked.

"This is my sable," Hardaway laughed as he walked outward to reveal the full length sable and stylish hat to match.

"Child, I only wear my mink for formal occasions and I refuse to give this guhl the privilege of believing or even thinking that one of his shin dings is a formal occasion," Bradley laughed.

"Child, I just wear my fur for warmth because I refuse to be cold," Hardaway laughed.

"Well, I prefer my leather," Melvin said.

Bradley noticed Melvin was wearing a brand new full-length leather coat.

"When did you get that?" Bradley asked as the line slowly moved forward.

"Child, I bought it this summer on a clearance sell," Melvin laughed. "You know I'm not going to spend money on a new coat in the middle of winter."

The group laughed.

The group finally managed to make it inside the front door.

"Good evening and welcome to my home," Xavier said as a person entered before them.

The entire group forged its way in at once.

"Child, we know who you are and we refuse to wait out in that cold any longer," Melvin laughed as he hugged Xavier followed by Eric, Hardaway, Bradley, Desmond, Douglas, and Howard.

"Xavier, you have not met my new beaux," Melvin said as Eric stepped inside. "Xavier this is Eric Curbie, Eric this is Xavier."

"Welcome to my home," Xavier said as he extended his hand to Eric.

An attendant took the groups' coats.

"You all go on in and mingle and I will be in shortly. William is somewhere in the house but there is food and drink all around the place. Just make yourselves welcome," Xavier said as he went back to the door to greet the guest.

Everyone in the group began to mingle in the spacious foyer. Slowly they made their way to the great room and the formal dining room. Eric was impressed with the splendor typeface the villa. Men and women of all shades, creeds, and colors traveled from room to room in the great halls of the house in constant chatter mingled with laughter and glee. The party could be considered nothing more than a success. By eight- thirty, the entire assembly had gathered in the great room, sang a round of "happy birthday" to Xavier and had begun to sit down for lighthearted conversation.

"Child, it has not always been like this," Xavier laughed. "If anybody in the room could tell you about the good old days of struggling, Melvin, Douglas, Desmond and Hardaway can tell you."

"Hell, yeah," Hardaway laughed. "You know I remember the road days right after you met William."

"I did love the company we traveled with," Xavier said as he thought about years that had gone by.

"It's still a bitch, child," Hardaway laughed.

"Will you sing a song with me for old time sakes?" Xavier asked Hardaway in a boyish, childlike manner.

Hardaway looked at him and couldn't resist.

Xavier and Hardaway stood beside the baby grand piano as a musician began to play. "Xavier whispered in his ear and he soon began to play a traditional gospel tune with a slight beat to it.

Together, Xavier and Hardaway began to bellow out a very blues rendition of *Just A Closer Walk With Thee*. Hardaway sang in a very heartfelt strong and powerful tenor while Xavier matched his voice harmonically in both alto and soprano at certain intervals.

No one noticed when William and Howard exited the room.

"This is a very nice bedroom," Howard laughed.

"Many things occur in this room," William taunted.

"I'm sure they do," Howard chuckled.

William walked closer to Howard and began to stroke the back of his neck.

"You are a married man," Howard reminded William although William's touch had begun to spark energy within him that he could not control. "What will your man think?"

"Xavier and I have not had sex in over a year now," William confided. "I just need to know how it feels to hold a man, touch a man, feel a man, make love to a man again."

"What makes you think you can handle this man?" Howard teased.

William kissed him hotly.

Howard lost all of his senses. He could not control his emotions as a new fire kindled within his soul.

"We may be discovered," Howard said in an attempt to break free of William's caresses.

"The doors are locked and this is a sound proof room," William whispered as he continued to kiss Howard on his neck, on his ear, on his cheek, in his mouth.

William and Howard lost control of themselves and allowed their passion to take full control of them- disregarding everything else about them.

They had hot, wild, passionate sex across the entire bedroom - on the bed, on the floor, on the nightstand, on a chair beside the bed. The sex did not stop there but went further into the master bathroom adjacent to the bedroom - in the bath tub, on the toilet seat, on the counter top. The energy was so high in the room until they completely forgot about where they were, who they were with, how they ever became attracted to one another.

Howard, down through the years, had made it a point not to date ministers. To him, there was a terrible consequence in dating them.

William had cheated on Xavier only once prior to this but there was something about Howard's smile, his appearance, his energy that sparked a fire in his heart that had left him long ago. Howard was so much like the Xavier William had met years ago.

They passed out in the bathtub briefly.

"We'd better get back down there after a quick shower," William whispered sadly.

"I agree," Howard said as he turned the shower on. William took a bath sponge, applied bath gel to it and gently washed Howard. Howard returned the favor.

William kissed Howard again as he dried Howard's body from the water and moisture left behind on his body.

Howard entered the great room from one end. A few minutes later William entered from another end.

Xavier and Hardaway sang their finale as William and Howard entered and stood at separate corners of the room.

"*Never Grow Old,*" the two sang as tears gently flowed from Xavier's eyes. Hardaway hugged Xavier gently when the song ended.

Tears streamed down Melvin's face as he thought about Frederick and Gramps Jeremiah.

Bradley, on the other hand, sat in silence with a slightly twisted mouth. He seemed rather pissed about something as he sat silently until the end of the song.

"Child, are you all right?" Melvin whispered when the crowd resumed to conversation, laughter, and noise again.

"I can't believe Howard fucked Xavier's man in Xavier's home," Bradley raged softly.

"What?"

"Didn't you see them leave together?"

"Hell, no," Melvin confessed. "I was listening to the music."

"The Bible says to watch as well as pray," Bradley said wryly.

"That I'd rather not see and I'm trying to digest it all," Melvin said as Eric approached.

"Are we still going out, boo?"

"Yeah, I'm ready," Melvin said.

"Would it be an inconvenience if I rode home with you guys?" Bradley asked Eric.

"I don't see why not if you don't mind coming to the club with us," Eric said.

"Good," Bradley said. "Let me go and give my regards to Xavier."

Bradley searched the crowd until he found Xavier.

"What's wrong with him?" Eric asked.

"Oh, he just saw something that really disturbed him."

"You mean William and Howard getting together tonight?"

Melvin looked strangely at Eric.

"We gotta go," Melvin said as he went to the coatroom to retrieve his coat.

Melvin, Eric, and Bradley met Desmond, Douglas and Hardaway at the door with Xavier following closely behind the group.

"Well, I'm sorry that all of you guys are leaving at the same time," Xavier said.

"Well, child, you know I have my mission work to accomplish tonight," Hardaway laughed as he hugged Xavier. Xavier held onto Hardaway a little longer than Hardaway expected. Hardaway looked up at him and noticed water forming in his eyes.

"Are you all right?" Hardaway asked.

"Just happy to see you all come and sad to see you all go, that's all," Xavier said as the tears began to roll down his face.

Bradley, Desmond and Melvin all hugged Xavier at the same time and began to cry as well.

"I gotta go," Hardaway said suddenly. "I can't take this."

Eric and Douglas laughed.

The group finally left.

Bradley and Melvin walked so quickly to the car until Eric could barely keep up with their stride. Even with his long legs.

As soon as the three were comfortably settled in the car, Bradley broke the silence.

"That wench is too devious for me," Bradley grumbled.

"I'm curious to know, Eric, how did you know what happened?" Melvin asked as Eric drove swiftly onto I240.

"First, they were making innuendoes all evening at one another," Eric said.

"I thought I was the only person who saw that," Bradley said.

"Hell, I was completely oblivious to it," Melvin confessed.

"I saw them when they went up the stairs even," Eric said. "I knew right then what time it was."

"Well, I didn't see them go up the stairs but I sure as hell saw when they left the room," Bradley said.

"Child, child, child," Melvin giggled. "My people."

"I just cannot believe that Howard slept with that man in the man's house with his lover and guest downstairs," Bradley said.

"Maybe that's what the tears were about when we left," Eric said softly.

"Nah, I doubt it," Melvin laughed. "Xavier would have stopped the party to kick ass, believe that."

"Sometimes I get a little worried about him," Bradley confessed. "He certainly doesn't look all that great anymore. I guess this gospel music and entertaining people year round has finally gotten to him."

"Probably so," Melvin agreed. "Probably so."

Chapter Fifteen
A Stranger In The City

Eric pulled the Lincoln *Town car* onto Vance Street and parked. They had arrived. A strange sensation befell Melvin as ghost from the past began to haunt him. It has been years since he had been out. The last club he had gone to was *The Apartment Club*. He didn't know if he was ready for the club scene again as he thought he had put the club scene behind him. He was secure now in his relationship and did not want to jeopardize that in any shape, form or fashion. Attending the club used to be the thing. Although he still maintain his cute shape and sexy figure, he knew that he was no longer the fresh, hot, young African-American gay man that he was when he first went to a gay club many years before.

N-Cognito was not *The Apartment Club* but like *The Apartment Club*, *N-Cognito* served as the gate for young African-American gay men in the West Tennessee area to discover themselves with like individuals like them. The new club offered the same unique qualities that the old club had offered. Young African-American gay men and women who wore the latest fad, had nice tight bodies, and wanted to be young, black, and gay. Nothing changes, only the faces.

Melvin noticed a beautiful black door that led to the entrance of the club. This was a plus in one aspect whereas you could see the street after you walked outside. It had its disadvantage whereas in the old club there was nothing but a huge wooden door that was the entrance that led, like the new door, down a small hallway. Melvin paid his money, allowed the attendant to stamp his hand, and then was scanned by security that stood at the door. Security was actually nicer than he remembered at *The Apartment Club*. They were courteous young men who handled business professionally and did not tolerate foolishness of any kind.

The club was a single level club. To the left, as you entered, was a raised platform where tables were arranged neatly. The bar was to the right directly behind two pool tables and a few scattered arcade games and pinball machine. The dance floor was directly in the middle of the club. Behind the dance floor was a stage where the drag show occurred. Melvin did not know that behind the stage to the right was a door that led to an outside patio.

When the group entered the club they were pleased with the findings of the gay club for the new era. The group walked to the bar. Melvin and Bradley ordered juice while Eric ordered a beer. They looked up and to the left as the club began to fill with young black gay men from out of nowhere so it seemed and to their surprise they saw Hardaway setting up some type of informational table.

"Hey, chilren'," Hardaway laughed as he noted the shocked yet expressionless faces on the three.

"What are you doing?" Melvin laughed.

"My mission work, child," Hardaway laughed as he continued to set up his table.

Bradley and Melvin walked over to the table to investigate. The table was an HIV/AIDS prevention table.

"Well, this is nice," Bradley said. "How long have you been doing this?"

"Child, since so many of my friends kept dying from AIDS," Hardaway said with sadness in his voice. "Somebody has to educate the children before it's too late for us all. Just look around the club. You seldom see a familiar face that was at the Apartment Club just ten years ago."

Both Melvin and Bradley quickly scanned the room. He was absolutely correct. Many of the familiar faces that once danced, romanced, and were the divas of the decade no longer roamed the club in joy, peace, and happiness with the assurance that everyone else at the club was exactly like them... gay!

It was a sad but shocking fact. So many of the "children" had gone on to meet their Eternal Maker and there was only fragments left of the people who made gay life in the eighties and nineties worthwhile.

But, it was a new day. New faces, new entertainers, and a new sense of gay pride all in a new club... *N-Cognito!*

The music roared as the club slowly filled up. Melvin could not get into the Rapp music that was played for what seemed an eternity. He noticed that Eric swayed from here to there on certain songs as they played.

At midnight, a show tune began to play. A strobe light twirled which made the light dance about the entire dance floor. People began to gather around the dance floor leaving it completely open. Melvin wondered for a moment if there was some couple who was about to dance for the crowd until the voice of the announcer broke through the silence.

"Good evening and welcome to *N-Cognito*," the voice rang through the crowd with such professionalism until one would have never believed the voice belonged to one of the entertainers.

"Who is the announcer?" Melvin quickly asked Hardaway who continued to fuss about his table without inasmuch as noticing what was about to occur.

"Oh, that's Alicia Kelly," Hardaway said. "She will perform in a few minutes. She's nationally known now."

"Really?" Melvin asked in great anticipation of who this person could be.

Several new entertainers performed. Many were from the House of Dupree, St. John, St. James, Cassadine or any of the other famous legendary drag queens who seldom performed any more but trained the new and upcoming entertainers the dos and don'ts of the entertainment world.

When the last act came, the famous Alicia Kelley took the stage and rocked the entire club with a gospel tune.

Melvin was shocked that anyone would dare do a drag number to a gospel hit. He looked around the room and noticed how many of the people began to clap, rock, or sway to the music as if they were in church. The reality of the situation hit Melvin like a ton of bricks. Alicia Kelley had provided something to the masses that many of them would not be able to enjoy comfortably again for years until a funeral. Alicia sang for the "children" who had been criticized, talked about, or basically banned from the church. In a smoke filled, dark, club Alicia spread hope into lives of young men and young women who had abandoned the one thing that traditionally kept all black people bound together... the church.

Unfortunately, even in the year 1998, the one thing that all black people once treasured as the most sacred place on earth was still no safe haven for African-American same gender loving people. Regardless of the amount of tithes paid or offerings raised to build cathedrals grand and tall, bulging with people from corner to corner, "Homosexuality was a sin and would not be tolerated" in the very congregations where homosexuals where the catalyst for churches growing. Melvin, like so many other African-American gay men, felt sad beyond all price. He simply refused to leave Mt. Carmel regardless nor would he tolerate anyone sitting in the pulpit preaching hatred. He felt sorry for the many men who suffered in silence while the church constantly mistreated them. Yes, they were the musicians, choir directors, ushers, trustees, deacons and even ministers who toiled and labored with other parishioners to build cathedrals to worship the Lord and Savior Jesus Christ in. When Melvin thought about how so many of his kindred brothers and sisters were beat down until they lost all faith in the God, he became furious from within. He, like so many others, was taught that God was a God of love yet this God hated did not love them. Total bullshit and a terrible propaganda technique used to keep the members under the rule and thumb of people who refused to read the Bible for themselves or refused to seek a personal relationship with God. Because of this, many African-American same gender loving people laughed at the coinage of the use of even being "gay." Who feels happy? So many strikes until it sometimes become easier to yield to the abyss of darkness. A life filled with casual and uncommitted sex attempting to find love. It had become a life filled with one trick after the next until life's fleeting moments pass away. It had become a life hidden in the darkness far away from God, far away from a church that hates so viciously.

Melvin's eyes misted at the completion of Alicia Kelly's performance. The applause was thunderous as the adoring fans paid tribute to the one voice who freed their souls from the mundane realities of day-to-day life. And then there was the darkness of the club and the life… again and again!

The music began to whirl through the club. Instantly, the dance floor filled with people. Melvin and Eric danced for a while until Melvin tired. To Melvin's amazement, Eric never tired. He danced and danced and danced for hours. Bradley mingled with the crowd until the club began to bore him.

When finally Eric tired from dancing, he found Melvin and Bradley standing at Hardaway's table talking. He also noticed a strange new face at the table as well.

"Are you all ready?" he asked as Melvin smiled and Bradley gave him a *Please help me!* look.

"Yes," Bradley commented before Melvin could say a word.

The three exchanged pleasantries with Hardaway and began walking to the car followed by the stranger.

"Can I get your phone number," he asked.

"Man, who are you talking to" Eric asked as he turned around. The man jumped a bit at the suddenness of Eric's turn.

"Dude," the guy pointed toward Bradley.

"I'll take your number but I'm involved right now," Bradley lied. Melvin's mouth flew open wide. Eric tugged at Melvin's shoulder.

Bradley kept a straight face. The guy was attractive but not at all what Bradley was looking for in a man if he was dating. The man was shorter than Bradley. He still wore a Jherri curl which was an immediate turn off to Bradley. The final strike was that as cold as it was outside, the man wore a tank top to reveal an extremely hairy chest. What made matters worse; his chest had gray hair in it.

"*Lord, why tonight, Father?*" Bradley thought. "*I don't want to meet anyone and certainly don't want to meet this guy. He's too short, too hairy, too damned old and too damned worn out!*"

"Where do you work?" Bradley asked coldly.

"I work at *McDonalds*," the guy said as he smiled to reveal a mouth full of gold.

"Oh, hell no," Bradley said aloud before he realized it.

"What's wrong, you don't like me 'cause I work at a restaurant?"

"Child," Bradley said as the group began to enter the car. "I'm happy that you are employed but again I just don't have the time nor patience for a relationship, a one night stand, or even friendship right now. So, you are really wasting your time."

"You a cold bitch," the man said.

"But a good one," Bradley replied. "Now you have a good night and go on back into the club before you catch cold out here. Where is your coat anyway?"

"I didn't wear nan," the man said as he began to walk back toward the club.

"Well that automatically is against you in regards to me, then," Bradley said. "Honey, I need a healthy man and you out here trying to catch a cold. You go on and have a good night, OK?"

"Fuck you," he said.

"Good night to you too," Bradley said as Eric started the car.

"That was cold as hell, Bradley," Eric laughed.

"Child, now what could he do for me with his hairy ass?" Bradley said as his lips twisted into a *reading* position. "Hell, I didn't fuck with folk who worked at McDonalds when I was a teenager why would I digress? Further, that Jherri curl and that gold ain't hitting on shit."

"Child, that curl is what got me," Melvin laughed.

"This is Memphis," Eric laughed.

"Home of the curl," Bradley laughed. "But I digress."

They all laughed as Eric turned the volume up on the radio as Patti LaBelle began to swoon *You Are My Friend* in the background.

"Sang it guhl," Bradley yelled.

Chapter Sixteen

Think About Heaven Later

When Bradley arrived home from the club, he decided that a nice hot bubble bath would be in order. His body was now tired and he knew that the best way for him to relax was to take a hot bath. He walked to the bathroom, turned the water on hot with a little cold water mixed in where he would not scald. He reached into a nearby cabinet and found his *Calgon* and poured half the bottle into the water.

"*Hell, I need to be taken away,*" he thought to himself as the bubbles began to rise high into the bathtub.

He walked into the kitchen and poured himself a glass of *Hawaiian* punch, gulped down a glass and poured a second for the bath.

He found a copy of Aretha Franklin's *Respect* CD and put it into the CD player.

"*Yeah, guhl, you need to sang to me tonight, child,*" he smiled and thought fondly about his infatuation with the artist.

He quickly slipped out of his clothes and went back into the bathroom. Just as he turned the water off and was getting ready to get into the bathtub, there was a beat at the door. The knock was too hard and rapid to be a knock, it was a beat.

"Now what the hell is going on," he said as he threw a pair of boxer shorts and tank top tee shirt on. "It is four o'clock in the fucking morning."

He walked to the door.

"This had better be important," he said as he flung the door open.

"Bradley, please let me in, I need to talk to you,"

"At four o'clock in the morning Jeremy," Bradley asked. "What in the hell do you have to talk about at four o'clock in the morning."

"Just let me in, man," he said.

Bradley's first mind said: *"Don't do it"* while another voice said *"See what this mothafucka is trying to pull at this time of night."*

"You have about five minutes to tell me whatever it is you need to tell me," Bradley said as he opened the door for Jeremy.

Jeremy walked into the house and a foul odor followed him.

"Ooo, child," Bradley said. "I can't take this smell. You have to talk fast."

"Well, if you can't take this smell then let me take a shower. I just got off work but I needed to talk with you," he claimed.

"If you want to take a bath, fine, but niggah you ain't worked in years and you know it."

He laughed as he walked further into the house.

Bradley led him directly into the guest bathroom, gave him a new bar of *Lever 2000* soap, a wash cloth and drying towel.

"Do you have anything to change into?" Bradley asked as he looked at Jeremy. He pitied him but knew that he was not getting ready to take in a drug addict. He didn't mind feeding him, clothing him, but for him to live with him, never. Sex certainly was not an option!

"No, I left them at home because I was in a hurry when I left work to talk to you," he said sheepishly.

"Just go on in there and take a bath," Bradley grumbled. "I'm sure that I can find you something to put on."

"Thanks, man," he said as he went into the guest bathroom and began to shower.

Bradley postponed his bath because he refused to allow this man to roam freely around in his home. He found an old pair of jeans, an old tank top, and an old sweater for Jeremy. Fortunately, they were close to the same size. He placed them on a stool on the inside of the guest bathroom while Jeremy showered. He silently closed the door.

He sat down and listened to Aretha Franklin sing. And sang she did, rendering testimonials to Bradley. *Like A Bridge Over Troubled Water* filled the room.

"You got any beer?" Jeremy asked when he returned to the living room where Bradley sat with his legs crossed and arms folded

"I don't drink alcoholic beverages," Bradley said. "They are bad for you. You need to stop drinking them!" Bradley noticed that Jeremy had failed to put the clothes on that he had given him or perhaps he just wanted a drink so bad until he felt it necessary to tell Bradley while he had a bath towel wrapped around himself. He had a nice body but Bradley was not in any way, shape, form, or fashion falling for the old trick of allowing a crack head to undress and become goo goo eyed. He was not that desperate and like the crack head, he got paid for sex, if there was any sex to be rendered.

Suddenly, Jeremy dropped the bath towel exposing his naked body. He then began to stroke on his manhood.

"If you don't go in there and put your damned clothes on niggah, you better," Bradley said. "Now I don't know what the hell is going through your mind but whatever it is you had better reconsider it."

"How come you won't let me have a piece of dat ass like you let my brother?" he grumbled as he stood in the middle of the floor stroking on his penis.

"Because your brother had a bigger dick! Now put your gotdamned clothes on mothafucka," Bradley yelled.

"You just like that other trick," Jeremy said. "Scary as hell."

"First, I'm not the damned trick," Bradley laughed. "My clothes are on!"

"Is you getting smart with me, bitch," Jeremy grumbled as he walked toward Bradley.

"Niggah, you in my house," Bradley said as he stood up.

"I'll fuck you up and then kill you like I kilt your friend," Jeremy said as he pushed Bradley back onto the sofa.

Bradley attempted to digest what Jeremy had said before his temper began to flare. Jeremy had done the one thing Bradley did not tolerate… Jeremy put his hands on Bradley.

"I know you didn't just put your mothafuckin hands on me in my mothafuckin house, you bald headed bastard" Bradley said as his eyes began to flicker with raged.

"That ain't all I'mma put on yo ass tonight, bitch," Jeremy growled as he yanked Bradley from the sofa towards him. "You gonna gimme that ass just like Fred did and then you ain't gonna live to tell about it."

Bradley lost full control of his emotions at this point. First, this man completely disrespected his home. Second, this was the man who had killed his friend and now he was coming back to talk shit. ***"Hell the fuck no!"***

Before Jeremy realized it, Bradley had swung a punch into his nose. This stunned Jeremy because no homosexual man had ever fought him back. Everyone was always afraid of him. Where he usually would have become uncontrollably angry he became sexually charged and more excited. He liked the challenge.

"Oh, so you a ruff bitch," he mused.

"No, you a psychotic mothafucka who is getting ready to get his motha fuckin ass whipped and kicked out side butt naked in the cold," Bradley said as he began to fight Jeremy with everything that he had. The punches that Bradley packed took Jeremy by surprise. Jeremy did not know that this man could fight. He was now sorry that he had even bothered to come by the house. His only true purpose was to come by and get money for a fix and now he was getting his ass kicked by a faggot. Enough was enough!

"You forget you fuckin with Psycho," Jeremy yelled as he punched Bradley back which knocked Bradley behind the sofa.

Bradley jumped up from behind the sofa with a vase in his hand. As he jumped up he hurled the vase into Jeremy's face.

Jeremy screamed like an injured animal as the vase crashed squarely into his face.

Before he could get over the initial shock of the vase, Bradley was punching him again - in the head, in the back, in the face, anywhere his fist would land.

Jeremy was being hit by so much so quickly until he didn't know what to do. His eyes were bleeding from the glass that hit into his face, his lips were bleeding from the punches that Bradley were giving him, his back was beginning to get sore from more punches. He turned to face Bradley and punched Bradley again. This time he knocked Bradley into a nearby open closet.

"That's your ass mothafucka," Bradley said as he jumped to his feet with a baseball bat in hand.

Bradley beat Jeremy mercilessly. Bradley did not stop until he basically tired from it.

Jeremy passed out from the beating. He could withstand the punches but the baseball bat was too big and too aluminum for him to handle.

Bradley immediately called three people: The police, Josh, and Melvin.

When he hung the telephone up, he sat down on the sofa beside Jeremy. The baseball bat sat beside him just in case Jeremy stood up again.

Tears began to stream down Bradley's face when the police, Melvin, Eric, and Josh all arrived at the same time.

Melvin rushed into the house before the police could.

"Child, are you all right?" Melvin asked Bradley as he looked at Bradley sitting on the sofa and Jeremy lying totally naked on the floor.

"At this moment, I am," Bradley said. "In a few minutes I won't be."

"What's going on here?" the police officer asked as he attempted to understand the sight that he saw. There was a bloody man lying on the floor totally naked. Another man sat on a sofa with an aluminum baseball bat next to him.

"This mothafucka was gonna tryin to rape me and he confessed to killing my friend," Bradley said.

"What?" both Melvin and Eric said at the same time too stunned to understand the full concept of what had happened.

The police called for backup. Within five minutes, six police cars had surrounded Bradley's house. Jeremy slowly began to wake up... groaning from the beating that Bradley had given him.

"Sir, you have the right to remain silent, anything you say or do can be held against you in a court of law..." the police began.

"Shut up, mothafucka," Jeremy said as he hit the policeman in the face before he could be hand cuffed. He grabbed the policeman's gun and held it to the officer's temple.

"This mothafucka is stone crazy," Eric said as he watched Jeremy in disbelief.

Melvin held onto Bradley and Eric in complete fear. He did not know what to expect.

"Put the gotdamned gun down, Jeremy!" Josh barked. "We'll get you out in the morning."

"You lying!" Jeremy said. "Before I let you mothafuckas take me out I'm a take as many of yall as I can wit me."

"What would momma say?" Josh pleaded. "To think that you killed a police officer and some other people?"

"What is she gonna say when she finds out that I killed Frederick or those other six mothafuckas in dat house?"

"Jeremy!" Josh said as his eyes grew large. "Shut, up, all of this can be used against you, man. Let me help you, please."

Josh began to walk slowly toward Jeremy with his hand stretched forward in anticipation of retrieving the gun from Jeremy.

"Fuck you, niggah," Jeremy said as he pulled the trigger. "You ain't for no damned body but yourself cause you knew what I did! Yeah, I saw your ass talkin to that snitch ass Ace."

Melvin screamed as Josh hit the floor and a spray of bullets tore into Jeremy's arm causing him to fall backward. The police immediately seized Jeremy, cuffed him, naked and all, and took him to a police car.

Eric rushed to the floor beside Josh and held him in his arms.

"Hang in there, Josh," he said softly as the first tears Melvin ever saw in Eric's eyes began to fall. "You're gonna make it."

Five minutes later two ambulances came.

"Child, what a morning," Bradley said as two ambulances sped off with Josh and Jeremy followed by the police.

"You all give me time to get dressed again," Bradley said. "I was just getting ready to take a bath when that crazy somebitch showed up at my door with all of this bull shit."

"I need to call LaKeisha," Eric said as he picked up the telephone and dialed LaKeisha to inform her of what had happened.

"You wanna ride with us?" Melvin asked Bradley when he returned to the living room.

"Hell, might as well cause I know you all want to know what in the hell happened," Bradley laughed as he looked at the blood on his carpet.

"Yeah, this looks pretty bizarre to me," Melvin said.

"Shit, well it looks like I got the damned award money for turning in the bastard who murdered Frederick," Bradley said wryly.

"Well, at least you did fight him," Eric said. "It never even appeared that Frederick even put up a struggle."

"Even if Frederick had put up a struggle," Bradley said. "Look at how big that niggah is and how small Frederick was. The only reason I could hang with him is because I lift weights my damned self and I come from a sho nuff fightin family. If you didn't fight when I was growing up you got your ass whipped."

The three jumped into Melvin's car and headed for the hospital. Mixed emotions swelled within all of their minds, hearts, and souls for various reasons.

"My only question is this," Eric asked vaguely. "If Josh knew, why the hell didn't he come forward?"

"That was his brother," Melvin said grimly.

"I don't give a damn if that's his mammy," Bradley raged. "If he knew he should have at least told me. The bastard!"

"Well, we'll all know the deal soon," Eric said.

"I'm sorry, Eric, I forgot Jeremy is your cousin," Bradley said.

"My fuck up, cousin," Eric laughed.

"Did you know, Eric?" Melvin asked.

"Now what kind of stupid question is that?" Eric yelled. "If I had known I would have turned the mothafucka in for the hundred grand reward my damned self."

"Is that what the reward was?" Bradley chuckled.

"Bitch, you were the one who had them up it to that," Melvin laughed.

"Money just keeps calling me, children," Bradley grinned.

"Well at least now we know who it was," Melvin said wryly. "Someone who knew the murder victim."

"That's normal," Eric said. "I just wonder what the final outcome will be."

"I hope they fry that bastard!" Bradley said firmly. "If I hadn't gotten tired of kickin his ass I would have killed him my damned self."

"Well, would that have made you any better than him?" Eric asked.

"Would it have made me any less than Frederick if he had killed me?" Bradley asked.

"Where was Josh shot at?" Melvin asked attempting to diffuse a possible argument although his feelings were still hurt from a previous statement by Eric.

"Jeremy got him in the stomach, I think," Eric stated. "He should live though if they hurry up and get him there."

I should have kicked that motha suckas behind too," Bradley grumbled. "Every time that I think that he knew I get furious! No, I get mad as hell!"

"Well, he might have just found out about it," Eric said.

"Did you just find out about it?" Melvin asked.

"Melvin, I don't know what you are trying to ask me," Eric roared. "But if you want to know if I knew if Jeremy killed Frederick then forget it. I didn't know. I didn't know that he killed those six people that burned down in that house the other night either. Josh wanted to talk about it on Saturday to see what I knew or had heard."

"Well why didn't you tell me about that, then?"

"Because I forgot about it, damn it, I just found out yesterday when Josh and I talked."

"Yall really need to quit," Bradley said as the car sped into the emergency room entrance parking lot.

"Why?" Melvin grumbled.

"Because you are arguing over senseless shit!" Bradley explained.

"Well, I don't think so," Melvin said as Eric looked at him in disbelief. "If he will hide that from me then what else will he hide from me?"

"Fuck you," Eric said as he slammed the car door and walked swiftly into the emergency room entrance.

"All right, guhl," Bradley said softly. "Don't you lose no good man over silly shit. Let it go, guhl."

"I'm not going to lose him," Melvin said confidently. "I just want to know that he is going to be real with me in everything even if it does hurt me. I want to know."

"Melvin, now that wasn't none of your damned business what Eric and Josh discussed yesterday about Jeremy. Was it?"

"Well, no, but..."

"Then it really doesn't concern you then, does it?"

"Well, no, but..."

"Then let it go!" Bradley said firmly. "He ain't Justin, guhl. Justin wouldn't have told you this much and you know it, guhl!"

Melvin was speechless as Bradley got out of the car, opened Melvin's car door up for him, and they both walked into the emergency room entrance together.

The emergency room was a farce. LaKeisha and Adrienne were both there as well as Trish Ann Curbie. To everyone's amazement, Hortence Perry was also there.

"What the fuck is *this* bitch here for?" Melvin asked Bradley as they sat on the opposite side of the emergency room waiting room.

"Tone down, guhl, you know news travels quickly," Bradley laughed.

An officer approached Bradley and Melvin before Melvin could begin a line of questioning to Bradley.

"Are you Mister Bradley Kelley," the officer asked.

"Yes, I am," Bradley confirmed.

"We need for you to come down to the police department to fill out an incident report and make a statement," he said.

Bradley didn't hesitate. He jumped straight up and began to walk out of the door almost leaving the officer.

Melvin searched through the crowded Waiting Room and found Eric.

"Baby," Melvin whispered. "I'm headed to the police station with Bradley. Is that fine with you?"

Eric gently hugged Melvin.

"Yeah," he said. Melvin noticed a tired and weary expression on his face. "Go on, Bradley needs your support right now. I'll be there as quickly as possible."

"Are you sure you don't need me here, baby?" Melvin asked as he looked into Eric's puppy dog eyes.

"Go on before I say yes, boo!" Eric said as he led Melvin toward the exit.

"Come on, here," Bradley yelled. "Hell, I wanna get this shit over so I can go home and go to bed."

Eric laughed.

"Yeah, you better hurry, Bradley is getting tired," Eric laughed.

"That heffa will be all right," Melvin laughed as he held Eric's hand firmly for support. Melvin knew that trying times were definitely ahead yet he wanted Eric to always know that he was there for him.

"I love you, baby," Eric said gently as a slight smile creased his face exposing a small glint of his pearly white teeth that Melvin adored and cherished so.

"I love you too, baby," Melvin grinned as he gently released his hand and walked to the car where Bradley was now blowing the horn.

"Bitch, shut up!" Melvin yelled. "You are gonna get our asses arrested for disturbing the peace at the damned hospital."

"Then come the hell on!" Bradley yelled.

Melvin quickly walked to the car and jumped in.

"Damn, bitch, we're gonna get there so you can cash in on your coins," Melvin laughed as he cranked the car up and pulled behind the police car that escorted them to the police station.

"Child, I just couldn't digest looking at Hortence Perry in that damned hospital room."

"I wonder why she was there anyway."

"We will certainly find out in the upcoming months why."

"Do you think she knew that Psycho killed Frederick?"

"I thought she and Psycho were fuckin, child."

Melvin did not hear that correctly.

"I beg your pardon?"

"I did not stutter, guhl."

"But he is *our* age?"

"And I hear he is horse hung and plenty of those old bitches that want their coochies worked out have been with Jeremy Curbie."

"But I don't understand the connection."

"Child, wait a few months," Bradley said wryly. "I bet you that it all comes out in court. Hortence has always been a messy bitch. That's why the whole town knows about her affair with her preacher. She ain't never had nothing and ain't never been taught how to be a ho and she sure as hell ain't in the parade."

"Well that is your department, last I heard, guhl, I wouldn't know," Melvin laughed.

"You damned skippy," Bradley laughed. "I had a good teacher and she still attends Mt. Carmel every Sunday."

"Who, child?"

"You know Mrs. Ables has always been a damned good ho."

"Mrs. Ables?" Melvin asked thinking about one of the most respected women in his congregation. Although she was every bit of eighty-five or ninety, she still wore five inch spiked pumps, the latest fashioned attire for any lady of the day, and the woman gave you fur in the winter.

"Yes, Mrs. Ables," Bradley chuckled. "I overheard a conversation one day that she was having with this young lady and I became her best buddy ever since that day. Honey, when she said told that girl: Stop giving your pussy up for nothing! Having all those damn nappy-headed babies. You ain't gonna do nothing but get old and have nothing but a wet pussy. Look at me. Every man I have ever had supplied me with a car, all my clothes, and all of my furs, plus money in my bank account. As a matter of fact, this sable that I have on my back right now was purchased by some other woman's husband. And you sitting up here with a damned *Catos* special on thinking you cute. Humph! Remember, you better get some meat on your head girl, and stop giving it up for free. Mark my words, he don't want nothing that ain't hard to get. See, I am a widow woman - a rather convenient title that gave me my seat on the Mother Board. I'm still one of the most respected women up in this congregation and ain't nobody gonna mess with me too quick."

Melvin screamed with laughter as he watched Bradley re-enact the entire episode with Mrs. Ables.

"Child, I became her best friend and pupil ever since," Bradley laughed. "I'm just like Mrs. Ables… one of the most respected ladies in church."

Melvin roared.

"You laughing now, bitch, but watch what I wear to church tomorrow morning and watch how those folk respond."

"You going to church tomorrow?"

"I go every Sunday just like you, child."

"Well, I do go to Mt. Carmel," Melvin chuckled.

"And I do go to St. James CPC!" Bradley laughed. "If we get out early I might run by Mt. Carmel. You know we don't worry the Lord as long as you Baptist folk do."

"As long as we don't go to the cross, I'm fine," Melvin laughed. "We haven't been up there since Easter, so I'm rather pleased with my pastor."

"Oh, I've heard about him and his messages," Bradley said. "I don't know if I want to do Miss Mt. Carmel tomorrow in my outfit."

"Child, you leave my pastor alone. You know what the Bible says about touching the Anointed of God."

"I sure do and that's why I'm contemplating on whether or not I should do Miss Mt. Carmel or not in my new outfit cause St. James can take me."

"Child, I already know about your new fur," Melvin laughed. "They give you fur at Mt. Carmel too, you know. As a matter of fact, we probably taught you country hos over at St. James how to wear them."

"I don't know who taught what," Bradley laughed. "The only thing that I know is that Mrs. Ables taught me how to wear my fur, budget my money, and work my men and make people respect me all the more. So I could care less."

"Well, she never says or does much at Mt. Carmel," Melvin admitted.

"Hell, she ain't gonna," Bradley laughed. "She says she never attends a meeting but just writes out a check and attends the event."

"And she's a beat bitch at the annual event too."

"And you know it," Bradley laughed. "She told me that she wasn't getting on any committees with a pack of women because the only thing they had to discuss was snotty nosed children and the success of snotty nosed children. She wasn't with that. So, she just attends the event and sends her five hundred dollar check every year."

"And she never ever sends a covered dish."

"That's because she can't cook."

"You lyin."

"Child if you eat that woman's cooking you'll be out there at the emergency room because it'll kill you. She'll be the first to tell you the Lord did not make Betty Crocker when he made her."

"I just love the elegance that she has when she puts some of those girls in their places," Melvin laughed as he thought about the previous Annual Women's day Program. "My mom was chairperson last year and she was co-chairperson. My mom had begged people to participate. Mrs. Ables said she refused to beg niggahs to do what they know they are supposed to do. On the day of the event, when things seemed as if they were falling apart, Mrs. Ables sat right next to mother. And when those girls started complaining, Mrs. Ables said:

Well, our chair lady asked us to do certain things but since we were more concerned with how pretty our outfits were going to look today we forgot about the program. I really don't see why you all try to compete with buying white dresses when you all know that you'll never beat mine anyway. So, why not go on and get you program together. Then she titled her head and all the plumes on that wide brimmed white hat swirled in the wind and she smiled."

"Child, I know there were some mad folk up in the camp on that day," Bradley laughed.

"No, they were too outdone when five minutes before the program began, the church Mrs. Ables invited from Memphis strolled in, packed the church out, and gave us women in white like they had never seen it before."

"I bet they did," Bradley chuckled.

"You talking about a hat parade," Melvin grinned. "Child, Memphis brought two tour bus loads of women in white to Mt. Carmel."

"I bet they were too outdone because they thought they had stopped progress," Bradley laughed.

"They should have known that Henrietta Ables always has a ram in the bush and if her name is on something, child please...."

They pulled up to the police station.

Bradley sighed and then stepped out of the car.

He and Melvin walked into the police station to begin a new journey of completion to an old unsolved mystery that seemed to unravel in more crazy and uncertain ways than they had ever anticipated.

Chapter Seventeen

What Is This?

Eight months of press releases, newsreels, and grape vine versions of **The Murder of Frederick Perry** taunted those individuals most closely associated with the case. Constantly, it seemed as if people had become uptight in dealing with a very unique and extraordinary situation. Jeremy "Psycho" Curbie had pleaded **not guilty** to the murders of Frederick Perry, Henry Tiss, Bill Butcher, Jake Minor, Alice Wish, KaKetrianna Puss, and Joy Day. In order to appease anyone, the trial was definitely sent to jury. Bets were made all day and all night at all of the gambling holes, bars, and pool halls on whether or not Psycho would be set free. One person dared say that it was a ploy of "the white man" to punish this man for this crime. Through it all, life was essential to be maintained.

Melvin opened his mail after a tedious day of work, to receive a very beautiful card of some sort in the mail. He suspected that Eric had mailed him another surprise card or something and decided to open it immediately. He wanted to feel good for at least a moment. Their relationship had definitely been under a strain as Eric seemed torn between family and a quest for truth.

Your presence is cordially requested to attend the

Engagement Celebration

Of Mister Maxwell Quest & The Rev

At Seven O'clock in the evening

Friday, The Eighth Day of October

In the Year of Our Lord Nineteen Hundred Ninety-Nine

At The Romachandra, RoEllen, Tennessee

Melvin secretly thanked God that there was a knock at the door and the telephone had begun to ring.

"Hello," he said as he picked up the telephone and walked to answer the door.

"Hey, baby, I'll be late getting over tonight," Eric said. "I've got some extra work to do tonight at the paper."

"O.K." he said as he opened the door. "But I'm on my way to frat meeting tonight and I may be a little late getting home but you have the key."

"I may have a surprise for you tonight," Eric said in a very deep yet sexy voice. The kind that Melvin had grown accustomed to that always tended to send chills down his spine.

"I like surprises…"

His heart stopped completely when he looked directly into the face of Julian Jordan.

"Hello, Melvin," Julian said.

"Except this one. Talk with you later," Melvin said as he hung the telephone up and literally stared at Julian before words would actually come to his mouth.

"Is that the greeting I get?" Julian asked. "I thought you like surprises."

"What on earth are you doing here?" Melvin finally managed to say.

"Oh, I was in the area and I just thought I would stop by."

"I am totally committed to another man who can actually love me for who I am, Julian!" Melvin said as he stood at the door. "I have a fraternity meeting tonight and I just got off of work and I am actually rather tired right now."

"Please, just hear me out!" Julian said as he held the door before Melvin could shut it in his face.

"I don't have time for this," Melvin said. "This is becoming too much to deal with in one day. Come in, sit down, say whatever it is you have to say but remember: I am involved with someone else."

Julian walked into Melvin's home and sat on the sofa in the great room.

"Would you like a drink?" Melvin asked. "Please excuse me as I move around. Again, I have a meeting tonight."

"I just thought about you and wanted to just see you again," Julian said.

"Well, you accomplished that," Melvin said as he walked into his bedroom, pulled out his fraternity insignia and placed it on the bed.

"Are you sure that you don't want anything to drink?"

"Just you," Julian said as he lowered his voice attempting sexiness.

"How is your wife?" Melvin asked as he then loosened his tie and took it off. He searched for his navy blue V-necked sweater.

"She's fine," Julian answered. "She's off to Europe this week."

"How nice," Melvin replied as he pulled the sweater over his head. He then placed his insignia on the required positions on the sweater.

"You are so beautiful still," Julian said as he scooped Melvin up in his arms from behind.

"Get your hands off of me, Julian," Melvin warned. "Why the hell are you in my bedroom?"

"I have missed holding you,"

"The feeling is not mutual, Julian."

"So many nights I've thought about you…"

"Get your mothafuckin hands off *my* man," Eric roared.

"Thank the Lord Jesus!" Melvin said as he broke free from Julian's tight grip.

Julian turned around and then looked up at Eric.

"**You** are Melvin's man?"

"Man, you got ten seconds to get out of this house before I give you a country ass whippin like you've never had before!."

"Man, I just came by to see an old friend," Julian lied.

"So you have seen him, now get the fuck outta here, niggah."

"I can't stand black assed niggahs," Julian grumbled as he walked toward the door. "Melvin, I thought you would have done better than this."

Eric nearly charged Julian but Melvin held on to him.

"Julian, I did better than you so what does it matter?"

"Oh, so it's like that?" Julian asked as he looked at Eric and then at Melvin.

"It's like that," Melvin said with pride. "I'm finally over you and I feel damn good about it."

"But why somebody so damned black?"

"You are the color struck one," Melvin laughed as he held onto Eric for dear life. "I love my black berry. Believe me, he has sweet juices. Now you take your ass to Europe with your little white wifey and fair skinned children. We have a life and we are happy with it."

Julian slammed the door as he left.

Melvin immediately turned around; tip toed and kissed Eric passionately.

"What was that for? Eric grinned as he looked down into Melvin's loving eyes.

"For sweet surprises just when I need them most," Melvin giggled as he hugged Eric gently again. "The last person I ever wanted to see standing at my front door was Julian Jordan."

"He's a trip," Eric laughed softly.

"A very pitiful man," Melvin sighed. "He married a white woman thinking his career would be boosted. Now, he works his ass off in DC to support the lifestyle of a political analyst."

"I thought he wanted to be a politician," Eric grinned.

"Be for real," Melvin said as he stepped back and looked directly at Eric. "This is still America! Although we are at the threshold of a totally new century it still leaves a bad taste in white and black people's mouths to see a black man with a white woman."

"I hear you, baby," Eric laughed. "Black women say there's a shortage of black men and white men are generally furious over the subject."

"And baby," Melvin smiled as he looked deeply into Eric's eyes. "I'm so glad you are growing. Regardless of what anyone says, I love you as you are and your skin color excites me still."

"Boo," Eric grinned as he picked Melvin up and twirled him around in a circle about the living room. "I put that light skinned-dark skinned shit behind me a long time ago. There is absolutely nothing that people can say to me now that has not already been said. But guess what, boo?"

"What?"

"I love me! I love you! We've been through the storm and yet we are still making it. Who cares about how dark I am or how light you are as long as you love Eric for Eric and Eric loves you for you!"

Melvin kissed him again.

"Are you still going to frat meeting tonight?" Eric finally asked as he managed to release Melvin.

"Yeah," Melvin sighed. "But I have a feeling that it is going to be a trip tonight."

"Why?"

Melvin walked to the stand where he keeps his incoming mail and produced the invitation to The Rev's Engagement Party.

"Read it," Melvin said as he passed the invitation to Eric.

Eric read it. His eyes widened.

"When have they set the date?"

"We'll find out October 8th."

"I meant to ask The Rev if he had finally completed building The Ramachandra," Melvin laughed as he thought about how happy The Rev was when his father had finally given him two acres of family land in Rock Spring, Tennessee. The Rev vowed to build a plantation house to symbolize the fact that his family had overcome slavery.

"Well, I talked to Maxwell and he said that when the house was complete he would be married and become the matron of the estate and The Rev had until the turn of the century to propose and marry him."

"Child, these folk are getting ready to turn the South upside down," Melvin complained.

"Are they in love?"

"Well, yeah, but..."

"Would you marry me if I proposed to you?"

"Well, yeah, but…"

"Then I support them," Eric terminated the conversation. "What did you cook for dinner tonight?"

"Man, I didn't cook a thing," Melvin chuckled. "You know my grocery bill has tripled since you moved in. There is a roast in there from yesterday. Make a sandwich."

"Ah, boo, left-over's again?" Eric teased as he walked into the kitchen pulled out the roast beef, a loaf of bread, and a jar of mayonnaise. To top off this litany he pulled the gallon sized pickle jar that had been emptied of the pickles but filled with *Kool-Aid.*

"You so country!" Melvin laughed.

The Omega Complex had not had as many cars surrounding its building in years as it had on this slightly warm October Tuesday evening in 1999. Melvin noticed the license plates from Dyer, Obion, Lake, Gibson, Haywood, Crockett, Madison, Lauderdale, and Tipton Counties. The organization was now just an organization for Alumni members. No chapter had pledged a new member since 1992 because of lack of interest from high school students. So, on January 1, 1995, it became law after a vote from the Great Council during the previous year that the Omega Phi Theta Fraternity would no longer pledge any new members. It would from that day forward serve as a Fraternal Order of Alumni and members who wished to join the organization would have to come before a review Board with credentials, learn the history, and pay a sum of no less than $500.00 to join. This did not deter some people as the fraternity continued to grow with African-American men who attended high school during the 1980s.

The Rev still held the position as Moderator while Grimlock was Vice-Moderator, Light Bulb was Dean of Admissions, D.D. was Stated Clerk, The Skull was Dean of Ethnic & Cultural Affairs, J.C. was Dean of Religious Affairs, Snake was Chief Justice of The Supreme Council, Smurf was Director of Social Affairs and The Sponge was Dean of Education & Scholarship Distribution. Melvin, Bradley, Howard, and Desmond still held positions as Senators.

The Rev took the podium after the anthem was played by Howard. Somehow, Melvin knew that things would forever change in the fraternal structure on this evening after receiving the invitation on the same day. OPT was indeed a loving organization and fraternity but The Rev was sending a very powerful message to the fraternity.

The Rev conducted a very normal meeting, delegating responsibility to the various chairpersons of various committees. A hush came over the assembly when he made his final announcement.

"Elections will be held for the Executive Boards on November first of this year," The Rev said nonchalantly. "We need all officers of the New Millennium turned in by December 1st to this office. For the first time in years, The Senate has called for a vote of the Great Council. We thank you and election will be held as stated in our Constitution on the first week in May in the year two thousand."

"I demand an election in December," someone who sat in the Trenton's section yelled.

"Why?" Grimlock asked before The Rev could utter a word.

"Because, I have the right to request that," the man yelled.

"Mothafucka, you ain't got the right to shit," Grimlock spit his words out with such contempt of the member until a hush fell across the room. "My memory hasn't failed me yet. You really ain't supposed to even be in the very chair you are sitting in because of the money that you have yet replaced from 1986. Just because you paid $500 to get back up in hear doesn't mean you don't owe us, niggah!"

"Well, what's the problem?" Snake, the Chief Justice who knew the laws of the fraternity backwards and forwards because he was one of the founding members, asked gregariously.

"I ain't supporting no fag as the leader of my frat," the man yelled.

A thunderous murmur immediately enveloped the room. *"Now it begins."* Melvin thought.

Snake pounded on his gavel for order in an attempt to silence the noise within the hall. Tempers had begun to flare as an exchange of unpleasantness filled the room.

The room went silent as The Rev cleared his throat over the microphone.

"Gentlemen," The Rev said. "If a vote is what you want, a vote is what you shall have. As Moderator, you may have your election the second Tuesday in January but that means you have two weeks to submit the name of the person you wish to run against me because I will not resign my position. You will have to vote me out of office if that is what you want to do. I have served this fraternity for almost fifteen years now. I have lived to see a lot of great accomplishments during my tenure as Moderator. As a matter of fact, I believe that for years you all would not even vote for anyone else because no one else wanted to do the work. But if you want an election, you certainly shall have one. If there is no further business, may I have a motion to adjourn?"

"So moved," Melvin yelled.

"Second," Bradley yelled.

"The meeting is adjourned."

Melvin, Bradley, Desmond, and Howard immediately found one another after the meeting concluded. Some of the members left the premises while others dispersed to the bar. Other members decided they wanted to sample a little of the food at *Ann's House of Wings* before they headed home.

"Child, the shit is getting ready to hit the fan," Melvin said as Desmond, Bradley, and Howard matched his stride in walking out of the Omega Complex.

"I honestly don't see the problem," Howard said. "Those bastards didn't have a problem with The Rev as long as he was writing grants and shit for their communities and school districts."

"They surely didn't have a problem when he made sure that some of those fuckas went to college," Desmond interjected.

"How about the folk he helped to get out of jail," Bradley added.

"It's not about that," Melvin said. "They just can't see the leader being gay and certainly can't see him married to a *man*."

"The mothafuckas didn't mind being married to a *woman* and paying me for sex," Bradley incredulously added.

"You had sex with some of the brothers?" Desmond asked in disbelief.

"Bitch, how do you think I could afford to go to Atlanta when I left Dyer County years ago," Bradley said. "I told you, I wasn't giving up anything for free. Now you other bitches can have broken hearts and broke pocket books and broken down pussies if you want to but not I."

"Spoken like a true ho," Howard laughed.

"I wouldn't go there if I were you, sugar," Bradley commented wryly as the group continued to walk to their various vehicles.

"Excuse me?" Howard asked somewhat surprised.

"The only thing that I have to say, Howard, is get paid for anything you do, child, and I'll leave it alone," Bradley said as he got into his car and drove off.

Desmond and Melvin did not give Howard time enough to question them in regards to what Bradley was talking about.

Immediately, the followed Bradley's lead and got into their vehicles and left.

"That was not good advice!" Melvin raged over the telephone.

"Melvin, just because you are the mushy bitch doesn't mean everybody else is," Bradley stated firmly.

"So, you are saying you support Howard in fucking William?"

"No, I said exactly what the hell I meant! Get paid if you are going to be a ho!"

"So does that mean that you would fuck my man too if he paid you?"

"Wait a minute, bitch," Bradley said furiously. "First of all, it's not that type of party. Second of all, I don't want your damned man. Third of all, he could not afford me if he *did* want me. Last of all, I have never come within two million miles of any of the men that you have dated or been with. The closest we have ever been to fucking one another's men is by dating cousins. I had relations with Josh years ago and you are fucking his cousin Eric now! That's it!"

"I just do not condone Howard and William's affair," Melvin stated firmly.

"It's none of your damned business," Bradley said. "I don't support it either but I'm not the one to concern myself with that shit. You better believe that Xavier ain't crazy, honey."

Before Melvin could answer Bradley there was a beep on his line.

"Hold on, let me answer this," he said as he clicked flash. "Hello."

"Melvin, this is William. I need all of you all in Memphis immediately. Xavier is asking for you. He's leaving us."

"What?"

"Please get in touch with everyone for me and get here in a hurry," William said and hung up.

Melvin clicked back over to Bradley.

"Child, Xavier is dying and is calling for all of us. We got to go to Memphis tonight!"

"Come pick me up and I'll call Desmond on his cell phone before he makes it to Jackson," Bradley said as he hung up the telephone.

Melvin could not believe what William had just stated. Xavier was dying? From what? How long had he been sick? *Jesus, Jesus Jesus!* "Eric!"

Eric jumped out of the bed and ran into the living room where Melvin was. He was a bit distorted as he stood in his T-shirt and boxers watching a crying Melvin.

"What is going on, boo?" he asked as he went to cradle Melvin in his arms.

"We have to go to Memphis! Xavier is dying and has called for all of his friends and wants us to be there with him tonight."

A frown creased Eric's face as he held Melvin.

"Boo, you need to go on and get it out of your system right now," Eric said as he held a sobbing Melvin. "If Xavier is dying, he will not need to see you all tore up before he transitions on."

"But we just..."

"Shh..."

Eric held Melvin for what seemed an eternity as he grieved for his friend. The years of life in the dorm at Lane College flashed before Melvin's eyes as he thought about Xavier. The years of trials and tribulations as the entire eighties generation grew, lived, loved, and died flowed through Melvin. Xavier was only thirty. He was only thirty.

Eric, Melvin, and Bradley walked quietly into Xavier's bedroom at his home. This was the one room Melvin remembered the door being locked on during the birthday bash months earlier. He never thought about it but wondered why there was a locked room on the first floor of such an exquisite home. Now he knew. When he entered, he saw his friend lying there in a hospital bed. An IV was in his arm. His flesh was ghostly pale. He no longer looked like the jovial little high yella boy from Louisiana with the sharp tongue and gorgeous features. Melvin squeezed Eric's hand as they entered the room.

"You made it," Xavier said weakly.

"Child, I didn't know," Melvin said as he released Eric's hand and softly grabbed Xavier's.

"Well, I've been going through, child, and my body is just tired," Xavier whispered.

Desmond and Douglas entered followed by Hardaway.

Desmond cried loudly as he walked into the room.

"Is everybody here, William?" Xavier struggled.

"Everyone's here, darling," William said.

Xavier struggled as he attempted to raise himself upward. William assisted him until he was in a sitting position in his bed.

"I know you all didn't know," Xavier said. "The only people who did know were Hardaway and William."

"Know what, Xavier," Melvin said as tears streamed down his face.

"I have the virus and I'm leaving here," Xavier said softly.

Desmond wailed even louder this time.

"Child, can't you be quiet with all of that damned loud as cryin?" Bradley asked Desmond as he strained to hear Xavier.

For the first time, Xavier smiled briefly.

"I just have a few things I wanted to tell you all before I leave you for a little while," he said gently.

"Oh, Xavier, please don't give up now," Melvin sobbed.

"I've fought for years, Melvin! I can't go on any further," he said gently. "Life has been good to me. William has been wonderful to me. Yeah, I admit, I have been a bitch at times but he has been a wonderful man to me down through the years."

At this, tears began to sting Bradley's eyes.

"William," Xavier said as he looked directly into William's eyes.

"Yes, darling," William said as he held Xavier's hand.

"I know about your affair," he said gently.

Desmond, Melvin, and Douglas began to sniffle. Desmond couldn't contain himself as he let out yet another wailing moan.

"This guhl is too many thangs for me!" Bradley whispered angrily to Hardaway as he looked at Desmond's hunched shoulders and body moving up and down as he continued a litany of tears. "She just refuses to let this man have a peaceful exit."

"Child, hush," Hardaway said softly.

"Make it last if you can," Xavier continued. "But keep *him* out of this house from now on! My money helped to make you what you are today. Respect my memory if nothing else."

William fell down onto the bed in tears sobbing.

Eric rubbed his hand gently up and down William's back.

"Just know that if he comes back in this house after I'm gone, I'll haunt you all until the place burns down to the ground."

A chill went down everyone's back at those words. They had heard of voodoo curses and Xavier was, after all, from Louisiana. If nothing else, he had the connections to make this come true.

"I'll respect your memory, darling, I promise."

"Hardaway," Xavier motioned.

Hardaway approached the bed and grabbed Xavier's hand.

"Teach the children," he whispered. "Don't let Brothers United die. Tell Dwayne I thank him for his vision and please don't stop now."

"I will," Hardaway said as tears began to stream down his face.

"We had a lot of good days on stage together in the old days," Xavier smiled. "You know that you have to sing for me at my funeral and don't be singing no *Trouble Of This World* either! I have my funeral planned like I want it. Give me a good send off, child."

"I will," Hardaway said as he softly pulled away from the bed and went into the hallway in tears.

"Desmond and Douglas," Xavier smiled. "You all have had the relationship that I have dreamed of for years. Stay together and continue to love regardless of what the world may say or do."

Desmond wailed louder as Douglas finally took him out of the room.

"Bradley, you have been my only equal for years," Xavier smiled. "Thank you for the love and friendship."

"Thank you for being in my life, Xavier," Bradley said softly.

"Melvin," he said gently. "You finally got the right one. Promise me you'll stay with him…"

The lump in Melvin's throat would not allow him to speak.

"Promise me!" Xavier said with all of the strength that he had.

"I promise," Melvin said as tears streamed down his face.

"I love you all," he said softly. "I'm just so tired…"

Melvin heard his last breath and screamed uncontrollably. William cried as he held on to Xavier's hand. Eric dialed 911 and requested an ambulance.

Desmond screamed and yelled and walked back and forth down the hall into the room and then outside of the room and then back into the room and then back into the hall way and then down the hall way and then back into the room until the ambulance arrived to remove the body of their beloved friend.

Bradley walked down the long hallway that led to the kitchen, found coffee and tea and began to brew them both. He then found Danishes and fruit. He looked up to see Hardaway in the kitchen beside him.

"Are you O.K.?" Bradley asked as he continued to prepare his refreshments.

"I will be in a little bit," Hardaway said as he busied himself as well in the kitchen.

They both listened to Desmond scream and cry for what seemed an eternity.

"Child, I would be all right if that bitch in there would shut up," Bradley said as he picked up a cup that he had accidentally dropped onto the floor. "Ooo he's really beginning to rattle my damned nerves with all of that shit! Heavens forbid if I die. The hollin ho probably wouldn't shed a damned tear!"

Hardaway laughed.

"Yeah, he has been going on and on for the past hour now," Hardaway laughed as he helped Bradley pick up the broken pieces of the cup and throw it away.

"What is Brothers United?" Bradley asked.

"Oh, it's a statewide organization," Hardaway said. "I chair the Memphis Chapter. Would you like to come to our annual retreat this year? It only cost $35.00"

"Child, money is no problem, just let me in on the details," Bradley laughed. "I'll need something to help me get over this."

"In time we will all have to get over it but that is one of the main reasons we have Brothers United. We have to stop the dying in silence. It is surprising to me that you all were that close to Xavier and did not even know that he was dying of AIDS."

"Child, with all of the shit going on in Dyer County, the last thing we even thought about was a friend of ours dying of AIDS," Bradley commented. "But, the year has not ended yet and I'm certain that we have many more hills to climb."

"What is this?" Melvin asked as he entered the kitchen to see hot coffee and hot tea as well as Danishes, donuts, and fruit on the table.

"We all need a break," Bradley said. "Get you some but keep that hollin wench out of here."

"He'll be all right," Melvin grinned grimly. "You know Desmond doesn't handle death well."

"That bitch just likes to work a room," Bradley remarked. "I have never understood why he **must** work a room with his melodramatic scenes?"

"Child, you know he's worse at funerals," Melvin interjected. "But you have been known to work a couple of funerals yourself."

"Touché, bitch," Bradley laughed. "But those were my husbands! I was supposed to work the room!"

Chapter Eighteen
In My Home Over There

Like any celebrity funeral in the city of Memphis, Tennessee, The Universal Morning Star Nondenominational Church was packed completely out for the funeral of its co-founder, Xavier André Thompson. He had planned the entire funeral out months before he died. William saw to it that the funeral did not deviate one letter from where it had been written by Xavier.

The white and gold trimmed casket was draped in a floral spray that seemed as if it were actually a flag. Flowers and plants were so plentiful in the church until it required six uncovered floral cars to bring them to the church and take them to the cemetery. People were to sit according to Xavier's bereavement cards posted. One hundred men were to dress in black and sit in the area that had black ribbons on the side of the pew. One hundred men were to wear white who sat behind those in black. One hundred men were to wear gold and they would sit behind those in white. Basically, the men in black were Xavier's 100 closest friends. Those in white were business associates. Those in gold were his "diva" section of men who were older; some had even been flown out to the funeral, and had earned Xavier's admiration and respect.

Melvin, Eric, Bradley, Desmond, Douglas, and Hardaway sat together dressed in black and on the front pew. William sat with the family on the opposite side of the congregation. A memorial musical had been given in Xavier's honor two night's prior to the funeral. The wake lasted from noon until nine in the evening. The Universal Morning Star Nondenominational Church Gospel Choir sang several of the songs that Xavier had taught them. Gospel Recording artist from around the country paid their respects to Xavier by attendance or by a floral arrangement.

Hardaway took the podium and a hush fell over the crowd. No one ever knew what to expect when Hardaway took the podium.

"Praise the Lord, Saints!" he greeted.

"Praise the Lord!" the congregation responded.

"This is really hard and I wouldn't do it if Xavier had not left explicit instructions on what he wanted me to do. It's just good to know that he had his house in order..."

"Amen," the crowd thundered as the music began to play a sad old gospel song written by H.J. Ford that Mahalia Jackson made famous years ago.

"You all pray with me," he said. "My mind wonders back to the time when Xavier and I would be out on the road. My mind wonders back to the night our tour bus caught fire and burned up everything we had. Through it all, Xavier kept the faith and said: "We still have each other those clothes don't mean a thing. And then he looked at my black suit and had the nerve enough to tell me, you can keep that, child and make a shorts set out of it."

The crowd laughed.

He began to sing in a deep, sultry, tenor voice. His voice bellowed out a life of pain, hurt, and grief that has been overcome through the grace of a loving God who watches over us all.

> *"When my work on earth is done at the setting of the sun,*
> *I am going to my home over there.*
> *I will walk the golden stair, and be free from every care.*
> *I'll be happy in my home over there..."*

Melvin attempted to resist crying because Desmond screamed and shouted at every interval throughout the entire funeral. Bradley's lips were poked out a mile long because he suffered sitting beside Desmond and listened throughout the entire services to Desmond's sniffles, screams, and boo hoos.

"In my home over there that my Lord, He did prepare. There is peace, there is joy everywhere." Hardaway sang.

By the time he reached *"I will see His face so fair and a starry crown I'll wear"* almost everyone in the congregation were either shouting, crying, or standing up to sway, clap, and testify to the power, the very essence of soul that flowed from out of this man's mouth.

"I'll be happy, happy, happy, in my home over there!"

The minister on the roster allowed the congregation a good fifteen minutes to shout, dance, and rejoice as the *Spirit* ushered its way into the midst of the funeral.

To everyone's surprise, the minister who eulogized Xavier did not put Xavier in hell nor did he put Xavier in Heaven. It was a refreshing feeling to actually hear a sermon for once about the deceased and everyone knew who was being eulogized. So often, in the South especially, ministers would dare preach over the corpse of people they did not know and everyone in the audience wondered who on earth the minister was talking about which only added to the grief when the casket was opened to be viewed or rolled down the aisles for the last time. A person would wonder if they had attended the correct funeral.

Xavier's funeral was not like this and he vowed until his last day: *"Don't let anybody speak over me who will not give you the real me. Tell them I was a bitch at times but I could be sweet when I wanted to be,"* he would exclaim.

William made certain that Xavier's wish was granted and throughout the sermon people did cry tears of remembrance and dedication.

Memphis was not fully prepared for the grandeur of Xavier Thompson's recessional. Six white horses draped in royal colors carried wagon draped in flowers on which Xavier's body was laid. In front of these horses was a team of African dancers who danced a native dance four city blocks long until they reached the cemetery where Xavier would rest. Behind the six white horses and Xavier's body was a brass band that slowly played Dr. W. Herbert Brewster's *Pay Day, Some Day* as the procession slowly marched forward to the cemetery. Following the band there came six floral cars followed by the 100 men in black, the 100 men in white, and the 100 men in gold. William and a host of ministers followed the men in gold. Gospel Recording Artists followed the ministers. The Thompson family followed Gospel Recording Artists. And the crowd followed the family. After Xavier was buried, the band struck up a New Orleans tune of *When The Saints Go Marching In* and the crowd danced in the streets.

Xavier André Thompson went on to glory as requested. No tears of sorrow but tears of joy. Another fine soldier had gone on to receive a great reward.

As Eric drove home Melvin and Bradley sat in silence.

"Why y'all so quiet," Eric asked.

"I'm quiet because that hollin ass Desmond has given me one of the worst headaches in the world," Bradley said vociferously. "That bitch hollered throughout the whole service. Why on earth do

yall always put me beside him at funerals?"

This broke the silence for certain.

Melvin bent down laughing so hard until his sides began to ache..

Eric could barely drive the car as Bradley complained all of the way home which kept the two of them in stitches for the full one hour and thirty minute drive.

Chapter Nineteen

On Our Way To Convention

The first weekend in December marked a very remarkable time in everyone's life. Melvin and Eric were personally invited to participate in The Rev and Maxwell's Holy Union Ceremony as well as attend The Brothers United Network of Tennessee 3rd Annual Retreat. Melvin did not know that the organization even existed but was proud to be in the number that attended. The coordinator, Dwayne from Nashville, had organized a group named Brothers United of Nashville in 1996. Soon, Brothers United of Chattanooga joined the association. Later, Brothers United of Memphis under Hardaway's leadership was added to the organization and later Brothers United of Knoxville and last Brothers United of West Tennessee. Each chapter made Brothers United Network of Tennessee. Dwayne had a vision after seeing so many African-American gay men die from HIV/AIDS to do something to educate African-American gay men. His vision spread quickly. He surprised the entire organization by including on the itinerary for the event... Commitment Ceremony. Everyone had a different opinion on what the ceremony would be. Some felt that it would be a time where the brothers would commit themselves and their hearts to Brothers United. Others, like Melvin and Eric, knew the "tea" but he was just happy to be doing something productive. After the death of Xavier, they felt they too needed to finally get involved in the fight against HIV/AIDS rather than fight with people who were infected with the virus.

"Hell, it will be a good get away from these crazy ass folk down here," Bradley said as he threw his bags in the trunk.

"Bradley," Eric asked seriously. "Why don't you ever drive?"

"Hell," Bradley laughed. "Because I have yall."

Eric laughed and threw his bags into the car as well.

They drove to Paris Landing State Park and had a blast on the way. Several times Eric got lost but it was fun just getting away.

"I bet Maxwell and The Rev are as nervous as hos in church about right now," Bradley laughed.

"Probably not," Eric said. "Knowing them they are packing their cars down with everything but the kitchen sink."

"So you know The Rev too?" Bradley chuckled.

"I've heard about him," Eric laughed.

People arrived at the cabins from around the country at different times throughout that Friday afternoon and evening but there was a feeling of pride and dignity as each individual arrived. A sense of hope even in dismal times was as sweet in the air as the smells of honey suckle on a spring morning.

The members of Brothers United Network of Tennessee were an impressive group. Melvin was amazed that none of the men were unattractive. Every shade of color was at the retreat: every size and every height. It was the most beautiful thing Melvin had ever seen in his life beside Eric. For the first time since pledging the fraternity, he finally found a group of individuals who through their various issues found time to put those issues aside, come together in brotherhood, and attempt to work toward a common goal.

The first person Eric and Melvin saw when they arrived was Hardaway.

Hardaway had pulled up in his spanking brand new, fully loaded, shiny black trimmed in gold, signature series *Fleetwood Cadillac*. As he stepped out of his car, his black mink draped the ground slightly as he busied himself unloading box after box after box of hats, furs, clothes, cameras, video equipment, and material to pass out.

"Hey saints of the Lord," he yelled as Eric and Melvin stood back to absorb the full effect of Hardaway in action.

"Hey, Hardaway," Melvin called out. "Why are you in such a rush?"

"I'm on the welcoming committee and I was detained in Memphis so now I'm late and that doesn't sit well with me, child," he said as his boots quickly moved about the area. "But, thank God, everybody is just getting here."

"Did you bring enough furs?" Melvin laughed.

"Child, these are just a few," Hardaway laughed as his black fur hat tilted slightly on his head as he ducked inside of the car to retrieve a stand for one of the video cameras that he had. "The sables and foxes are all at home."

"Is this a new car?" Eric asked as he admired the rather lengthy car.

"Ain't the Lord good, child?" Hardaway laughed. "Now lift those hands and tell the Lord thank you!"

Eric and Melvin automatically lifted their hands and told the Lord: "Thank You" before they ever realized a thing.

Before the end of the day and night had begun to settle in, the cabins began to slowly fill and each person from near or far began to warm to one another slowly.

Hardaway's welcoming committee welcomed the guest to the Annual "convention/retreat" 1999. The count for the year was 65 men strong. Dwayne then gave his famous HIV/AIDS presentation. Slowly the group began to warm to one another.

After dinner was served the group reconvened for a seminar entitled *BREATHE* by the famous author J. Ricc Rollins.

"Child, these folk have clout," Bradley whispered. "They have all these authors here, you know that cost them some money."

"Stop seeing dollar signs and enjoy what the man has to say," Melvin chastised softly.

After Mr. Rollin's presentation, the group split into several smaller groups. A choir rehearsal was called under the direction of a guy named Flex while solos were being rendered by a guy named Dilworth who had such a gleam in his eye when people sang until it made everyone want to sing. And sing the children did on that evening.

"Child, don't you all let Dilworth hear you sing too much," Hardaway warned. "He'll have you singing all night. You know that's Mahalia Jackson incarnate."

"Shut up, Clara Ward, you just jealous," Dilworth teased.

The most interesting thing to Melvin, however, was that the most prevalent name throughout the event was the name of Anthony or Dwayne. There were so many in attendance until the founding Dwayne began to number them or they were called by their last names.

Melvin, Bradley, and Eric were shocked the next morning to discover R. Bryant Smith in attendance. He presented a seminar entitled "When The Children Get Together" which somehow became a battle cry throughout the remainder of the conference.

During his seminar, a spark ignited, and it seemed as if everyone began to talk. He laughed when Dwayne told him that he had to end the seminar because it had run over the time limit.

"Well, all I got to say is I ain't takin the same shit I took last year," one attractive man had said during both seminars.

"O.K." Bradley said. "So he's not going to take any shit out of you queens this year."

"I can't take you nowhere," Melvin laughed.

A very important thing that touched Melvin's heart was how Smith, during the seminar, brought his own life into focus and used it as the tool for conversation throughout the seminar. Feathers were ruffled a bit when the discussion of how African-American gay men were treated in church slipped into the discussion.

"Well, I think it is terrible how gay men can sit up in church and take a lot of mess from these preachers when they don't have to..."

"That's sho right..."

"Well, I have a pretty good relationship with my church and with my pastor, so I don't understand the hubbub..."

"Well, I think it is crazy that we make up everythang from the pulpit to the choir but will be subject to criticism every Sunday. I think it's crazy..."

"Well," Smith says. "One thing I want everyone to remember is St. John 3:16. Let's repeat it together."

Everyone in the building recited from memory:

For God so loved the world that He gave His only begotten Son that whosoever believeth on Him shall not perish but have everlasting life."

"What is the key to what you just said, guys?" he asked.

There was silence in the room.

"**Whosoever** is the key word," Smith said.

"Child, that's my cousin," Bradley laughed.

"Who?"

"R. Bryant."

"Really?"

"He's a descendant of Rock Spring."

"Get outta here," Melvin said softly.

"Have you bought his book yet?"

"It hasn't come out yet but I have to get it, you know."

"Well, yes, as I look at him, he and The Rev do look remarkably alike."

"Smith blood, honey, it runs deep."

The "convention" as Hardaway had named it (the name took form and spread like wild fire) recessed and met again with yet another famous author, Sundiata Alaye who discussed his novel *Empty Promises, Private Pain - A Light Out of Darkness*.

"Child, I didn't know there were this many gay black authors in print," Bradley smiled with pride after Sundiata's seminar.

"It's a new age," Eric said. "But I have read most all of these guys' works."

Melvin was shocked. He didn't realize Eric ever read even though he was a journalist for a newspaper.

"Well you go then," Melvin laughed. "Child, I didn't even realize that half of the shit these folks are talking about this weekend has really made me want to re-evaluate a few things."

"So your gonna stop hoin'?" Eric teased.

"I sure am," Bradley laughed. "When Jesus comes back."

"All right Saint of the Lord," Hardaway said in passing as he snapped a photo of Melvin, Eric, and Bradley. "That's pretty close to blasphemy."

"Well I ain't gonna quit hoin' until Jesus comes back," Bradley laughed. Hardaway was forced to laugh as well. "Child, I don't screw for free. So, if *hoin* is what they want to call it, so be it. But here lately, I haven't found any participant who could afford me."

"So I guess you are in semi- retirement, then," Hardaway laughed.

"I sure am," Bradley laughed. "Now can I come and sit beside you on the Mother Board, First Lady?"

"You have to be holy to sit by me, child," Hardaway teased.

"Child, I'm holy," Bradley mused. "So holy you can see straight through me."

"Be gone, child," Hardaway laughed. "Are you all coming to the Holy Union Ceremony this afternoon?"

"We have to we are in it," Melvin laughed.

"Well, good, then," Hardaway laughed. "Because I am too."

"Duh?" Eric teased. "Maid of Honor Hardaway."

"I hope I brought the right pumps, honey," Hardaway teased.

"You'll do fine," Bradley assured. "I've seen you work a church, it's the same difference. Make the most of it."

At five thirty, Celine Dion's voice rang over the small but very quaint chapel/hospitality room. *"Ava Maria"*

A small crowd gathered inside of the room and took their seats as the music played.

The Rev followed by his best friend and best man, Lemont, and Dwayne the wedding coordinator entered behind J. Ricc Rollins.

"Child, I didn't know he was a minister," Desmond whispered to Bradley who had been recently seated in the second row of chairs from the front of the make shift altar.

"Read his bio on his book, better yet, buy a book and then you will discover a few things," Bradley whispered.

"They got books for sale? I thought this was only a wedding?" Desmond whispered.

"This is a retreat, idiot!" Bradley grumbled. "Child are you gonna give me a damned headache like you did at Xavier's funeral?"

"I seldom cry at weddings, guhl," Desmond mumbled and crossed his legs.

"Why aren't you and Douglas not married yet anyway?"

"We do fine as a couple," Desmond said as he stood up and moved totally away from Bradley.

"Thank you, Jesus," Bradley said softly.

Celine finally mellowed out and *Learn to Respect the Power of Love* began to play.

Bradley turned to figure out why he heard so much giggling behind him. When he looked up he saw Hardaway in one of the largest black hats he had ever seen on a man. Hardaway was gliding down the aisle like a black panther.

"You better walk, bitch!" someone in the audience yelled.

By this time, Hardaway stopped, posed and picked one leg up behind the next and continued his slow march down the aisle.

He was followed by Eric and Melvin arm in arm.

Bradley noticed the tears streaming down Melvin's eyes.

The Wedding March from the Opera Lohegrin began to play. The audience stood up. Bradley was shocked that Dilworth marched Maxwell down the aisle as they had just recently met.

"Well, this retreat is at least bringing us together in ways that we never even knew," Bradley thought.

When the music stopped, Maxwell stood on the altar in front of The Rev.

J. Ricc Rollins then explained the very nature and essence of the meaning behind love and why the couple, the audience, everyone was blessed to participate in the celebration of Holy Union of The Rev and Maxwell. He explained that, no, the couple were not married, but in the eyes of God, they were taking a solemn oath to coexist with one another as partners for the duration of their lives.

Bradley remembered the same vows when he and Arthur took Holy Union Vows. Against his will, tears began to flow down his face in a constant stream.

Maxwell glowed like an angel as he stood before the Rev in his black tuxedo. A constant flow of tears streamed down The Rev, Lemont, Melvin, and Eric's face as Rollins read the very lengthy vows chosen by The Rev and Maxwell.

Bradley felt proud that he could witness a union between two people he knew, respected, and loved. They had a right to love one another and if they were brave enough to dare love one another in the Rural South, Bradley certainly prayed to God that they would have an everlasting love.

The Rev and Maxwell exchanged rings.

Bradley once again was shocked into tears when he saw the surprise and gleam in Maxwell's eyes when The Rev revealed the wedding band that held a karat diamond in it. Bradley was also surprised that The Rev chose only a simple band for himself.

"O.K. Kiss each other and let's be finished," Bradley thought as ghosts from the past began to creep upon him. He remembered how wonderful it was to be young, black, gay, and in love with someone who loved you even though you had your many faults.

Rollins continued with a reading from *I Corinthians Thirteenth Chapter.*

Tears streamed down Bradley's face as he listened intently to the words being spoken.

Suddenly, he looked up and Maxwell had fainted.

Bradley attempted to choke his laughter when he watched Hardaway. First Lady Hardaway picks no one up off of the floor even if First Lady Hardaway is your Maid of Honor.

"I'll go and get a glass of water," he said as he rushed out to fetch a glass of cool water.

The Rev stood on the altar shocked beyond belief.

"Um, Mr. Dilworth will feature us with a rendition of *The Lord's Prayer* while we give Maxwell an opportunity to regain his composure. Indeed any event like this can be overwhelming."

Dilworth stood and sang his rendition of *The Lord's Prayer*.

Maxwell, who was layered in clothes upon top of clothes, had actually gotten too hot during this lengthy ceremony.

After, the song, the two stood back up and Maxwell fell into The Rev's arms.

"Yeah, I love it," Bradley thought. *"All of the poise and grace and eloquence in the world can't help now."*

But when Rollins pronounced the couple "partners for life", Maxwell straightened up as if he had never fainted and kissed The Rev.

The broom jumping ceremony was postponed until the reception that was held at one of the cabins.

Bradley joined in the laughter, tears of joy, hugs, and fellowship that preceded the ceremony. He was so elated to be black, gay, and alive until he became energized with a renewed sense of hope amidst the craziness of Dyer County.

The Rev had furnished one of the biggest wedding cakes imaginable for such a small and private affair. There were no more than fifty people to attend one of the major events of his life yet he had enough cake served to feed an army. But the wedding punch was a blast. It was a mixture of fresh raspberries, sherbet, and ginger ale. The members of Brothers United helped to celebrate as well as host the regular party.

Bradley danced with both grooms and the entire wedding party including First Lady Hardaway.

Maxwell threw a bouquet and Hardaway caught it.

The Rev threw a bouquet and Lemont caught it.

The weekend ended with a worship celebration. The Brothers United Network Choir sang a rendition of *"I Know It Was The Blood,"* and *"Blessed Assurance"*. Bradley was impressed. It was the first time he had ever attended any type of worship service with African-American gay men who were confident of who they were, certain about their faith, and had no hang ups. A young man sang a medley entitled *Because He Lives/I Sing Because I'm Happy*. It was sweet and the young man was very attractive. Hardaway took the podium and sang *"If I Can Help somebody"* which made half of the audience shout and cry. The Rev was heard above everyone else- crying like a baby. It was something about the power that Hardaway sang with. The message in song reminded the entire group of the reason they had come together... to help somebody as they passed along whereas living will not be in vain. Hardaway was followed by another power house who sang *"I Won't Complain."* Bradley had maintained his composure until The Rev and Maxwell took the podium and sang *"Sweet, Sweet, Spirit."* Bradley forgot that The Rev had a rich tenor but did not know that Maxwell could sing first soprano. And first soprano he sang. When they completed their song, a box of tissue was passed around the room as most everyone was in tears including Bradley.

There was a sweet Spirit in the room. It was a spirit of unity and brotherhood; a spirit of overcoming self-hatred and destructiveness; a spirit of knowing that it was absolutely grand to love what God had made... unique individuals who did not mind praising their Creator.

Dilworth came behind the duet with an old Southern gospel and took the assembly to a higher height when he sang *"The Lord Will Make A Way Somehow."*

Now they knew they were in church. Brothers began to shout at this time. Not cute and dignified shouting but old fashioned rural and Southern foot stomping, hand clapping, hands in the air shouting to a God who was certainly worthy to be praise because indeed He will make a way out of no way.

When the assembly calmed down a bit, a brother named Lemont broke into the old fashioned "Sanctified" dance which riled the crowd once more.

Bradley was amazed. These men really did not mind praising God in the manner in which they praised Him in their own congregations in their own churches in their own hometowns. For the first time in years Bradley felt at peace with the God of his creation. Flex sang *"I Have Faith"* before Rollins delivered the sermon.

Bradley learned a lot about excess baggage although he knew that he wouldn't have to worry about that problem any time soon. He wasn't looking for a relationship therefore he did not need anyone to clean out his bags. He certainly didn't have time to assist anyone else.

The choir sang *"I'll Never Turn Back"* and Bradley was ready to go home at this point. Although the service only lasted the regular length of service for him... one hour and a half, he was ready for church to end.

The organization presented its founder with a plaque for dedication and hard work. Bradley was honored the organization realized the gold mine they had in their leader. The South did work in the HIV/AIDS education but the rural South was the last on the totem pole. Ignorance prevailed even in the midst of education.

Bradley yet thanked God that he knew there was now hope!

"Did you enjoy your weekend, Bradley," Eric asked as he drove home.

"Immensely," Bradley said.

"I don't think that I have been so exhilarated in all of my life," Melvin said.

"Well, all hell breaks loose next week in court," Eric reminded Melvin and Bradley.

"Don't I know it."

"We'll understand that better by and by," Melvin sighed.

"Indeed."

Chapter Twenty
And the Battle Is Fought

Delores Kelly stood outside of Flora's Beauty Salon in Newbern smoking a *Virginia Slim 120*. Although the weather was cold and brisk as it normally is in January of any year, she could care less. The only thing she knew was that she wanted to smoke a cigarette and the shop sign specifically stated *No Smoking*. She did not have a problem with non-smokers as long as they did not have a problem with her. She paid $3.36 per pack for her cigarettes and no one could tell her, an African-American woman who lived in the rural South before, during, and after integration, whether or not she could or could not smoke her cigarettes. Yes, she knew all of the statistics that came with smoking. She knew that it was now becoming a dying art when it was ever so popular to do when she first began over thirty years before that moment. The only thing she knew was that she needed her nicotine right then and right there and she would not let the cold weather or anything else prevents her from taking a draw off what she had paid her money for.

As she lit the cigarette, her mind drifted back to years that seemed as if they were good years. The 1960s were not so bad although they were terrible. No, black people could not eat, pee, or sleep where ever they pleased but they were certainly a together people back in the day. She thought about just how Dyer County had begrudgingly changed with integration. She remembered being with the group that decided to protest against the lunch counter at *W.W. Woolworth's* in downtown Dyersburg against the protests of the church, the one and only black school, and the more feared... the parents. Yes, Dr. King preached a mighty good message on freedom and equality but Dyer County was going to abide new laws in its own time. The African-American Dyersburg that she remembered was not too fond of giving up Bruce High School to integration. It had been the only school in the state to rank Class "A" for over fifty years. Yes, Bruce High School had beat out many schools for a coveted prize in 1922 by being the only black school in the state of Tennessee to have a faculty of over 40 members and student enrollment of over 1,000. Through the strength of the church and Bruce High School, the Bruce

Community relied on itself for most everything. Hence, you were a member of the elite class if you became an educator or minister. If you were a farmer your wealth was measured by the acres you owned and the amount of children you had to work your own fields as well as the many other white owned cotton fields in the South. The school's calendar year was abbreviated to accommodate for harvest in the fall and planting in the spring and summer. Parents who either owned or worked in the fields could care less about a child obtaining an education when food had to be placed on the table. Hence, no one attended school during planting season or Bruce never would have had an enrollment of over 1,000 students.

Delores thought fondly back to those days when the nucleus of black life in Dyer County surrounded Bruce and those black churches. The churches supported education therefore supported the school. Even though many churches built one story, one-roomed schoolhouses on their property for the purpose of educating their congregation, all children attended Bruce High School after the elementary school years. The most surprising thing to Delores, however, was that it was The Colored Cumberland Presbyterians in Dyer County who did not mind building a school beside their church and cemetery. Rock Spring, Hopewell, Fairview, and Beech Grove all had schools on their properties yet all were family owned congregations.

Black business flourished during this time as well. Beside the train tracks in Dyersburg, directly in front of the station itself, the Bruce Community sat with dusty streets and bustling activity. The infamous *Hill* was the club that legendary singers at one point in time, for whatever reasons, performed in along with *The Purple Palace, and The Field.* Because there were so few white owned businesses that would accommodate blacks in or around Dyersburg, the black inhabitants forged their own future by building hotels, gas stations, taxi services, Laundromats, grocery stores, fish houses, and, of course, the famous underground bootleg society of an evening drink.

Delores shook her head at the thought of the new slogan of *The White Man Holds Me Back* during this present age and even in the new millennium. It seemed foreign to even hear those words when black people had far less then but far more now. It was simple, black people knew they were not going to be treated as a human in white Dyersburg, so rather than buck against the tradition and system, black men and black women became self-reliant. Hence, Dr. King's message was a bit strange to the people of Dyer County during the 1960s because they had their own hassle-free world whereas they were forced to deal with white Dyersburg only during working hours. Working hours lasted only for a little while.

It was hard to give Bruce High School up to integration. Over the ninety-year span from the 1880s when the school was established until 1972 when the school closed its doors forever, a reputation of excellence had developed within its confines. Bruce had an award-winning band that could easily stop a parade. People from miles around would come to Dyersburg's Christmas Parade just to watch this marching band perform the rich sultry music strung by an African beat. Led by the majorettes whose beautiful black legs would kick high into the sky as they plowed the way the Bruce High School Marching Band seemed to render melodies from heaven. Segregation could not grip Dyersburg when the Bruce Marching Band descended upon Dyersburg. If music calms the savage beast, certainly the Bruce Marching Band calmed the beast of segregation in Dyer County for everyone in the city proudly called the band its own after any performance. No one liked to face the Bruce Bull Dogs on the football field or basketball court either. Seldom did this team have a losing season if ever. People actually thought they had attended a Broadway play after attending the Annual end of the year school plays by the various Drama departments at Bruce.

Yes, it was sometimes a hard pill to swallow when the textbooks obtained for studies were the "hand-me-downs" from Dyersburg High School and often the word *Nigger* would be found on the pages. But Bruce was more than a facility to teach algebra and economics, Bruce taught morals and values as well as social and survival skills. Yes, Dr. King's dream of integration was an eloquent one. It was indeed a dream to be embraced. Yes, Bruce needed to become a learning facility equivalent to white schools of the day only when academia was applied. But it did not. Instead, it, much like Frederick Perry, was raped and murdered. As life oozed slowly from the depths of Frederick so did life ooze from the halls of Bruce when its doors closed for good in 1972.

"Girl, you look deep," Jean said as she joined Delores for a cigarette on the outside of Flora's Beauty salon.

"Child, I was just thinking about how things have really changed," Delores said with such an emphatic melancholy until Jean knew that she was reflecting on life from years gone by.

"Girl," Delores chuckled as she lit a second *Virginia Slim 120* and passed her lighter to Jean who lit a *Newport 100*. "I was just reflecting on the past and thinking about this trial that is coming up tomorrow."

"Well, Delores," Jean said as she sat down beside Delores, "The only thing I can tell you which is a simple truth is that nothing changes only the faces."

"Shit, Dyersburg has changed," Delores said. "I don't ever remember black people being as pitiful as we are now."

"Well, Delores, black people have never had the opportunities that they have now. Of course they are going to change."

"Are you telling me that we were better in bondage?"

"No," Jean laughed. "I'm saying that when we were not allowed across the tracks after a certain time we were furious enough to get off of our behinds and make a very similar life to those who lived across the tracks."

"And your point?"

"When was the last time that you saw a black man own a service station or taxi service or hotel anywhere in Dyer County?"

"Child, don't even ask that," Delores laughed.

"But, hey," Jean laughed. Your son is trying; he has his own store now."

"Well, that is a start," Delores laughed. "His prices are high as hell to me."

"Are you shopping there for *Wal-Mart* clothes or for a nice garment that will last you for several years?"

"Now you know Bradley is not going to sell anything cheap," Delores chuckled. "But I'm worried that he'll go out of business at the rate he's going."

"If he goes out of business, at least he tried," Jean assured. "I give him credit for just trying."

"His overhead is terrible," Delores complained.

"Any man in business outside of his home is going to have overhead. But Bradley doesn't look too worried about it to me," Jean laughed. "Didn't he just buy you a new car?"

"Child, I didn't want a new car or new house," Delores laughed. "But that's my baby; he's going to have it his way or no way."

"You don't have to tell me a thing," Jean laughed as she thought about her son, Maxwell. "These kids are no longer kids anymore. They are fully grown men now."

"How did you deal with Maxwell getting married, if I may ask?" Delores said as she dumped a long line of ashes onto the ground and took another drag from her cigarette.

"How was I supposed to deal with it?" Jean laughed. "I could have played crazy and told him I wasn't going to love him and lost him forever or I could love him as my son and keep on living."

"You got a point," Delores chuckled. "I know Bradley is definitely no angel but he is still my baby."

Ellen pulled up to the salon in her candy apple red *Mazda 626*. She stepped out of the car and cussed at something.

"Girl, what are you cussin' about?" Jean laughed as she inquired what it was that had Ellen in deep thought.

"I have been driving around all day with my belt in the door and now it's all wet," she said as she walked quickly up the small steps that led to the massive porch in front of the salon. "How are you all today?"

"Fine," Jean said as she stood and hugged Ellen. "How else is life treating my sister?"

"Sister?" Delores inquired. "Aren't you all bound now by your sons as mother-in-law and mother-in-law?"

Ellen and Jean laughed.

"That made us seem too old, girl," Ellen grinned. "Maxwell and Rev had us over for dinner before they took vows and asked us what they wanted us to call them."

"I immediately said call me Momma," Jean laughed. "I don't like that mother-in-law stuff."

"And I said call me Mother as I've been called all of these years," Ellen said.

"But why do you all call one another sister?" Delores asked.

"Because Ellen seems more like a sister to me and now that she is family, that is how I see her," Jean laughed as she lit another cigarette.

"Well, girls," Ellen said. "I'm sorry to leave you all but it's cold out here and I need to have a manicure done today."

"Go on in, somebody will get to you in a minute," Delores laughed. "Are you going to the trial tomorrow?"

"I doubt it," Ellen said as she walked into the salon. "I just hope justice is served."

"We shall see," Jean said. "We shall see."

The courtroom was filled on that cold January day in the new millennium! Melvin had praised God with millions of other people as the end of the century closed and the new millennium ushered its way in. There was no Y2K bug to shut down the entire world nor did the world end as prophesied by so many other people. On January 3rd, he had to report to work for business as usual. The last thing he wanted to do on this day, however, was to attend the trial of Jeremy "Psycho" Curbie. It was the second week in the year and the fraternity was already in an uproar over the nuptials of The Rev. Now, he, Eric, Bradley, Desmond, Douglas, Eric, Howard, William, Maxwell, and The Rev sat in a courtroom listening to the ugly details of the trial.

Jeremy sat in his chair as if he could care less. The prosecution called witness after witness but no one could testify to seeing him murder Frederick or the other people. Each and every person who was called to the witness stand was discredited by the Defense lawyer who had been hired by Hortence Perry to defend Jeremy.

Feelings were on edge as the case seemed as if it were a losing battle for the prosecution. All seemed as if Jeremy was going to walk free even after his testimony in Melvin's living room. The entire courtroom grumbled when the judge dismissed the police report as inadmissible evidence to the case.

Melvin attempted to digest the court case as well as it proceeded to linger on step by step making the entire prosecution look ridiculous. Finally, the prosecution rested and behold, the defense called Hortence Perry as its first witness.

"Do you swear to tell the truth, the whole truth, and nothing but the truth? The bailiff asked as Hortence placed her hand on the Bible.

"I attest," she said.

"I attest," Bradley grumbled softly. "We are in for a righteous sermon now, yall. This doesn't look good."

"Please state your full name for the court records," the judge instructed.

"Hortence Melvira Perry," she said as she stared into the faces of Frederick's friends as well as Jeremy's family.

"How long have you known the defendant, Ms. Perry?" the lawyer for the defense asked.

"All of his life," she said. "As a matter of fact, his mother and I used to hang out together."

Melvin praised God that the prosecuting attorney motioned for a recess after about thirty minutes of Hortence's jabber. Melvin could not stand much more of her long tedious Holy Ghost filled speech on how she loved the Lord with all of her mind, soul, and body. The judge granted the request and court was adjourned for the remainder of the day and scheduled to reconvene the following day.

As Melvin walked out of the courtroom, he caught The Rev before The Rev could get out of his sight.

"I just wanted to tell you that you know you have my vote tonight," Melvin said as he welcomed the thought of another subject besides the trial. "You know they have it out for you tonight."

"It won't be the first time, Melvin," The Rev said grimly. "You know, I actually welcome whatever God has in store for the evening. If they choose to vote me out of office, so be it but they will never get a resignation."

"Yeah, I heard that when we returned from Paris Landing several members had sent a petition around requesting your resignation."

"Well, I received the petition and you should have the letter of response in your mail," The Rev grinned. "If you didn't get it then it simply stated that I refuse to resign. They will have to vote me out."

"Some of the people were talking about splitting the fraternity if you remained in as the head official."

"I won't allow that," The Rev said. "But they will get an election."

"You are just as stubborn as your cousin who wrote *The Book*," Melvin laughed as he thought about R. Bryant Smith and the stir that he had caused in Dyer County as well because of his novel *"When The Children Get Together."*

"We are hard headed Smiths," The Rev laughed. "I hear he has to face a similar situation on tomorrow with one of the church groups that he works with."

"I don't understand the crisis," Melvin admitted. "People act as if there has never been a gay person here before."

"That's not really the problem," The Rev smiled. "The problem is not being gay or living gay it is about being free. People would rather you live a lie than to be who you really are."

"Yeah, that's our culture," Melvin sighed. "We love to look through the glass darkly but truth we cannot deal with."

"Do you know that one of my preacher friends actually told me that he could tolerate me being in the closet or out of the closet but could not support me being married to a man?" The Rev laughed.

"What kind of shit is that?" Melvin growled.

"Child, the rural South," The Rev chuckled. "He went on to say that he had a total disbelief in my life style but that because he was a Christian he loved me and God loves me and I was yet welcomed to attend his church."

"Please tell me the name of the church," Melvin begged.

"I will not reveal that," The Rev commented. "The only thing that I know is this. These are the days where our everything will be tested. I cannot change the fact that I love Maxwell enough to commit myself to him for life. Because it is illegal to actually marry, I chose to honor him with the only possible means that I can, a Holy Union. I will be damned if I will allow people to make me choose between loving him or living a lie full of pretense. This is a new millennium and to live in silence is to die in suffering"

"I feel you," Melvin said as he thought about the ceaseless arguments he and Eric had about how they could or could not act in public. Melvin did not want to show any type of affection in public where Eric felt it was his God given right to do what he felt. Many quarrels had ensued between the two of them because of it and now, once again, his hero was making sense of the situation.

Melvin could barely find a parking space when he pulled up to the Omega Complex for the Election of 2000. He could not remember a time in the history of the fraternity when this many members attended any event much less an election. The word was obviously out and about and tonight was about to be a witch-hunt. Melvin could feel it in his veins.

He passed the Council Chambers where all of the present officers were getting robed up for the election. Because this would be a momentous election, everyone was required to wear dress uniforms. Melvin went to the Senate chambers, grabbed his sash, and walked into the Congressional Hall and took his seat.

"This is a waste of time," Bradley said as Melvin took his seat beside him. "The Senate has to vote before the election can ever hit the floor anyway."

"These folk are out for blood," Melvin said as he eyed the ugly expressions that were twisted about many of the members faces. "And to think, The Rev has served for three consecutive terms without fail. That's six whole years."

Chief Justice Snake entered the room followed by the other high-ranking officials. The anthem was sung and the meeting began.

The Rev took the podium and spoke.

"Gentlemen, brothers, and friends," he said. "It has truly been an honor and a privilege serving you as the highest ranking official of this organization for three consecutive terms since graduation from high school and two before then. The years have certainly toiled along since the early days of OPT. I have heard the cry of the people and I have heard the gossip filled with malicious rumor as well. As I look around the room, I am proud that I have actually managed to get the full cooperation of the fraternity and every member is present tonight. That certainly deserves a round of applaud for yourselves."

The assembly applauded. A few members actually chuckled at The Rev's comments because they had not been to a fraternity meeting in years but could not dare miss the show down on this evening.

"I have in my hand a petition requesting my resignation," he continued. "When I consider the work established by my own hands within this organization, I am inclined to know that it would be a discredit to my character and disservice to the organization for me to honor this request. Many of you went to colleges across the nation thanks to my work here in this very building. The work from my office stood between starvation for many of you. I cannot count the endless nights when my home phone would ring for me to come and bail many of you out of jail or your brothers, sisters, cousins, and some of your children as well. As Moderator, I have attempted to preserve a culture of being an African-American man from the South that has taught me how to love, how to keep morals and values, and how to serve a just God. I've asked you gentlemen to produce a name to run against me and there is not a name to this day yet you ask for an election. Some of you have dared called my home and speak obscenities as if you were attempting to frighten me. It didn't work! Last, there is a rumor that some of you plan to split the organization if I remain as Moderator. I remind you all, gentlemen, you may leave this organization but you can leave with what you came with... nothing! Saying all of this, I bid you God's speed as I declare all office of The Omega Phi Theta Fraternity vacant until filled upon this evening. We shall elect every office from the head to the tail until all offices have been filled if it takes us all evening or this election will be declared unconstitutional."

The Rev took his seat after a great murmur began throughout the assembly. The Chief Justice called a recess.

Five hours later, the results were returned to the Chief Justice who took the podium. He read the names of all of the Senators who retained a seat. Melvin and Bradley were shocked to discover they no longer held a position nor did Desmond nor did Howard. They were being exterminated from an organization that they helped to build from the ground up.

"Child, I don't give a damn," Bradley said as he took his sash off and returned it to the Chief Justice. "I have held this position now for what seems an eternity. Even when I wasn't here to attend the meetings, I held the position. If it means this much to these folks they can have it."

The Chief Justice then read the tallies for the election of The Great Council Seats. Grimlock replaced The Rev as Moderator by a vote of 89-88. Melvin attempted to review in his mind who had not voted. One person did not vote because it would have been a tie vote.

The Rev's name was called as Vice - Moderator.

"I decline the nomination or acceptance of the position," he said and took the podium again. "Thanks guys but no thanks. I appreciate the vote of confidence for all of you who voted for me and thank you."

"The Rev did not vote," Grimlock said as he took the podium. "As Moderator, I declare a tie vote. All future votes will be held among the Great Council. Good evening."

"We'll tear this joint up, niggah," the same man from Trenton yelled.

"As Moderator," Grimlock said as he looked at the man. "The first thing I will do for the few hours that I will hold this office is this. You are hereby stripped of all rank and everything else. Get out of this building before I throw you out personally. You were never supposed to come back but The Rev allowed you back in! I ain't gotta do it!"

The man left the room in tears.

The Great Council met in a private meeting for another hour and then produced a new roster.

"Grimlock will remain as Moderator and The Rev will be our new Chief Justice if he will accept the position," the Stated Clerk said.

The audience applauded.

The Rev waved and took the podium again.

"I'm trying to give all of this hard work over to you guys," The Rev laughed. "I know some of you have a problem with who I love and I don't want to interfere with your mission. The Lord knows I really would love to sit and review all of that paper work and stuff and..."

"Man, shut up," Skull laughed. "Just take the position. Will you?"

"What about Snake?" The Rev asked.

"He was elected to serve as Dean of Education," Grimlock said as he reviewed the tallies again. "Your office will be right next door to mine or better yet you keep your same office and I will take the one next door."

"But the paper work..."

"The paper work is something you have always loved to do anyway, now show us how to do it since you used to always complain about Snake's paperwork," Grimlock laughed.

"Bet," The Rev said as the audience applauded. "I don't understand you guys nor will I ever."

"It's not what you do, Rev," Grimlock said. "It's just what you do."

As Chief Justice, The Rev would be responsible for processing all historical data of the organization as well as reviewing all scholarship papers submitted. To some, it seemed as if it were a less important position, yet it was ideal for The Rev. It would mean more time to devote to Maxwell and less time to devote to a dying organization that was holding on by threads. His old problem was now Grimlock's new problem. For the next two years he could sit back, relax, and enjoy a vacation while Grimlock began his personal witch-hunt as Moderator. Grimlock had always been totally opposed to the renewal of several members' membership. On that very night that Grimlock was elected Moderator of The Omega Phi Theta Fraternity, he canceled the memberships of many who had voted him into office.

With a cigar in Grimlock's mouth and a cloud of smoke about him, The Rev laughed as he passed Grimlock's dusty office as Grimlock searched each member's file in search of anything that would discredit that member's membership. By the following meeting, there were only 105 members left in the entire organization. Melvin and Bradley were restored to their former positions as Senators because they had been replaced by known drug addicts. The

Great Council approved every cancellation made by Grimlock. To the discredit of those who sought out The Rev, they had forgotten, The Rev's ties went back far in OPT history but Grimlock had not. The Rev planned his honeymoon to the Bahamas with Maxwell as things were back to normal because OPT had a new leader with a new zeal.

"Fuck 'em," Grimlock grumbled as he stamped CANCELLED on the next file.

Chapter Twenty-One

It's Over Now

Melvin sat in stitches beside Eric during the tedious trial of Jeremy "Psycho" Curbie on that rainy Tuesday morning in February. The courtroom was filled to its capacity as it had been for all of the days the case was heard. Everyone wanted to hear what Hortence Perry would actually say in the defense of the murderer of her son. She had bored the courtroom to death with her oaths of salvation and how God had touched Jeremy's life during a tent revival under her ministry of her church. There was no way this fine individual could have murdered anyone, in her best judgment.

"Mrs. Perry," the prosecuting attorney asked. "Did you have a relationship with Jeremy "Psycho" Curbie?"

"I don't understand the question," Hortence said as sweat began to pour down her face.

"It is a simple question, Mrs. Perry," the lawyer said as he walked directly to the witness stand and looked Hortence in the face.

The entire courtroom was as silent as a ghost town. Nothing could be heard within the courtroom. The only sounds available to the ear were the sounds of vehicles that passed the courthouse on that day and they were few and far between as it seemed to take Hortence forever to answer the simple question.

"Answer the question, please, Mrs. Perry," the judge said as he leaned over his desk curiously waiting to hear what she would say at this point.

"He's just a child," Hortence mumbled.

"The question again, Mrs. Perry," the lawyer badgered. "Did you have a relationship with Mr. Jeremy "Psycho" Curbie?"

Hortence wiped sweat, make-up, and hair grease from her brow as a lump developed in her throat.

"Well, Mrs. Perry?"

"Yes," she said and let out a long sigh.

Trish Ann screamed out "You bitch!" and was removed from the courtroom followed by a long line of other spectators.

"It was not my intention to date him." Hortence attempted to proceed. "He was not in my caliber but I was lonely and..."

"No further questions your honor," the lawyer said.

"But you don't understand," Hortence rattled on in tears as the bailiff removed her from the witness stand. "It was not what you think..."

Melvin was crushed in his Spirit yet he was determined to remain in the courtroom until the bitter end. So many things were beginning to unravel at this point and he never believed his little life in Fairhaven, Tennessee could be so detailed and complex as it had become over the past few months. He grabbed Bradley's hand that was now in tears. It took no rocket scientist to figure out what had happened, especially when the next person took the stand.

"Please state your full name," the bailiff said.

"My name is Howard Essary Avery," Howard said as he placed his right hand upon the Bible and his left hand in the air.

"Do you swear to tell the whole truth and nothing but the truth so help you God?"

"I swear," Howard said.

"You may be seated."

The defense lawyer thought it wise to call Howard to the stand but found it to be a fatal mistake. Realizing the mistake, he asked Howard's relationship to Jeremy and the deceased.

"Jeremy and I were friends years ago," Howard said. "Frederick and I were lovers for years."

"No further questions your honor," the defense lawyer said.

The prosecuting attorney stepped forward and began a barrage of questions that brought Howard full circle into a testimony that rocked the courthouse walls.

"Yes, I knew about Jeremy and Hortence," Howard revealed. "She dated Jeremy since we were in high school; for what reasons I will never know. Jeremy knew about Frederick and my relationship because many days in order for Jeremy to get to come to the house Frederick was used as the alibi for Hortence and Jeremy's affair. "

"Why do you think a mother would testify against her son in a trial of this nature?" the prosecuting attorney questioned.

"It's simple," Howard began. His words tore at the hearts of many because many people knew what he said was true but no one ever stepped forward. "Right before Frederick and I became an item, Frederick told me about how his mother's boyfriend had been taking him sexually at night against his will. When Hortence found out about it, she beat Frederick unbearably and told him that she was not raising punks, faggots, or sissies in her house and she would be damned if a child of hers would sleep with her man."

Tears flowed from Melvin's eyes at this point. This fact he never knew but he did know that there had always been a strain on Frederick and Hortence's relationship.

"Is the man in the court room today?" the lawyer asked.

"Yes, he is," Howard said as he looked over the crowd.

"Could you point him out to the court?"

"Yes, sir," Howard said as he pointed to the pastor of Hortence's church, the Bishop B.D. Ickles. "He's sitting right there with the loud green suit on."

All eyes turned on the Bishop. He was a middle-aged man with a slightly graying *Jheri* curl. He won no beauty contests but it was said that once upon a time he was indeed a handsome man. His clothes were always the flashiest, gaudiest, loudest pieces any man in the world could find. However, everything always matched. If he wore green, he would have green shoes, hat, gloves, and over coat or cape to match. When everyone looked at him, he had the audacity to smile which revealed seven gold teeth. He stroked his chin when he realized that Howard had just pegged him. On each finger were some of the most expensive diamond rings money could buy.

"So, you are saying that this man basically raped Frederick years ago and his mother said nothing?"

"He did," Howard said. "In fact, one night after the incident occurred, Frederick had called me because the Bishop was at his front door and he was afraid of him. When Hortence found out that the

Bishop had been by the house and Frederick did not let him in, she beat him again. And it was the Bishop who told Hortence to find a young man to have sex with. He even suggested that she date Jeremy."

The judge had to call a second recess when Howard left the witness stand.

"Guhl, this is too many thangs," Bradley said as he nudged Melvin as they walked down outside of the courthouse for a breath of fresh, cold, winter air.

"We are getting to the core of it all," Melvin shuttered.

"The preacher was having Frederick?" Desmond walked behind them and said in disbelief.

"Ain't that tired?" Bradley laughed when he thought about the image of the preacher.

"I wonder if he will be called to the stand." Melvin asked curiously.

"He may but I don't see how his testimony will be relevant at this point," Bradley said. "His tea just got spilled, that's all."

They looked up into the eyes of Trish Ann and were all horribly sorry that they had said a word for her to hear. Trish Ann, who was now fully gray headed, puffed on a *More* cigarette as if it were her Saving grace. Dark circles encompassed her eyes from years of worry from disobedient children and this endless court case.

"Hell, go on and talk," Trish Ann said as she puffed furiously. "I thought that bitch was my friend and she was fucking my child and trying to hide it because she was fucking that jackleg preacher."

"Do you think Jeremy is innocent?" Bradley asked honestly.

"Hell no," she said sadly. "But he is still my child. My fuck up, hard headed, child that was spoiled rotten by my mother-in-law. I couldn't afford to give him all of what she wanted and now it makes sense to me. That bitch was buying him all of these years."

Eric walked outside and for the first time ever, Melvin noticed a cigarette in his hand.

"What are you doing?" Melvin asked as he looked at Eric.

"Baby, I need something to settle my nerves, this shit is getting crazy," Eric said as he puffed away on a *Newport 100.*

"I only wish that half of my children had been like you, Eric," Trish Ann said as she looked up at Eric.

Eric stood still in disbelief.

"Yeah," she said as she puffed away attempting to warm herself as the cold wind blew gently as she swayed from side to side. "I know my children always got more than you did because you were who you were. But look at all of them. Every last one of them except Josh is in prison."

Eric was speechless as he watched tears begin to stream down Trish Ann's face.

"Who would have ever believed that I would have conceived a pack like this?" she cried. "I gave all I could and still that was not enough."

Eric placed his arm around her as she began to wail. Melvin, Bradley, and Desmond silently tipped to the other side of the railing and eyed the scene from the corner of their eyes in order to not disturb the two but discretely hear everything that was said.

"Well, Aunt Tee," Eric said as he wiped the tears away. "We cannot change the past, we can only live and learn during this present time we have."

"But why would he kill that poor child," Trish bawled.

Now, Melvin, Desmond, and Bradley were in tears.

"Drugs, money, who knows?" Eric said.

"Well, why did he kill the other folk, is it just in him to kill now?" Trish asked as someone announced court was reconvening.

"I don't know," Eric said as he walked Trish Ann inside.

The defense attorney called The Bishop B.D. Ickles to the stand. The Bishop condescended into the courtroom like a proud peacock in his loud green suit with suede shoes to match. There was so much gold draped on the lapels of the coat until the material seemed as if it were weighed down. His *Jheri* curl was freshly done and cut into a style called a Shag - short on the sides and top but long in the back. He took the stand and grinned revealing his gold crowns.

He denied a relationship with both Hortence and Frederick and told the jury, judge, and entire courtroom that he had never even seen Jeremy before in his life.

The prosecuting attorney looked at him, smiled, and asked the question:

"Mr. Ickles if you do not know this man then why are you paying for his attorney? That doesn't make sense to me."

The courtroom murmured.

"I object, your honor," the defense attorney yelled. "That question is irrelevant to the case."

"Over ruled," the judge said. "It seems to be a fair question to me."

The Bishop squirmed a bit in his seat, smiled, and said:

"I sponsor multiple charities and I always fund young black men who are in trouble who need good lawyers but cannot afford them. You know Jeremy wouldn't stand a chance in this court room if he had a lawyer from this area because the entire system is crooked and you know it."

"On the contrary, Mr. Ickles," the prosecuting attorney smiled. "I disagree."

The prosecuting attorney walked to his desk, retrieved a document, and brought it to the Bishop to view.

"Mr. Ickles," he said. "If you do not know Mrs. Perry or Mr. Curbie, then why would this statement show from your personal record a check in the amount of one thousand dollars to Mrs. Perry and one in the amount of four thousand dollars to Mr. Curbie two days after the murder of Frederick Perry?"

"I have no idea what you are talking about," The Bishop retorted.

"So, you are saying that someone else wrote checks from your account for this sum of money?"

"Well, no, I normally paid them in cash but I…"

"You didn't have it on you at the time?"

"I plead the Fifth Amendment," The Bishop said.

"I would too," the prosecuting attorney commented cunningly. "No further questions, your honor."

The moment arrived that had been awaited. Jeremy Curbie was called to the stand to testify in his own behalf. Melvin squeezed Bradley's hand as he marched slowly to the witness stand. The defense attorney asked trivial and basic questions, and finally, he asked:

"Mr. Curbie did you kill Frederick Perry or anyone else?"

"Naw," Jeremy said with his head bowed downward.

"No further questions your honor."

"Mr. Curbie," the prosecuting attorney smiled. "Do you know Mr. B. D. Ickles or Mrs. Hortence Perry or Mr. Frederick Perry?"

"Objection your honor, what's with the roll call?" the defense attorney roared.

"Please contain yourself and let the man ask his questions," the judge grumbled. "Overruled."

Jeremy looked up into the eyes of the audience. He had been prepared to say and do one thing yet he was tired of the lengthiness of the trial. Although his lawyer had done a good job at discrediting the prosecuting attorney's witnesses, he did a lousy job by putting Hortence, B. D., or him on the stand.

"Yes, I know them all," he answered softly.

"Excuse me," the attorney yelled. "I couldn't hear you?"

"I know all of them," he shouted.

"How do you know them?"

Jeremy looked into the crowd at The Bishop. The Bishop made a gesture that made Jeremy furious. A simple gesture of no more than winking his eye but Jeremy hated him at the moment for winking at him.

"Well," Jeremy said. "I first met B. D. years ago when I went to Chicago to visit my aunt one summer. He was the most awesome man I had ever met. He was pimpin' the hos and the niggahs and gettin' paid fat for it. Well, he got run out of Chicago and came down South. Somebody told him that the best way to pimp in the South was to be a preacher and so he made himself a preacher. Then he met

Hortence. Hortence was a fine woman then with some good pussy. He married some woman who knew the ropes of the church and she helped to make him a Bishop and get him a congregation and after he got big again, he kicked her to the curb. When she got out of line, he beat her for not being able to have children and when she got pregnant he beat her until she lost every one that she had. She finally went crazy and they had to send her to Bolivar...."

Again there was complete silence as Jeremy revealed the story. The Bishop, as dark as he was, began to turn red with rage as Jeremy continued the story.

"Did you know about an affair between Mr. Ickles and Mrs. Perry or Mr. Perry?" the prosecuting attorney asked as the defense attorney stared in disbelief as he watched his entire case unfold before his eyes.

"It started out an affair between Hortence and B. D.," Jeremy said. "But B. D. recognized the fact that Frederick was gay way before Frederick even recognized it. He told me that he fucked Frederick in order to make him one of his male hos like he had in Chicago. But honestly, he just got addicted to fuckin' Frederick, that's all. I was in the house the night that Hortence caught B.D. fuckin' Frederick and she hit the roof. She told him that the only reason he had to fuck a man was because he didn't have a big dick and that was the reason everybody called him B.D. or Big Dickless. That's when he kicked her ass all over her own house and told her to get into the bedroom and get undressed. He then told me that he would pay me a hundred dollars to go and fuck her and I took the money."

"You better work it out, boy!" Bradley yelled accidentally. He could not contain himself. He truly respected *The Ho Association of America* in its entirety.

"Order in the court," the judge said. "Anymore outburst like that one and you'll be held in contempt of court. Mr. Bailiff, please bar the doors. No one is to enter or exit from this point on."

A cold shiver went through Melvin. This was getting pretty serious.

"Continue," the judge instructed Jeremy.

"Well, I went in and fucked her and got my money but I didn't know that she was gonna like it," Jeremy said. "Well, this went on all through high school and when I went to college, both of them paid me to come home just to fuck her. He became impotent over the years and she needed her monthly supply of big dick."

Trish Ann cried during the testimony. She could not believe her ears. She, Hortence and Delores were the best of friends until Hortence supposedly "got saved." As it turns out, it was all a huge fabricated lie. Trish Ann had tried to attend Hortence's church but she always felt uncomfortable around this man, B.B. Ickles. Now she understood why. He was a ghetto pimp who had made a fool of southern people who never went anywhere beyond the confines of their own streets. Ignorance killed them worse than anything they could ever imagine.

"…When I got kicked out of college for selling dope that B. D. had given me to sell to make some extra money while I was there, he told me not to worry about it, he would take care of me as long as I took care of Hortence. But I got tired of her. She wanted more than what I could give her so I stopped going by as much. Then I went by one night and she gave me a rock and I smoked it for my first time and have been chasing the high I felt on that night forever. It was the first time I made love all night long. I fucked her so much until she begged me to stop but I couldn't ever get a nut so I kept going. Then, after that, I started to smoking the rocks that I was selling for B. D. and he got mad and threatened to kill me until I kicked his ass a couple of times just for GP…"

Melvin felt sick to his stomach as he listened to Jeremy. The testimony sounded as if it came from the voice of an innocent child yet it was coming from a man who had been screwed over by a world of pretense and social piety.

"… I had stopped going by Hortence's house so much after she had that operation that cut out her pussy. When we had sex then it just didn't feel right but the money kept getting better and the rocks kept coming until one night she said she had to go out of town with B.D. to some convention or something. Well, I was feigning hard and just needed some money or a rock. I first went over to Melvin's house but he had a lot of company at his house that night…"

Melvin almost fainted.

"Who is Melvin?" the attorney asked.

"Him," Jeremy said as he pointed Melvin out in the crowd.

Melvin's heart skipped an endless beat that seemed as if it had been engulfed in a timeless pit never to be found again.

"Why did you go to his house?" the attorney asked.

"Well," Jeremy explained. "I used to fuck him off and on after he came back from college. He always tried to be this sneaky little person. He would pay me to keep my mouth closed about fucking him..."

Melvin began to shake as he stared straight ahead at Jeremy. His foot began to tap a quick yet rhythmic beat in order to pass the time. Bradley's eyes grew as wide as saucers as he listened intently to the testimony, and then slowly turned to see the expression on Melvin's face. From the corner of his eyes, Bradley also looked into Eric's face. Bradley noticed the frown that began to appear on Eric's face as Jeremy continued his testimony. The frown on Eric's face became a permanent fixture for the remainder of the trial.

"Well, I caught a ride over to Howard's house then," Jeremy continued.

"Mr. Avery?" the attorney asked.

"Yeah," Jeremy said. "I used to fuck him too."

Melvin and Bradley both gasped as they looked over their shoulders at Howard whose head fell into his lap as he attempted to hide it from the eyes that now turned to look at him within the confines of the walls of the courtroom.

"Howard used to always try to compare himself to everybody else that he suspected me of fucking." Jeremy chuckled. "He always wanted to know if his ass was better than Frederick's, Melvin's Xavier's or even Desmond's..."

Desmond made a choking, gurgling noise as he began to grab and twist at the front of his sweater.

"It's interesting that those were the faggots that I used to sleep with. They suspected one another but would not dare tell because they were so afraid that I would kick their asses. I really didn't give a damn if they did tell..." Jeremy said as he continued his testimony as if it were a long conversation and confession with an old friend or priest.

Melvin's heart raced as the vessels within the temple of his head began to bulge in contracting motions. He wanted to kill Jeremy on the spot and in the witness stand. If Frederick has just said "NO" none of this would be happening.

If looks could kill, Howard's looks would have definitely killed Jeremy on that day. Howard glanced at Bradley who caught his gaze. A slight smirk formed on Bradley's lips. Howard wanted to slap Bradley silly but knew better than to open that can of worms.

Tears streamed down Desmond's face. He could not stop rubbing his hands together, shifting from one side of his seat to the next, and then rubbing the back of his neck.

"How can I ever face Douglas again?" Desmond asked himself repeatedly.

The one time in his life and relationship with Douglas that he decided to cheat was with Jeremy. He thought that he had picked a safe and secure person. It was to be a secret between the two of them only and now this man had just revealed this secret to the entire world.

"Anyway," Jeremy continued. "I used to tell Howard that he was the best just to get more money. He would always make sure that I had forty or fifty dollars neatly tucked away in my pants pocket before I left only if I told him that his ass was better than any of his friends' asses." Jeremy laughed slightly. "Once, I didn't tell him that he was better and there was no money in my pocket. I quickly learned to always lie to him. He really wasn't the best. He didn't know how to take dick. Frederick, Xavier and Melvin did though…"

Bradley coughed slightly in order to cover the roaring laughter that welled up deeply inside of him. Melvin's foot began to tap on the floor again. This time, however, he tapped so loudly until Eric placed his hand on Melvin's leg in order to stop the noise.

"Desmond was the best dick sucker out of all of them but he was too big and scary to fuck. Although he was good, he turned me off with his crying like a little bitch or something. He kept saying that he was in a relationship and I wasn't stuttin that. All I wanted was my damned money. He gave me sixty eight dollars and seventy-five cents to never return to him again. Hell, I thought that was real good even though he could suck a mean dick. But, I respected him and never went back after that one time. The other ones, I did go back for more.

They didn't pay as good as Desmond but if I humored Howard enough I could get fifty dollars and Melvin and Xavier always paid between thirty to forty dollars. I guess Frederick was the poor one out the bunch because he never gave more than twenty."

Bradley could barely contain his laughter. He grunted and attempted to clear his throat as Jeremy continued his testimony.

"Well, anyway," Jeremy continued. "Howard wasn't at home that night either. So, I got a ride over to Frederick's house. When I got there, he had just gotten dropped off by Bradley. I thought I could get the money from Frederick a little easier anyway. I knew that money wasn't gonna be as good as Howard or Melvin but Frederick knew how to fuck good. He could always keep me hard. The others really couldn't."

Melvin's hands began to tremble and sweat profusely as Jeremy continued to render all of the explicit details of his life. Melvin's hands were so wet until he had to retrieve a handkerchief from his pocket in order to dry them.

"So," Jeremy continued. "I went over to ask him for the money. He played this tired ass game about he wouldn't have no money until the next day after some punk pageant or something. I ain't never seen no punk pageant and I didn't believe him. So, I took my clothes off and stroked on my dick and he got weak. I started fucking him but it didn't seem right to me. His whole body seemed to be screaming out that he wanted more from me. All I wanted was my twenty dollars for a hit. I didn't want to fall in love with no damned body. Well, I always keep a pair of shoe strings in the bed with me because Hortence is a freaky bitch and likes to do wild things. I thought that since Frederick was her son, he was into it like that too. Then he started acting like I was hurting him and this began to piss me off when I know I wasn't hurting him. So, I was going to try the shoe string thing with him in order to make it a little more special. Then, he started twisting and it began to feel so good but he wasn't supposed to twist because I was pulling...."

Melvin could not contain the flow of tears that streamed down his cheeks like rivers. Bradley sat with his mouth wide open in astonishment. Desmond covered his mouth with both hands as tears streamed down his face. Desmond covered his mouth and shook his head "NO" continually.

Finally, the group understood what had happened. This finally explained why there was no crucial evidence of the murder and how their beloved friend died a senseless and needless death over twenty dollars - the price of a "hit."

"... The last thing I heard him whisper was "*Why*" and I was wondering what the hell was wrong with him. So, I thought he had gone to sleep. So, I put on my clothes and searched through his wallet and found ten dollars and then I left. I didn't know the mothafucka was dead until a day or two later when I went by Hortence's house. She was in an uproar because B.D. was tore up about it. So, I never told her what had happened because I still needed my money to get high. Well, I hit the streets and slanged a little cane but smoked most of it until B.D. just wouldn't let me have no mo unless I paid for it. Well, I started livin' out in an old abandoned house beside that big old church cemetery in Fairhaven. That's when the voices started always asking me: *"Why?"* I went out to apologize to Frederick for killin him because I didn't mean to kill him. I thought he liked it rough and passionate..."

Desmond hunched over and began to make muffled, snorkeling noises. Douglas embraced him slightly. The reality of Frederick's death mixed with closure was quite overwhelming. Melvin could not shed another tear. He had to hear the remainder of the twisted story for himself.

"... The night I went to visit him there was a big storm and from his grave Frederick keep screaming to me *"Why?"* The mothafucka wouldn't say nothin else but why and the next thang I knew the damned house was on fire. By the time I got back, the roof fell in on it and killed all of them people. B. D. was pissed again because he had pimped all of them and just made sure they had enough crack to keep them half-the-way satisfied. The rest, they had to rely on me to get. I was the one who would go and steal corn and beans and shit to feed 'em fit enough to do another hustle. But B. D. was floggin when he played this role of a saint and buried all of 'em with funerals at his church. Just when I thought it was all over I saw Ace talking to my brother and I know he was tellin' Josh everythang so that's the only mothafucka that I wanted to kill. The big-mouthed bastard. Now that's all I got to tell you." Jeremy said as he looked the prosecuting attorney directly in the eyes. "I don't give a damn about goin' to no jail 'cause it won't be my first time but yall ain't gonna sit here and try me for no murder when I didn't mean to kill nobody but Ace."

"I rest," the prosecuting attorney said.

The trial concluded on that day.

Silently, Melvin, Bradley, Howard, Douglas, Desmond, and Eric walked out of the courtroom. Howard attempted to break the silence but words would not come from his mouth.

Bradley began to laugh a loud yet wild and hysterical laugh.

"What's so damned funny?" Douglas asked as the group looked at Bradley.

"Just think," Bradley giggled. "All of these years I thought that I had it going on. I don't hold a key to any of you all! Especially in Jeremy's eyes!"

"You bitch!" Melvin growled as he grabbed Bradley's coat.

"I'm gonna tell you this once, Melvin," Bradley said as he looked into Melvin's eyes that were beginning to fill with tears. "Get your hands off of me. Your secret is out now. The only thing that I want to know from you is this…"

Bradley looked around into the eyes of Howard, Desmond, Douglas, and Eric.

"Was it worth it?" Bradley asked.

Desmond began to wail loudly.

"Can we be real, now?" Bradley asked.

"What?" Melvin asked.

"You heard him," Eric said as he looked at Melvin.

Tears filled Eric's eyes as he looked at Melvin. His bottom lip twitched. He folded his arms and rubbed upward and downward in an attempt to caress himself.

"Eric," Melvin cried as he grabbed Eric. "I love you!"

Melvin could not bear the thought of loosing anyone else from his life, especially Eric. He dearly wanted to turn back the hands of time but he knew that he could not. What had happened had happened. Melvin dearly wanted to hold on to the life in which he had made for himself and yet he wanted to be free of his past. Life, in

Melvin's rural Southern hometown had always been one great lie. It was a life where "don't ask – don't tell" was a way of life. Now, it did not matter to him. He only wanted to know if he could still love and be loved in return by the one true and real man of his heart.

"I love you too, Melvin," Eric muttered as tears streamed down his face. "But can you just let it be real? Can you be real?"

The jury found Jeremy "Psycho" Curbie guilty of first-degree murder on seven counts and sentenced him to death by electrocution. Unfortunately, he did not make the electric chair as his body was found in his cell the day before transport to prison. He had been strangled to death by a shoestring.

A rainy afternoon found Melvin sitting on his porch drinking a glass of iced tea… reflecting. Tears began to slowly stream down the cheeks of his face. Suddenly, the telephone rang.

He cleared his throat.

"Hello," he answered in a gruff, bass voice.

"What color is your draws, bitch?" the voice questioned.

"I don't wear them anymore," Melvin giggled. "It takes too much time for Eric to get them off of me."

"Guhl, that's too damned murch information for me," Bradley laughed. "What in the hell are y'all doing?"

"Not a damn thing," Melvin confessed. "I was just sitting on the porch, drinking a glass of iced tea… reflecting…"

"That's too damned murch information for me, guhl," Bradley teased. "What were you reflecting on anyway?"

"What a good friend you are," Melvin smiled. "And what a good man Eric is."

"And you know that," Bradley chuckled.

"What?" Melvin asked.

"Hell, that I am a good friend," Bradley laughed. "You better ask somebody."

"Yeah," Melvin confessed. "You've always kept it real."

"And you know that!"

The End

Critical Reviews

R. Bryant Smith has given our community a novel that radiates Southern charm, chronicles the lives of friends and guides us through a furtive journey into the hearts of those who were touched by the life and (more importantly) death of one of their own.

This story is told with wit, candor, laced with suspense as smith weaves a tale of how a small town and a cadre of friends grow and develop in the wake of tragedy in their small Tennessee hometown. The voice is hauntingly familiar as it calls the reader to examine his or her own relationships by the mystic rubric of unconditional love.

Alaric W. Blair, author
The End of Innocence: A Journey Into The Life

In Fairhaven, Tennessee, there are few choices for black gay men but they are epic and sweeping in their consequence: There is a lied life and there is a lived life. You are a witness or something to be witnessed. In the south of R. Bryant Smith's novel *Let It Be Real*, you can be a queen, educated, light or dark black, you are surely corn fed and you can be a king. You are an ingredient, sugar or lemon in his story, this sweet tea. Mr. Smith's most elegant entrance into the literary world is a front porch invitation extended to you to sit a spell and sip a while. You will not leave his presence, these men, this story, this meal unchanged nor unsatisfied.

Marvin K. White
Last Rights
Nothin' Ugly Fly

A powerful meditation on friendship, sexuality, and masculinity. R. Bryant Smith is a modern author who has found his voice.

Dr. Rudolph Byrd, author
Traps: African American Men on Gender and Sexuality
Essentials

The author captures the thick, rich complexities of religious faith, violence, death, friendship, and the comedic character of black gay life that balances the all too tragic realities of homophobia and violence in black communities. The book reminds us all that an injustice to one of us is an injustice to all of us despite our personal achievements.

Dr. Victor Anderson, author
Beyond Ontological Blackness
Pragmatic Theology
Creative Exchange

www.ingramcontent.com/pod-product-compliance
Lightning Source LLC
Chambersburg PA
CBHW020615260626
47157CB00003B/1021